Petra,
To my new
Enjoy the adventure
Susan
7-30-16

TOUCH the
MAYAN MOON

Susan LeMiles

Touch the Mayan Moon

Rio Bravo Books
South Padre Island, Texas

Touch the Mayan Moon
Published by Rio Bravo Books
South Padre Island, TX

This book is a work of fiction. Names, characters, places
and incidents either are the product of the author's
imagination or are used fictitiously. Any resemblance to
actual persons, living or dead, events, organizations or
locales is entirely coincidental.

Library of Congress Control Number : 2010905870

ISBN 978-0-9826166-0-4

Edited by Mari Okabayashi
Cover design by Ralph Ayres
Graphics by Toucan Graphics

For my Sweetest Heart

With love, all things are possible.

Chapter 1

The Migrant School

Catarina let the five gallon bucket full of water drop to the floor. She had carried it from an irrigation ditch a half a mile away. There were no consequences to the splashes that swept over the rim, for the water was absorbed immediately by the thirsty dirt floor; no clean up needed.

She struggled to lift open the weathered, unpainted wooden windows to let in some air. She was just barely strong enough, just barely tall enough to slide the old pieces of lumber in place that converted the so-called windows into awnings on three sides of the cinder block structure. The tin roof soaked up the heat of the sun all day and baked the dirt floor throughout the night. The stifling air hurt to breathe at two o'clock in the afternoon, and Catarina wondered if she could bake a cake in here.

The field store was operated by the farmer for whom Catarina worked. Migrant workers flocked to shacks like this on the sides of farm roads all over the Rio Grande Valley. Here, they would spend their

1

meager pay on the barest of life's necessities - pinto beans, masa for tortillas, white bread, soda, cough syrup. Sometimes there was cheap alcohol for those who desperately required it.

Families milked a goat, if they had one. Vegetables and fruit came from the generosity of any farmer who would allow them to keep a little of what they picked. Those farmers were the humane ones.

Takeo Ito was such a man; he was a Japanese American farmer from California. He provided workers with barracks, buildings that had wooden floors and windows that could be opened during sweltering nights and closed when it rained. Men and women who came from Mexico to work for him labored in the fields from dawn until dusk, had outside privies and cooked on open fires, but they never went hungry. Ito knew they didn't because he worked beside them.

Giving in to persistent campaigning and bargaining, Ito allowed Catarina to set up a school in the field shack on the days it was not in use as a store. Any children whose parents were willing to let them go could get instruction in letters, numbers and manners. Mostly the smallest children came. Anyone big enough to fill a one hundred pound sack of cotton and drag it to the weigh station worked.

In exchange for the privilege of holding class, Catarina helped Ito with the record keeping in the store. She accounted for inventory, compiled supply lists and guarded the cash box honestly.

At least one day a week, she washed and scrubbed chalk off the cinder block walls that served as a writing surface during lessons. Today, she took the time to draw a sketch of a man's face on the wall. With a few deft lines, she created a handsome, cruel face with eyes that looked directly at her. She whispered a breathy chant as she drew the figure. "I hate you. I hate you. I hate you. I hate you."

After stepping back to critique her work, she attacked the chore of cleaning the blocks with punches and slaps. She pretended she was grinding the wet towel into the face of her sometimes lover. In the beginning, she thought he was everything; she believed she loved him. The awakening of her young sensuality and the discovery of what a man could offer drew her deep into his clutches. When she discovered he was married, she tried to rid herself of him. But when she no longer went to him willingly, he changed. His advances were accompanied by vague threats against her and her family. Being with him grew into a sick, sucking quicksand she could not escape. Catarina felt she was living a nightmare.

Last night, he found her walking home alone. She hated that he seemed to know just how long she could go without sex and just how aggressive he needed to be to make her betray every promise she made to herself. This time, it had been months, and she berated herself for being so easily manipulated, so weak.

She took the dirty rag and mashed it into the mouth drawn on the blocks. She imagined stuffing it down his throat. His eyes bulged out and she could hear him as he started coughing, coughing, choking. She didn't stop because it felt so good. *Do it, just a little more!* Her fantasy evaporated when she heard someone behind her.

"Excuse me?"

Catarina whirled around. Although the murder of her cruel lover was committed only in her imagination, she felt as if someone actually caught her in the act. The pleasure she experienced was so real, she felt guilty. The stranger was a big imposing Anglo. Such a man intruding in the separate world of illegal workers could be a danger, for Catarina's life required anonymity, not notice.

This man was not dressed in a uniform, so he probably was not Border Patrol or police. Still, you never knew. Catarina stepped behind the bucket, kept the wet rag in her hand and slowly rotated her position to get herself closer to the door.

"I'm looking for the school." The stranger's size made the shack feel even smaller than it was; and his big voice reverberated off the low tin roof. Catarina pretended she spoke no English. That tactic was always the first line of defense. She shook her head to indicate she knew nothing.

"Mrs. García.....Señora García? I am supposed to meet her at the school."

At the mention of Señora Delores García's name, Catarina relaxed a bit. He was referring to the teacher that Father Garza had introduced to her. Delores was crushed at the waste of any human mind and especially distressed that a woman like Catarina de la Alvarado was working as a picker in a life that resembled nineteenth century slavery. Most people in America had no idea that this existed in 1964, one hundred years after the Civil War. It did; and it was a tough life with no promise.

Delores provided the chalk Catarina used to write on the cinderblock walls. Sometimes Delores taught the children herself. If no students showed up, she taught Catarina teaching technique. She was going to show Catarina how to get a student visa and help her pass college entrance exams. A dream was blooming; Catarina could see a possibility of doing what her heart told her she should do with her life, teach.

In spite of the way the man examined her, Catarina decided to speak. "Este es la escuela.....school." She opened her hands and indicated the four walls surrounding them. She watched his expression as he looked around. There were no desks, no chairs, no pencils, no paper, no books.

"I guess I expected more." He seemed apologetic. "I saw Mrs. García on television talking about a school for migrant children. I think she is raising money." The absence of understanding in Catarina's eyes told him there would be no conversation. "I'll wait."

Catarina's soft, dark eyes lingered on the man's startling blue ones. When she realized he noticed, she returned to washing the wall. She turned her back, but she could still smell him. He smelled of sunshine, vitality, physical confidence, and he was dressed as though he was going to the beach.

She cringed to think of what she must smell of, sweating from hauling the bucket of irrigation water to the field shack. Her clothes were abandoned things she found in the basement of the Catholic Church where migrants went to mass. She wore cotton pants, thin with wear and a white cotton over-shirt. Could he see through the loose weave? The touch of his stare felt as though he could.

She heard movement behind her. She felt him

pick up the other towel lying beside the bucket. He began to wash the wall at the far corner of the shack. He took care not to stand too close.

"No lave Las Mayas! Son para los niños." Catarina grabbed the rag away from him and spanked his hand with it. She repeated herself, "Las Mayas." She pointed to some faint etchings of yellow and white chalk on the grey cinder block. He stepped closer and tried to figure out what the drawings were. Catarina took a precious piece of chalk out of her pocket. She inserted herself between the man and the wall and began to redraw the parts of the figures he erased.

"This is Itzamna, the Father of Mayan Culture. He gave us calendars, medicine and chocolate." She flicked her eyes over her shoulder. "This is Chac, God of Rain and Thunder.....and.....this beautiful woman is Ix Chel, Goddess of the Moon and protector of women." Catarina smoothed a chalk line with her fingertips. "She tells us to take care of ourselves in the face of anything that hurts our sense of self." Catarina's English was accented, but perfect. She continued drawing. "The children need to know where they come from. Be proud. No?"

When she looked back at the stranger, she regretted it. She wished he hadn't smiled. In that instant her body recognized his appealing maleness. He was no longer an intruder with an over large voice who ruined her art work. She recognized the man, full of primal energy that reached out to the woman part of her. That part, which moments ago, she wished did not exist. Just seconds before he walked into the room, she vowed to put those urges away, never to acknowledge that side of being female again. What irony.

He stepped to another place on the wall and began to wash again. Catarina returned to the task as well. When his hand brushed hers, the jolt of electricity almost dropped her to her knees. He did not seem to notice.

She could not take her eyes off him. Stretching, washing. Thank God, the chances of never seeing him again were very good. She couldn't imagine why he was here in the first place or any reason why they would run into each other in the future.

A car slowed and pulled off the road next to the field store. "Mrs. García?" he asked.

"Sí." Catarina dipped her towel in the water and wrung it out.

"It's not nice to trick people into thinking you don't speak English," he said.

"You're scary."

"Humph."

Catarina followed him the few steps to the door and watched while Mrs. García walked around her car to the trunk and opened it. Her no-nonsense denim skirt swished around a broad beamed bottom as she struggled with something heavy. Case's long stride put him at her side in seconds. "Here, let me get that."

"Mr. Becker, I presume." Delores García was a short, round ball of welcoming energy. She turned to face the middle of his chest and had to look up another twelve inches to find his face. When she found his eyes, she laughed. "Well, look at you!"

"Can't help it. Just born this way." Case grinned and hefted a big box of books to rest under one arm while he closed the trunk with his other hand. They walked back to the shack together, and Catarina stepped out of the doorway to let them in.

"Oh, Catarina, you have met Case Becker." Delores's words fell on an awkward pause.

"We haven't been introduced.....he washed my Mayan drawings." Catarina's lowered gaze and fumbling words caused Mrs. García's eyebrows to rise into a question.

"Well, we can fix that. Señor Case Becker, this is Catarina de la Alvarado." The name rolled off her tongue in the Spanish way, Kah-tah-ree-nah. "She is the person behind the establishment of this new school. Catarina, this is Case Becker. He saw the television clip I did on your school for the news. He is interested in working with us, on reading improvement." Case shuffled his feet.

Catarina wondered why a man like this wanted to help migrant children learn to read. He looked like the type of gringo she knew protected the crops with guns at night from the organized hordes of bandidos that came across the river from Mexico. Crop robbers could strip a field bare long before dawn. They brought huge rubber rafts to float the ripe cantaloupe, watermelon and vegetables back across the border.

Gringo men and boys who enjoyed this kind of work were needed to "shoot them off" the farmer's property. Murder was not the objective. Protecting profits was a necessity.

When raiding activity was slow and boredom set in, the sharpshooters turned their attention to busting clay pots off the heads of Mexican women as they drew water from the Rio Grande to do their laundry. It was a nasty sport, too common an occurrence for the authorities to even acknowledge it as a crime.

Mrs. García clarified the immediate situation. "Mr. Becker needs some help overcoming a reading problem. You are going to see if you can figure out what can be done for him." It was as if a fire alarm went off in the little shack!

"No, Señora....." Catarina started.

Case dropped the box of books on the floor. "This was supposed to be confidential! I called you; you're the reading specialist!"

"No, Señora! I don't know what to do. I have a job.....and the school. He's.....he's.....por favor, I can't do this."

"Catarina, I'm already teaching twenty hours a week in overtime that I don't get paid for, plus the hours volunteering here. You say you want to be a teacher? Help people learn to read? Then do it!" She pointed at Case. Rowdy children started running through the door for class.

"Señora, this is not what I meant." Catarina was stunned. A little boy just tall enough to grab Catarina around the knees threw himself into her back side. She collapsed forward and Case automatically grabbed her outstretched hands to catch her. Another jolt of electricity! As soon as she caught her balance, she jerked away from his touch. She scolded the boy, "Cuidado Martin!"

Mrs. García took control of the room. "The kids are here. You two go outside and talk about this. Catarina, you are the smartest, most intuitive person I have ever met. You figured out how to educate yourself and if anyone can figure out this man's problem, you can." She turned to Case. "Señor Becker, what have you got to lose?" When there was no answer to her question, she physically pushed Catarina out the door. Case bent to pick up the bucket of dirty water and followed her. The little shack filled with children.

Once outside, Case walked to the lone tree struggling to survive in the heat. He slowly poured the water directly onto the roots of the suffering plant. He turned the bucket upside down and patted the bottom of it indicating that Catarina should sit down. She did not sit. He leaned against the tree and propped one foot against the trunk to support his weight.

"At least you are kind to plants." Catarina's sarcasm and distrust could not be missed. "What does intuitive mean?"

"It means you see things or maybe sense things that other people don't. Do you.....see things?" he asked.

She challenged him with her stance, her crossed arms, her chin in the air. "What's wrong with you?"

"I don't know. If you ask other people, I'm just lazy and don't give a shit."

"Do you.....give a shit?"

"I've spent a lot of time trying to make people think that I don't." Case looked at her scowling face, counted to ten and said, "Forget it! This was a stupid idea." He kicked the bucket against the wall of the field shack and stomped off to the monstrosity of a truck he was driving.

Catarina listened to the diesel engine belch, then roar to life. Case backed up briefly, shifted gears into forward and drove into his own dust to get away. It was strange to Catarina to meet a gringo this way, to see one as a person with a problem. People like this didn't have problems. They had power, comfort, an easy life. He probably was lazy. At least she wasn't going to have to deal with him. Still, she would empty her bucket of water on the roots of the tree from now on.

Catarina returned to the class and a disapproving look from Delores García. The two of them worked with the children until dinnertime. Today's lesson was about words that began with "M." Catarina helped little hands write on the wall, man, music, muscle, moon, maybe, more, map, Mexico. When it was time to quit, little fingers returned tiny pieces of left over chalk to a ragged cigar box.

"I see your conversation with Señor Becker was not successful." Delores García slammed the borrowed books back in the box.

"He doesn't want to learn. Even he says he is lazy. A man like that will probably be a beach bum for life anyway." Catarina tossed off Delores' displeasure with a shrug of her shoulders.

"A man like that," Delores parodied Catarina's words, "could get us books, supplies, money for this school. You've made a mistake." She was angry. "You think you don't need help? You're wrong. You've just blown your biggest chance to help these kids. I thought he might respond to a pretty, smart girl."

"What do you mean? Who is he?"

"Well, it doesn't matter now, does it?"

Chapter 2

Drowning

Case felt himself descending into an all too familiar state. He needed to escape the pressure of the decisions he would be forced to make soon. Human sharks with the taste of blood and profits in their mouths were after his family business. How could he make good decisions if he couldn't read the contracts? The failed attempt at contacting Mrs. García was his last feeble effort at reviving a long abandoned hope. His soul needed wind, sand, and water. The place to find them all was on South Padre Island.

His road trip was interrupted by a curious event; something was happening in Resaca Park. He slowed his brand new 1964 tow truck to watch from the highway through his open window. This was the park of the poor. The tropical oasis was nestled in the corner between the road and the waterway created when the Rio Grande River changed its course hundreds of years ago.

Barefoot children and Mexican women in faded dresses scrambled, deserting their Sunday afternoon leisure. They abandoned their picnics and ran through Resaca Park to hover at the place where the grass stopped growing and the water hyacinths floated, making an island of solid green leaves and profuse blue blossoms. If you didn't know, you would think that land extended far beyond the actual bank.

Case's instincts clicked in rapid deduction. It was a drowning.

Three men talked urgently in Spanish while they high stepped through the flowers. The water was up past their knees. They swished their arms back and forth and called someone's name, "Alberto!"

Two more men popped their heads out of the deeper water and gasped for breath. They screamed to each other in mixed languages, "No miro! I can't see!" Sounds of panic broke out among those on the bank.

Case spun his steering wheel to careen off the highway onto the lane that led into the little park. He shifted into four wheel drive, gunned the motor and ploughed the giant wrecker over every bush and mesquite tree less than five feet tall. Wood cracked, birds scattered and branches thunked against the protective grate on the front of the huge vehicle. The truck seemed to propel itself uncontrolled up to the brink of the water. Ripples lapped at the big tires as they sank into the spongy bank.

Case stepped out of his sandals as he dropped from the high cab. He stripped his yellow T-shirt off during the climb to the top of the truck's hood. From this height he could perform the shallow water dive that would take him past the hyacinth labyrinth. The hood bent and popped back into shape as the big man shot like an arrow through the air. The water barely

registered his smooth entry and his long body glided under the surface almost to the other side of the resaca.

The muddy water was stirred to blackness by the floundering rescuers. Case guessed visibility to be about an inch. He knew this water. This was the third time in two years he swam towards the pump that took water out of the resaca to irrigate adjacent fields of vegetables. The victim would be close to the sucking pump.

He surfaced and took a final breath before diving beneath the glassy black water. He had to be fast.....no time for feeling or thinking.....only reacting. He needed plenty of breath to investigate and maybe some oxygen left over to blow into the victim's mouth, if he was lucky. Case did not know how long the person they called Alberto had been under. He could feel the suction from the pump tugging at his shorts and legs. A man his size didn't have much to worry about, but a smaller person, a weaker swimmer, that was a different story.

Case sensed movement in the brown gloom. Yes, it was a body; and it was struggling. He wasn't too late! He grabbed the man around the neck and shoulder from behind as his life guard training dictated and pushed for the surface. A grip of steel was necessary to control the man's panicked flailing and prevent the rescuer from perishing along with the victim.

The resistance was no surprise, for Case had done this many times in these fresh waters, in swimming pools and in the salty Gulf of Mexico. If they had been in deeper water or farther from the bank, Case would have punched the man out to make him manageable. When they broke the surface, the man exploded with anger and accusation, not the panic or gratitude Case expected.

"Relax, Alberto, I've got you!" Case's voice was deep and commanding, designed to communicate calm control.

"No! No es mi! No es mi! Es un muchacho! Está muriendo!" The man who was *not* Alberto muscled his way free and delivered a fist to Case's nose just hard enough not to break it. The man took a rasping breath and disappeared back under the water.

Case shook stars out of his vision, checked his nose for blood and followed the man into the swirling mud. He saw the problem. There was a boy floating, much too still. The shredded strings of his cut off jeans were entangled in the pump mechanism. The man ripped the strings away from the pump and raised the boy into the sweet air he could no longer breathe. Case surfaced with them and watched the man pull Alberto to the bank. The boy's lips were tinged with blue. Now, Alberto's rescuer was working hard not to tip over the edge of panic.

From the opposite bank, a young mother screamed, "Alberto, mi Alberto! Dios! Dios! Mi Dios!" Friends and family restrained her when she tried to step into the hyacinths to splash her way to her son.

Case pulled himself through the thick cattails onto the bank. Mud tugged his feet when he pulled them from the water. Alberto's rescuer was trying to revive the boy by slapping his face. Case pushed the man away and rolled Alberto to lie on his back. He ignored the stinging insults spat at him in Spanish. He roughly compressed Alberto's ribs and forced air from his own mouth into the boy's still lungs. He listened for a heart beat. When he heard nothing, he pounded Alberto's chest with his fist and repeated rhythmic breathing and compression.

Alberto coughed water and began to cry the sounds of a frightened child. It was exactly what Case was looking for. He looked to give a "thumbs up" sign and a smile to the frantic mother on the other side. She ran around the low highway bridge to gather her son in her arms. She showered Alberto with both kisses and curses.

Case looked down to see muddy blood flowing from a cut on the side of his foot. He cursed vividly, addressing his foot and some unnamed careless bastard. Case was glad the Mexican man still standing beside him could not understand a word he said. He stank of silty mud and decaying vegetation. They both did.

Case slipped in wet grass when he walked down the bank to a huge willow tree. Against all odds, the tree grew horizontally, straight from the side of the bank. Its massive trunk hung inches above the water as far as fifteen feet out. He scrambled onto the trunk to rinse his feet and legs in the resaca.

Life teemed in the heat around him. Perch nibbled at his leg hair, wild parrots carried on a lively conversation, cicadas hummed. Even algae thrived, bright lime colored and alive. He felt the sensation of rough bark cutting into the backs of his thighs. Case always noticed life with such acuteness when some of it came close to slipping away.

"You saved Alberto." The words were heavily accented in Spanish.

Case shook his head at his own assumption that the man couldn't speak English. "No, *you* saved Alberto."

"I didn't know how to make him breathe. You did." The man's admiration and curiosity was apparent.

The man walked around the cattails and crossed the grass to join Case on the tree. The trunk sank a little closer to the water when he sat down. In silence, each bathed their slimy legs with their hands and tried to get the mud from underneath their fingernails. The morning sweltered. The bugs attacked. The life energy of the place slowed back to normal.

"I want to learn to make people breathe."

"You want to learn how to make people breathe." Case repeated the question, delaying the request he knew would come next.

"Sí. I want you to teach me."

Case rebelled internally. Getting involved with the families of people he saved or lost just wasn't a good idea for him. He preferred to keep his distance. All the tears, all the gratitude, all the fawning over him. It made him feel obligated to continue relationships he didn't want. He had to protect himself from that.

"Mi familia, mis amigos, we swim the Rio Grande sometimes. You know, for work."

A sideways glance told Case that the man was checking his reaction to the announcement that all these people were illegal workers. It was something that happened every day, but no one admitted it unnecessarily.

Case considered the man sitting beside him. He had been valiant today. He was strong enough to punch Case in the nose and slip away. He was brave enough to ask for help from someone who might report him to immigration, someone who clearly did not want to get involved.

What the hell, it would be a one time thing. Case swished his legs in the water in a circle of hesitant resignation. He waited a moment longer just to make this stranger wonder what the answer would be.

"OK. But I'm not touching you without a shower and shampoo." Case pointed to the sticky mud clinging to the man's legs and a bristling weed resting on top of his head. Case was punished with a broad smile from his new student. *Shit.* Case heard his personal "no involvement rule" crack under the charm of the stranger and was certain he would be sorry in the long run.

"Come to la casa de mi Abuelita, my grandmother. Mañana, at dinner time. She will pay you for the lesson with a feast. Tamales, bueno?" He spoke with the blended vocabulary that was common between browns and whites on the Texas border.

"No, no payment. I'll teach you because I think you can do it. I think you will be good at it, and someone will live if you know what to do. That's the payment." Case extended his hand to seal the agreement. "Adios." He came to his feet and the sway of the tree trunk challenged his balance. He stepped around his companion, jumped to the bank and walked around the highway bridge to his tow truck on the other side of the resaca.

The man raised his voice trying to reach Case for he was speaking to Case's back. "El Camino Ratama. The pink house. A las seis? My name is Sixto, Sixto Terrazos!" He waited for Case to return the courtesy and announce his name. Case never looked back to acknowledge Sixto. He didn't respond to the following words either.

"I guess your name is 'Gringo'!"

When Case reached his truck, he paused only to pick up his sandals and shirt. He slammed the door when he got in and turned the ignition. His vision clouded with the white mist of anger. He was through screwing with the bureaucracy of the local water district. Next week he was getting signs made to post at this pump site and every one like it in three counties. English and Spanish.

Those do-nothing jackasses on the district board had almost cost another life today. They couldn't get past bureaucracy to make a decision even when it was not going to cost them a dime. Case was personally funding the entire safety program. Because he was having difficulty completing the written paperwork necessary to place the proposal in front of the board, they wouldn't give him the time of day. If he got arrested for trespassing by putting up warning signs without permission, then so be it.

The decision made him feel better. His shoulders relaxed and he shifted the gears of the truck into reverse. He grimaced at the destruction of the park's landscaping when he backed across the rutted grass. The damage wouldn't be as bad as it looked in the long run. In the subtropics of the Rio Grande Valley, the grass would grow back in a couple of days. Those smashed banana trees would start popping new shoots in a week. He would send someone out to prune the rest of the trees he knocked down. Problem solved;

decision made. Too bad the other problem that plagued him was not so easily solved.

He returned to the highway that would lead him to the island. The water would relax him, clear his tangled mind, for a while. He hoped. The drive took exactly thirty three minutes if he obeyed the speed limits. The closer he got to the smell of salt water, the more he could feel its anticipated offer of peace.

Case had always managed to misdirect people with irresponsibility, humor and expert diversion tactics. He had been labeled everything from lazy to incorrigible. The truth was his secret. There was something wrong with him. No one ever knew but Case, before today.

He took a left onto State Highway 100. It was a symbolic turn towards his favorite place in the universe. It was time to let go of all the angers that plagued him.

In minutes, he reached the little fishing town of Port Isabel. The swing barge bridge to the island was open to boat traffic. A line of six cars waited for a shrimp boat to pass. It chugged slowly through the channel, riding low in the water with a big catch. Case took his place in line and waited. A grizzled captain doffed his sweat stained hat. The barge operator took his time reconnecting the bridge and finally, the line of cars rolled over the clackety swing section onto the longer bridge that actually spanned Laguna Madre. No one here was in a hurry. Case liked it that way.

He breathed in the salt air, checked the bay for white caps topping the surface of the water and looked for dolphin. It was windy enough to make for an exciting sail today. When he reached the island, he turned left on Padre Boulevard, one of the island's three streets, and headed for Skipper's Water Craft Rentals.

Gravel in the parking lot crunched under the truck's tires. Case left the keys in the ignition in case Skipper needed to move it while he was gone. A twenty-one foot catamaran rested in the sand, rigged and ready. Case trusted his friendship with Skipper would survive the act of piracy he was about to commit.

It took Case just under three minutes to fasten himself into a butt bucket and launch the sail boat. He was strong enough to slide the boat down the sand beach and into the Laguna Madre by himself. As the double hulls of the sleek craft glided into the bay, Skipper scrambled out of his shop.

"No! No! Case, you can't have it today! It's rented! Got a family gonna' be here in less than fifteen minutes! Hey, Case!"

Case stood on the transom, legs apart, salt spray wetting his tanned skin. He had the skills and presence of a Viking; and in his experienced hands, the main sail was already catching the breeze. The Hoby Cat gathered speed rapidly, as it was designed to do. Case attached his harness to the lines. The mainsail popped as it billowed, and one of the hulls rose in slow motion, tilting the mast deep into the wind. Case swung his body out over the water balancing the weight of the mast and allowing the other hull to skim like a razor through the water.

Skipper's bald head gleamed in the sun when he threw his Captain's hat in the sand and stomped on it. Case could read the impotent curse on Skipper's lips, "Dammit, Becker!"

* * * * *

Abuelita put every inch of her yard into flower production. There were roses of every color, gardenias, carnations, baby's breath and every conceivable flower that could be used in a funeral arrangement. She sold what she could to a local florist and enjoyed the rest. The tiny woman was invisible, working hunched under the giant sunflower stalks.

Catarina stormed through the garden gate, leaving it swinging and roughly banged the screen door to the house. It was an unmistakable announcement of her state of mind. Abuelita popped her head from under the heavy sunflower buds. Her straw hat was unraveling on one side and her hands were full of fresh plucked weeds.

"Catarina! What's the matter with you? What happened?" She dropped the weeds, closed the gate to the chain link fence and followed her granddaughter inside.

Abuelita stepped around a trail of discarded clothes from the front door to the bedroom. Catarina had striped to her underwear and thrown herself across the bed trying to cool off. Her temper was as hot as the weather. A little electric fan oscillated over her feverish skin.

"How am I supposed to work for Ito, set up a school, go to school and teach a lazy gringo how to read? This is not going to get me any closer to college! I won't do it."

Abuelita shook her head and opened her hands indicating she did not understand. "Today, Señora

García told me that if I wanted to be a teacher, I should try to teach this.....this man to read. He's a man for God's sake. He's got to be almost thirty years old and hasn't learned yet!"

Abuelita sat on the edge of the creaking bed next to Catarina and stroked her heavy, wavy hair. "Catarina, there is a reason you have been asked to do this. Remember, the strong must help the weak. This man, he asked for help?"

Catarina's exasperated answer was muffled by her pillow. "Sí, but he doesn't really want it."

"Ah, that is why Señora García chose you. He might listen to a pretty girl. Hmmm, is he handsome?" Catarina raised her head to look at her grandmother with disgust. "Well, you'll have to get over that little problem. And, I have to get back to the flowers. No one buys roses with bugs on them. Hurry, you need to help me prepare tamales for tomorrow night. We have to be ready when everyone arrives." Abuelita left the room, hiding a tiny, private smile breaking the corner of her mouth. From the kitchen she called out, "You should look pretty tomorrow night! Sixto has invited a guest!"

Chapter 3

Teaching CPR

El Camino Ratama was a dirt road just outside the reach of community zoning laws. Someone put up a hand painted sign that resembled the town's official ones. The street led to a neighborhood of tiny ramshackle houses where dogs, chickens and children ran loose. The nicest house had a leaning chain link fence surrounding the lot. A tall Mexican fan palm stood like a sentry at each corner. Together, the fence and the palms marked an oasis in the dust. It was filled with lovingly tended hibiscus, bougainvillea, gardenia, roses and sunflowers. The house was very pink.

Case knocked at the loose screen door. He planned on spending an hour showing Sixto the basics of CPR and making his excuses before dinner. He was truly irritated with himself for caving in so easily to this request. He thought about not showing up, but hell, he had no other plans tonight. So, here he was.

From the number of different voices he heard inside, he wondered how many people could live in 800 square feet. He was surprised by who rushed to the door to greet him. Three wild young boys bounced off the walls of a narrow entrance way. One of them announced, "Es El Gringo!" Case recognized Alberto. Instead of stepping back to make room for Case to enter, it seemed they pressed forward with eagerness only enjoyed by the very young. Sixto appeared behind the boys and elbowed his way to the door.

"We call them Los Lobos." He explained. On cue, the boys howled like wolves. A Chihuahua joined the song. He put so much energy into his bark that his little feet left the ground with every yap.

"Is Alberto your son?"

"No. He is my best friend. Right, Alberto?" Sixto gave a wolf howl of his own.

Just when Case found room to make his move to squeeze into the house, more people filled the hallway. The faces looked familiar and by the time he made it to the living room, he began to recognize many of these people from Sunday afternoon at the park. Their faces looked different with smiles on them.

Alberto shoved his pet box turtle in the air for Case to greet. He then came eye to eye with a Scarlet Macaw who introduced herself as Lola. Lola sat on a high rack attached to her owner's back. The homemade contraption that rested on his shoulders was decorated with well-chewed bird toys and hastily wiped bird droppings. Case shook the man's hand.

María Sanchez, Alberto's mother, tearfully thanked him over and over for rescuing her son. They were all so glad to see him. This was exactly what

Case hated, a party in his honor for doing something that anyone would do. Saving a life was not a conscious act of bravery. It was just a reaction, undeserving of such hullabaloo. How would he endure this?

That was when he saw Catarina de la Alvarado floating through the sea of faces with the grace of a ghost. She carried a cake. It had blue roses made of icing covering the top and circling the bottom. The single candle was a sparkler left over from some Cinco de Mayo past. Someone turned off the lights and Catarina started singing Las Mañanitas, the traditional birthday song. The glow from flying bits of light framed a snapshot of her face that would remain in Case's mind the rest of his life. Whenever he thought of her she would be floating in a golden halo of ethereal sparks just like this.

Catarina placed the fiery cake in front of an older woman. The sparkler sputtered out. The light flipped on again and eighteen people plus the ones hanging out the back door into the yard shouted, "Abuelita! Feliz Cumpleaños! Speech, speech!"

Case felt foolish. The party was not for him.

Small, lovely and brown, Abuelita curtsied and held up her hand to silence her subjects. "I declare we will eat the cake now, before dinner. Life is short. Dessert must come first!" The children cheered; the adults laughed and Case saw Catarina shake her head in adoring disapproval. Catarina must not believe in the "dessert first" philosophy. Case did. This little Abuelita was his kind of woman!

When Catarina turned to take the cake back to the kitchen, her brown eyes discovered Case's blue ones. He could see how unprepared she was for his presence. She registered recognition and did not look away at first. Just as when he had seen those eyes in the field store, he held them until she blushed. She looked away before he did and Case felt as if he had won some undeclared battle. Her graceful movements were gone. She bumped into a chair and did a dance of confusion with the people between the living area and the kitchen door.

Without taking his eyes off her, Case asked Sixto, "Isn't her name Catarina?"

"Sí."

"Is she your girlfriend?"

"You know her?" Sixto was surprised.

"Well, I don't know her. We met Sunday at that school she's starting." Case felt himself changing his mind about yesterday's events. Maybe he should convince this woman to work with him after all. He'd suspected there was something glorious under those old pants and shirt. He remembered the sparks that flew when they touched. But, he had no idea her body was this curvy, her skin this beautiful. He noticed his breathing was going shallow.

Sixto noticed it too. "Gringo, before you teach me to save people, I must teach you to keep your hands off my sister." Case flashed a smile at the news Catarina was Sixto's sister. Then he took a look at Sixto to see if the "hands off declaration" was a serious one, and what he saw did not reassure him.

The birthday cake was a cake of tres leches, three milks. It was a concoction of whole milk, heavy cream and boiled, sweetened concentrate. There was a little piece for everyone. The sugar roses and icing trim

27

stained everyone's teeth and lips blue. Alberto was the first to notice it on his friends. He looked closer in curiosity before he pointed and shrieked! In an instant, realization halted his giggles. He ran to the open bathroom door to look in the mirror. He shrieked again.

Alberto's friends crowded into the bathroom to fight for mirror space. Three blue tongues waggled between three sets of blue teeth. Los Lobos thought it was exciting. The adults caught on to the situation. The men roared, "Los dientes azules!" as they pointed at each other. The women covered their mouths in embarrassment.

Case's first bite was poised in front of his mouth. He carefully scraped the icing to the side of the plate and put the remaining cake into his mouth. He swallowed it whole, taking care that it did not touch anything but the back of his throat. Catarina grabbed her purse to get her mirror. She frantically started scrubbing her teeth with a paper napkin. She looked in the mirror again. Blue. Case smothered a laugh. She fought Los Lobos for the bathroom to brush her teeth. The toothpaste helped a little.

Dinner was wonderful. The crowd moved to tables set up in the back yard. The trees and shrubs were strung with colored Christmas lights. There were platters of succulent barbacoa, mangos, tomatoes, papaya, arroz con pollo, sweet leche que mada, grilled peppers, enchiladas. But, nothing surpassed the tamales. Abuelita's pride in her recipe would not let anyone else make them, so she made them herself for her own birthday party. Those who did not get in line quickly enough to get a plate ate from their hands. Licking their fingers was a treat.

There was one birthday gift from the whole group of family and friends. It was a ceramic cookie jar in the shape of cartoonish cow. Case thought it looked like some of the things his own grandmother had in the attic saved from the Great Depression. Ugly.

Once Abuelita opened the gift, the cow was passed around for everyone who could to drop spare money into its belly. From the clinking sound of the coins, no one had very much. Case slipped the ten dollar bill he held in his hand back into his pocket and searched for coins. His insides cringed at the thought of how conspicuous he would have been. Now seemed like a good time to go back to his truck for the equipment he needed to teach Sixto Cardiopulmonary Resuscitation.

He rounded the front of the house just as a Border Patrol unit cruised slowly by. Case knew the driver, Logan Dell. He was a local hard-ass bully turned law enforcement officer. His childhood playground behavior followed him into adulthood, and the man's reputation for abuse of his power was as nasty as any in The Valley. Logan pointed through his open window at someone standing inside Abuelita's front door. Case overheard Logan's words.

"I'll collect for this later."

Case craned his neck to see who was in the doorway. There was no one. Even gringos knew about the practice of "mordida." It was pay off money for looking the other way. Whoever owed something to Logan Dell had already disappeared.

When Case returned to the back yard, he found the crowd had grown. Sixto was standing in the middle of a circle of humanity making an announcement. Case spoke just enough Spanish to understand most of what Sixto said.

"Sunday afternoon, God gave us a miracle. He gave us back the life of Alberto Sanchez. He knew that we could not live without him. God did this miracle through a servant whose name we do not know, este gringo." He indicated Case. "I have asked him to show us how to make people breathe, like he did for Alberto. He has agreed to do this."

Case's mind raced through the facts. His informal lesson with Sixto had been publicized and turned into a neighborhood event. Although he was certified to teach CPR, he hated speaking before big groups. The rescue was medical science, not a miracle. These people all spoke Spanish. How did this all happen? The only good thing that could come out of doing this was the possibility of getting his lips on Catarina de la Alvarado. Sometimes he was amused at his single mindedness.

He leaned to Sixto's ear and spoke out of the side of his mouth. "What the hell is this? I told you I would teach you, not the neighborhood."

"They need to know this thing. We all cross over the border through the waters of the Rio Grande, to work. Sometimes there are floods, accidents. We need to know how to do this. Por favor." Sixto smiled at the gathering and nodded his head in assurance.

Case sighed and resigned himself. He was trapped. "OK. My Spanish is not good enough for this. You have to interpret."

"Sí, sí. No problema." Sixto stepped aside and Case became the center of attention.

"My name is Case Becker." Case nodded his head to blank faces. He hesitated while he evaluated the crowd and decided to change his tactics. He raised his eyebrows and said, "Gringo es mejor, sí? My name is 'Gringo.'" He nodded his head and the faces reacted. Yes, that was better. "Alberto, where are you? Come help me." A grinning Alberto materialized in front of Case. He still wore the ragged cut off jeans that had been tangled in the pump. Case reached into his pocket for his knife.

"I want to show every one what happened to Alberto. See these strings on Alberto's pants? This is bad, malo. They caught on the pump and held him under water. Alberto, you are a strong boy, right?" Alberto flexed his muscles in agreement. Case grabbed the strings. "Try to get away from me," Case instructed. Alberto pulled and twisted against the vice of Case's grip to no avail. When Case thought he had made his point, he cut the taut strings with his knife and let Alberto fall to the ground. Everyone laughed. "Don't wear things that can get caught and hold you under water."

Case dropped to one knee to move his repeat victim into position. He demonstrated how to check the neck for a pulse, how to position the body, clear the airway, and compress the chest. Next he needed to demonstrate how to blow air into a victim's lungs. When Alberto saw Case's open mouth coming towards his lips, he squeaked and wriggled to his feet.

"Aw, com'on Alberto, I'm not going to kiss you!"

"Yes you are!" Alberto took two steps back.

"You ever kissed a girl?" Case asked.

31

Alberto slowly scoped the room before confessing with pride, "Yes, I have kissed a girl."

"Then you will be able to tell what we are about to do is not a kiss. It won't feel like a kiss at all. I am going to blow air into your lungs. Then you have to tell everyone what it feels like. I already did it to you yesterday." Case beckoned for Alberto to come back.

With great reluctance, Alberto lay back down on the grass and allowed the demonstration to continue. As Case's body loomed over him again, Alberto turned his face to the audience and yelled, "It's not a kiss! No es un beso." He squenched his eyes, stiffened and waited.

Case had to laugh. "Relax, pretend you are unconscious; you won't feel a thing." With that, Case covered Alberto's mouth and a powerful surge of air from his lungs flowed through Alberto's chest.

Alberto coughed. "I can feel it! It works! It's his breath in me!" The crowd murmured approval and leaned in to hear the details regarding how many breaths to give in between pumping the chest.

"Now I want to make sure everyone gets to see what this feels like for themselves, as a rescuer and as a victim. Find someone you are comfortable with and I will take you through the demonstration again."

After extensive negotiation, the only people ready to go forward were married couples. No one would look at Case. Public physical contact of this kind was not acceptable in their culture.

"I was afraid you might feel this way, so lucky for you, my girlfriend, Lucy was able to come with me tonight. She will kiss anybody! 'Lu-cy, you got some 'splainin' to do!'" Case reached into his duffel bag and brought out a dummy of the upper torso of a life sized human. Its face had no features except for an open mouth. Its chest was open to expose plastic lungs that could expand and contract in a CPR demonstration.

For fun, Case dressed Lucy in a long red wig. He caressed her nylon tresses, did a couple of dance steps and dipped her backwards in a tango move. He kissed her vigorously. The antics were unexpected enough to make the nervous students laugh out loud. The atmosphere in the back yard was a little less tense and seriousness changed to play. Lucy was really great with crowds. Case prayed he could get the shadows of any blue icing stains off her face since the United States Coast Guard was unaware of Lucy's secret rendezvous tonight.

So this was Sixto's gringo, Catarina thought. The man she insulted yesterday afternoon was the man who saved Alberto's life yesterday evening. Catarina decided to clean up in the kitchen rather than watch a big clown with blue eyes demonstrating mouth to mouth resuscitation. Why she couldn't keep herself from peeking out the back door and over María's shoulder when Case mentioned a girlfriend, she would never know. It annoyed Catarina when she experienced relief that the red-haired hussy she saw enjoying Case's kisses was not a real woman.

María Sanchez twisted a lock of her hair and dreamily whispered to Catarina. "He has the body of a warrior and the lips of a poet."

"Shut up." Catarina's angry retort surprised them both.

Cleaning the kitchen didn't take long. María was anxious to join the fun in the back yard. Catarina stretched the work out as long as she could. She lingered to polish the sink, rearranged the spices. It was a mystery to her when she wandered to the bathroom to arrange her hair. She noticed her teeth were back to their normal color.

Now, there was nothing else to do but follow María into the yard. She assessed herself in the mirror and thought she looked blah. I'll just watch, she instructed herself. She didn't want El Gringo touching her.

Case was stepping over bodies, going from couple to couple. He repositioned "victim's" heads to maximize air flow. He demonstrated the correct amount of pressure and rhythm to use when compressing the chest. He waited for one girl to get over a ticklish spell. Someone took a deep breath and choked on a mosquito.

Catarina watched from the porch steps as El Gringo endured the display of twittering embarrassment. Some were so shy they wouldn't even touch Lucy. Catarina noted Case's deliberate patience. No one else could see his exasperation with all the silliness, but she could. Everyone seemed to crave his attention. He knew exactly when to correct and when to reward efforts.

El Gringo spent extra time with Sixto and three others who were serious. By the end of the evening, these men would be able to make a difference some dark night in the water.

They saw El Gringo as a hero, someone bigger than life. Catarina observed something different, a man with a vulnerability. However unintentional, he shared a secret with her, a secret he took great care to hide from everyone else in his world. The knowledge softened her. She watched him.

She wondered if he was purposefully ignoring her because of the secret or because she was of no interest to him. Usually, she knew exactly what men were thinking about her. Surely she wasn't the only one aware of the electric current snapping between them. As the evening came to an end without his speaking to her, she felt a distinct sting of disappointment.

After El Gringo answered all the questions he could, he felt his promise to Sixto to help people breathe had been generously fulfilled.

It was completely dark. Children had to be found and sorted. The neighborhood echoed with friends calling to each other, "Buenas noches, good night." Abuelita's chatter with Sixto drifted from the kitchen. Dishes rattled as he put them in a cupboard too high for her to reach.

Only Case, Catarina and Alberto remained in the yard. Alberto was looking at a pamphlet on CPR. It was written in English.

"What does this word mean?" Alberto extended the booklet for Case to see. Catarina noticed he didn't even look at the paper.

"I'm busy with Lucy here. Got to get her home before her parents know she went out on a date without permission. Ask Catarina."

Alberto didn't get the joke but Catarina did. She was actually delighted to know that Case knew she was alive!

"Catarina, what's this word?" Alberto asked.

She carefully spelled it aloud. "c-a-p-s-i-z-e-d. kahp-seez-ed?" Her accent affected the pronunciation.

"Capsized; it means your boat sank. You know, went under the water," Case explained. "If you didn't learn to swim and your boat capsized, someone better know CPR." He reached out to ruffle Alberto's hair in affection.

Catarina swallowed a catch in her throat. Now that the CPR demonstration was over and the opportunity was gone, she wondered what El Gringo's touch would feel like. She *wanted* to know. "Alberto, you better get home. Your mother will be worried. Vamanos."

"Can I keep this?" He held up the pamphlet.

"Sure you can." Case unzipped his duffel bag to tuck in a wisp of red wig. He slung the bag over his shoulder. Alberto gave Catarina a goodbye hug and ran to the edge of the yard. He turned abruptly and ran back to fling his arms around Case. Alberto said nothing, just squeezed as tight as little boy arms could. Then he was gone. Case adjusted his duffel.

"I will walk with you," Catarina began. There was no protest, so she fell into step beside him. She felt small. He held the bushes back to make way for her to pass around the side of the house. "You helped my family tonight. If you still want my help, I'll do it."

"Tonight was a lot more than I bargained for." Case said.

"That Sixto." She laughed a musical laugh. "He can over-do things. You still want to work with me?"

"I don't think it's going to make a difference."

"It might. You knew what capsized meant."

"Yeah, but you had to read it. Sometimes I think maybe letters don't look the same to me as they do to other people."

Catarina considered the man and encouraged him. "I believe you want to do this."

"I have to." He threw his bag in the truck.

"Who is making you?"

Case grunted and shrugged, "No one."

It occurred to Catarina that she and this gringo had something in common after all, an inner drive to do something no one else thought you could do. She knew this was the moment for her to decide. "At Resaca Park, tomorrow, at six. Bring lots of paper and pencils, for the school."

"Sure." He got inside and slammed the door to the truck. Now there was a metal barrier between them. Finally, finally, he looked at her. "I'm sorry I ignored you tonight. I didn't really know how to handle seeing you."

His meaningful stare and his words arrested her. She struggled to come up with something to say. The best she could do was, "I'm sorry about yesterday. I didn't really know how to handle seeing you either." They broke into simultaneous smiles. It was a truce.

"Can I ask you something?" Case began carefully.

"Sí."

"You don't seem like the kind of person I would expect. Your English is good; you are a teacher; why are you working picking fruit?"

Even though she had given her permission, the question felt blunt and intrusive. "I am not an

American citizen. I come from a poor family. We have to work."

"How did you learn?"

"Everything I am, all the good parts, anyway, come from mi Abuelita. She taught me. I am curious; I don't know; it is so easy for me. Maybe it's like Señora García says, intuitive."

The screen on the front door squeaked, and Case looked up to see Abuelita and Sixto making their way through the flowers. Abuelita carried a dozen of her tamales wrapped in newspapers.

"Muchas gracias. You are a blessing." She handed him the gift through his open window. She covered his huge hand with her tiny one as he accepted her offering.

Case responded simply, "Adios." As he drove away, Sixto's words followed him.

"Adios mi amigo! Go with God my friend. You will find us if we need you!"

* * * * *

Catarina went to bed that night feeling more alive than she had in ages. The energy kept her awake. Images of the evening swirled in her head. She smiled remembering the shock of seeing El Gringo at the party. She pictured him dancing with Lucy, pictured the strength in his arms as they cradled the nervous victims to lie in the grass. In her mind's eye, she watched him clown with the kids and shake Sixto's hand in friendship.

Her grandmother called him "un benedictión," a blessing. What a thought. What did Sixto mean when he said, "You will find us when we need you?" That was strange.

It was easy for her to sense the ways of men. After their private conversation, she knew one thing. She could have this gringo if she wanted him. But, she wouldn't. The man she chose needed to be of Mexican descent, more familiar, more predictable. Her only physical affair was a horrifying venture into the Anglo world. She would never let it happen again. Working with this gringo would be a means to an end, some supplies for the school. It was going to be brief, but interesting. She would make the best of it.

Catarina started going over the things El Gringo said that might give her a clue as to why he couldn't grab the words off a page and put them in his mind. Eventually, she calmed and drifted into the first shallow stages of sleep. She sensed a warrior's body hovering over her bed. He had blue, blue eyes and poet's lips that made an otherwise rugged face pretty.

Chapter 4

First Lesson

The next morning, Case woke to awareness that he had been missing something in life lately. The feeling grew from a vague sensation to clear, raging lust for Catarina de la Alvarado. He couldn't remember the last time he wanted a woman like this. It felt good. He closed his eyes and let himself savor the hunger. *Wow! I need some of that!*

He eased into a morning ritual that started while he was still in between the sheets. He stretched his arms over his head towards one corner of the bed and extended his legs to hang off the opposite corner. He brought the heels of his palms to rub the sleep from his eyes. His hands traveled down his chest and stomach, waking every inch of his skin. He reached his groin and rearranged his male parts. He stretched again. He wondered if Catarina slept in the nude. *Probably not!*

He looked at the alarm clock. He never set it; there was no need. He simply decided the night before what time he wanted to wake. His body clock did the rest. It was seven a.m., eleven hours until he saw Catarina again.

Case's house was modest; he kept it clean. He didn't need much because he didn't stay there much. It was simply shelter to him. His living room furniture consisted of all the necessities of outdoor life - surfboard, sleeping bag, scuba tanks and his extensive collection of salt water fishing tackle. There was an extra drift anchor for a bay boat, just in case some friend needed one. Last time a woman was here, it was his mother. She sat on a case of marine motor oil and asked him, "How's your love life?"

For Case, planning his day usually meant brushing his teeth and waiting for an emergency. He loved being in places where he did not feel confined by thought. He liked to feel a good adrenaline pop. The chemical would surge through his veins and he would react. It was what people admired about him and what scared them to death. It was what made Case watch his drinking. He wasn't a mean man, but he didn't like to loose control.

He remembered that he promised Catarina he would bring school supplies and his thoughts turned to the people he met last night - the uncles, cousins and neighbors of Sixto Terrazos. Case felt the tug of an unexpected connection. He always knew that there was a separate society living next door, an underworld of poverty and powerlessness. He got to see it up close for the first time, at the field shack and in Abuelita's back yard. He knew himself and his tendency to care too much. Caring about these people could be a costly hobby. He would have to be careful with Catarina too.

She might be different, educated, but she was still part of a world he knew little about.

* * * * *

Case arrived at Resaca Park early. He identified the picnic table with the most shade and the least bird poop. He washed it down with a gallon of water he brought in a milk jug. He dried the table with one of the old beach towels he kept behind the seat in the truck and set out mosquito repellant. Then he retrieved the box of school supplies and reminded himself that this meeting was not a date.

Case hadn't really dated in a long time. The girls he took out as a younger man tired of waiting on him, married others, got divorced and were back on the market again. He was starting to get occasional phone calls. If he wanted to settle down, a couple of them were actual possibilities. What would his family think if they knew he was falling for a beautiful, smart, illegal alien fruit picker instead. Maybe she wouldn't show up. He settled against the table to watch some turtles bask on a rotting log.

"Hola, Gringo!"

The voice behind him was the voice Case was waiting to hear. It did make his heart skip a beat. He looked over his shoulder and saw her. *I wish this was a date.* She must have gone home to clean up after work. She looked fresh, soft, touchable. Her hair was pulled back into a ponytail. Her sleeveless shirt showed creamy coco colored shoulders he had not seen before.

"Hey. I cleaned up a table for us." The hair on Case's legs raised a bit as Catarina chose to sit beside him on the bench instead of across the table. "It's hot! Can we pick a place with air conditioning next time?" He lifted the front of his T-shirt away from his skin and fanned the fabric.

"Sissy," she called him. "We need to meet some place open, proper. This is as good as any. Are these mine?" Catarina looked inside the box of supplies.

"Yeah. You didn't say what to get, so I stuck to the basics."

There were pencils, a sharpener, chalk, crayons, notebooks and enough paper to last a year. "So much! Thank you!" Her fingers caressed the items one by one. "You are generous."

She called him generous! Case flushed and stammered. "Uh, it's nothing. A lot of it was in the closet at my office."

"You keep crayons at work?"

"Well, no, I bought those....." His sentence trailed off, for she was absolutely radiant and he felt like it was the first time he ever talked to a girl.

Catarina opened a package of paper and tested a pencil. "I've been thinking, and I may have an answer to your question."

"What?" Case felt himself jerked back into the moment.

She printed the word "capsized" on the paper and passed it to Case. "Copy that," she commanded. "Not like letters, like art. I want to see what you see."

Case flushed again. There went his budding romantic fantasy! She was all business and pressuring him from the start. All his negative feelings about himself rose like bile to this throat. The familiar emotions of resentment, shame and anger tasted bad. He snatched the paper, picked up the pencil and painstakingly started copying the word. He gripped the pencil so tightly, his knuckles were white. He wrote so hard the table wiggled under his efforts. Concentration clouded his face. He tossed the paper back at Catarina. The scratching looked like, "ooq ziz od."

In the most matter of fact tone, Catarina announced, "You're right. You don't see what other people see."

Case's tension exploded! He slapped the table so hard it made Catarina jump back. The bile in his throat retreated and his eyes stung. "I knew it! I just knew it! Why is this?"

"I don't know why. Why do you have blue eyes and I have brown ones.....God made it so."

Case stared at the paper. "No one has ever believed me. Now, at least I can quit trying so hard."

"Quit? Oh, no." Catarina was challenged. "If God made you like this, it can't be a bad thing. Let's work together some and see what happens."

"You will be disappointed, Catarina. Need me to pull you out of the river? Sail you to the Yucatan Peninsula? Kill a shark? I'm your man." Case leaned back from the table. With his chest out, he struck an unconscious pose to let her see how virile he was.

"I know it's your 'thing'; but I don't need saving."

Was that disdain in her voice? Case felt a little power struggle begin. He said nothing, letting her win because he desperately needed to sit beside her.

They stayed in the park until dusk. They devised a system of communication that developed into a cadence of rapid exchange between the two of them. They discovered that Case could usually get the word when Catarina verbally spelled it rather than his looking at it on paper. They practiced on the names of the living things in the park around them. "B-a-n-a-n-a."

"Banana!" Case said.

"C-a-t-t-a-i-l-s."

"Cattails!"

"H-i-g-h-w-a-y."

"Highway."

They graduated to words that Case told her he needed to recognize: maintenance, bank account, profit. Together, they started making a list of words written the way they appeared to Case so he could recognize them in the future. Case began to sense there was possibility behind the veil of twisted, garbled scratchings in books.

When the study session was over and Catarina started stacking papers, Case stopped her. "Wait, let's watch the sunset."

"I don't have time for things like that. I've got to go."

"Everyone has time for the most beautiful event on earth." Case grabbed her arm with one hand and gently put her elbow on the table. He reached for the back of her head with his other hand, tenderly forced her to put her chin on her fist and turned her head towards the west. She watched the glowing colors while Case watched her. He began to wonder about her, as a person. "How did you figure this out for me when no one else could?"

"I guess I just look at the world a little differently. You live in a world where everybody can read. I live in one where almost no one can. After that, it's about listening and using imagination. I know there's always a reason. Sometimes, it's simple; you just have to look for it."

"You're smart."

"Maybe, we'll see when I get to college." A look of doubt crossed Case's face. It seemed to make Catarina a little defensive. "Señora García is helping me get a visa. I'm going to college; then I'll become a U.S. citizen and then I'll teach for real. Make a difference for people like me."

"It takes seven years to be a citizen." Case looked at Catarina's hands. They were a fieldworker's hands. Tiny lines of permanent grime were embedded under the delicate nails and around her cuticles. Little nicks and scratches scattered up to her elbows. He knew she didn't have any money for school. He wondered if she had any idea of how hard it would be for her. Catarina's dream was a long, long way away.

Case folded one of his lists of words and put it in his pocket. He treated the paper with the reverence of a talisman. "Tomorrow?" He asked.

"If it doesn't rain. Let's work together for a month and see what we can do." She picked up the box of supplies and flashed him the smile he had been waiting for. It was as blinding as the smile in his memory, the one framed by the light bits of the sparkler.

"Adios," she said flippantly.

"That box is heavy. Let me drive you home."

"No."

"Why not?"

"Because, I don't want you to." Catarina shifted the box of school supplies to her hip and waved goodbye.

Case watched her walk away. He wasn't nervous any more; but he felt that pleasing her was of paramount importance. For the first time in a long time, he decided to try hard.

* * * * *

That night, Case dreamed of giving CPR to Catarina. They were alone, lying on a strange island beach. He had never been there before. Her hair dripped with sea water and a wet, thin, white cotton cloth was all that protected her skin from his hot hands. He could see beaded, deep rose circles pressing through the fabric. He didn't touch them. The sound of waves hissed softly in the background. He breathed air deep into her lungs. Her chest rose and fell to the rhythm his hips were making when he started to wake.

He fought to get back to sleep, back to holding Catarina. When the battle was lost, he smiled and began his morning stretch. When he rearranged his man parts, his mind wandered. *I'm going to have to start wearing tighter underwear or baggier shorts when I see Catarina!* Neither solution seemed ideal, but what a nice problem to have. These next few weeks might end up being fun!

Chapter 5

Waiting

Three weeks of waiting was killing Catarina. Today, it was official. Her period was late. Was she crying just because her emotions were going through the inevitable cycle of her body's whims? Or was it time to start thinking of how her future was about to collapse? An unwanted child fathered by an unwanted lover. In Catarina's world, saying no to sex was a woman's job. Failing one time could be one time too many. Another tear slid down her cheek.

Catarina's thoughts shot from lamenting her failure as the guardian against premarital sex to feeling betrayed by her secret lover, to feeling helpless against the cravings of her woman's body. She knew it was time to stop pretending they didn't exist or that she would always control them.....She needed to talk to María.

* * * * *

María Sanchez's house was in the same neighborhood as Abuelita's, just down Camino Ratama. Sitting on cinder blocks like all the other houses, it consisted of three tiny rooms stacked end to end against a front door. The first room served as the living area and Alberto's bedroom. It was strewn with rocks and sticks that little boys collect. His clothes were folded and stored in a cardboard box that was stashed between the wall and a couch that rested on legs of red bricks. Late afternoon sun shone on the windowsill where a limp aloevera plant teetered in a clay pot waiting to be knocked over again.

An open space served as a kitchen; a curtain hid a bathroom off to the side. The last room, a bedroom, had a door with a lock. María was lucky to have her own house. She was the only single woman who did.

Catarina's knock had an urgency that brought María to the door quickly. She wore a flowered, cotton wrapper that she held closed with her hands.

"Hola, cousin. What's wrong?"

All the preparation Catarina made to be brave when she faced María couldn't hide the red rims around her eyes or the tension in her face. "Is Alberto here?"

"No, he's playing outside with Carlos."

Catarina stepped inside the door. "I need to talk to you, about private things, woman things."

".....Now? I'm getting ready to go to Mass."

"Sí. Now. The church can't help with this." Catarina grabbed María's hand and led her to the bedroom. She closed the door and locked the flimsy hook latch. She leaned against the door with her eyes closed until María asked again. "What's wrong,

Catarina? Talk to me. That's why you are here, to talk, no?"

Catarina opened her eyes and sank to the edge of the bed. She took María's hand and drew her down beside her. She stared at their clasped hands as if there was an answer to her problems held within them. "You have lived as an unmarried woman a long time. You only have Alberto."

"Sí, Alberto is my life."

"I know, but how did you keep from getting pregnant other times?" Catarina removed her hands from María's.

"Ahhh. You are in love."

"No, I'm not, but I need to know if there is a way, for the future," Catarina hedged.

María patted Catarina's hand. "Tell me; is it El Gringo, eh? You have been spending a lot of time with him. Are you falling for that lovely body? I would.....fall right over backwards."

Catarina shrugged off the insinuation. "No! He's just a student.....he's nothing."

María smiled a wise woman's smile. "I don't think so. I saw you laughing together. It's good to see you laugh. And the other night, when you were in the kitchen, you were singing.....like when we were children? Is he the one making you smile?"

Catarina fought back a wave of new tears, because what María said was true. And the man making her smile was not going to be in her life much longer. "Yes, he makes me laugh, but this isn't about him. Help me, María; don't ask questions, por favor."

María unlocked the door and went to her bathroom. She came back with a small black cloth bag with a draw string. "I remember feeling the way you do. The responsibilities of being a woman in this way are not fair. No one takes care of us except each other." She hugged Catarina's stiff shoulders. "Here." She dumped the contents of the bag on the bed. "Nothing is guaranteed." María spread the items apart. "These little things in this package are condoms. They go over a man's, you know.....thing, like a balloon. It catches his juice when it comes inside you. Here, take it, for emergencies."

Catarina winced at María's bluntness. "What's that round rubber thing?"

"This is a diaphragm. If you use it and the condom, you're even safer. You are supposed to get this from a doctor." She held the cup in her hand for Catarina to examine.

Catarina could hear the doubt in her own voice. "Then the doctor, he would have to know....."

"Don't worry; I'll get you one. You put it inside yourself. Cover the place where his stuff could get into your womb. Afterwards, wash yourself very good before you take it out."

Catarina dropped her face into María's lap and sobbed. She felt so alone and miserable. María held her and rocked her until she was quiet again. Catarina sat up to face her cousin. Her voice trembled with the next question. "What if it is too late for these things? What will I do? Do I have the baby, like you did Alberto?" She watched María's face cloud with concern and turn hot with emotion.

"If it's that big gringo, you get him to give you money! I see him look at you. He will."

"It's not him." Catarina shook her head. She didn't want Case's help in any way. The last thing she wanted from El Gringo was the obligation that would come with taking his money.

"Who?"

Catarina continued shaking her head. She would never tell. Her shoulders shook with another sob; she reached for tissue to wipe her nose.

Compassion filled María; she hugged her cousin again. She held her tight enough for both of them to feel safe for just a moment. "I know someone in Matamoros who can help. Are you sure?"

"I'm pretty sure. I've never been this late before. Guess I won't need that student visa for college."

"Let's give it a few more days to see what happens. Then you can decide. I'll be with you; you won't be alone. I promise. Do you want to go to church with me? You could confess, ask for a miracle?"

Catarina threaded a strand of wayward hair behind her ear. "No. You have to be sorry for confession. There are reasons I can't be sorry."

"Catarina!" María was alarmed.

"Don't worry; I'll be fine. I need to go. I have another lesson scheduled with that gringo you lust after. You should flirt with him. I definitely think he is horny." Catarina purposefully destroyed the intimate moment between the two of them.

When Catarina got back to Abuelita's house, her grandmother had not returned from mass. She had the house to herself; Sixto was still at work.

Catarina stepped into the shower. She let the tepid water run in rivulets through her hair and down the crevice of her back. She soaped her breasts searching for tenderness that would indicate she was with child. She kneaded her belly, feeling for any swelling; there was none yet. She let her hair dry in waves, too apathetic to try to control it. She pulled on a simple blue cotton shift, grabbed a notebook and the papers she needed, then smiled at herself in the mirror. The smile was forced, but it helped a little.

On the way out the front door, she stooped to pick a gardenia and slipped it behind her ear. She breathed in the soothing perfume. The flower was pretty; it made her feel better. She usually wondered what El Gringo thought of her appearance, though it hardly mattered now that her life was going to change so dramatically. She was going to be so late to their meeting; he may not have waited.

* * * * *

Case waited in Resaca Park. The sun was going down. Catarina was never this late. The grass his truck destroyed during Alberto's rescue three weeks ago was completely grown back. The banana trees not only had new shoots, but big broad leaves. A sign had mysteriously appeared on the pump mechanism across the resaca. In big red letters, both English and Spanish, it warned, "DANGER! – PELIGROSO!"

Case wondered what Catarina thought about him. He was frustrated. She did not send the signals he got from other females. Her smile did not invite him to lean into her, to protect her or possess her. She was so controlled. It couldn't possibly be that she was immune to him. Could it? He supposed there could always be a first time. *Nah, she's not immune; she's controlling herself.* This felt weird, gouging his curiosity and frazzling his nerves.

When he looked at Catarina, he saw someone who gave freely of herself to everyone, the children at her school, her family, even him. It was confusing as to why she showed so little of what was inside of her. He didn't know if he would have time to find out what was there; their agreement was only for a month and three of those weeks were already gone. His reading progress astounded him. His lack of progress with Catarina confounded him.

Catarina was impossible not to look at. Her hips swayed with unconscious sensuality when she moved. Maybe that is why he always wanted to be at the park first, just as he was tonight. He could watch her come towards him. He closed his eyes to indulge in visualization. Hmmm. He liked it best when she wore her hair down. It fell soft and heavy past her shoulders. He tried to remember if he had ever touched it or just created the memory of doing so in his own mind. On the hottest days, Catarina twisted her hair up and fastened it with a tortes shell clasp. Case liked this too, because wavy tendrils fell out of the clasp and he could watch them dangle down, caressing her neck like he wanted to do. Very arousing.

How could she not acknowledge the electricity that jumped from his skin to hers when they sat next to each other? He had started counting the times they brushed arms and legs sitting at the picnic table at each meeting. It was cat and mouse. He chased.....created opportunities. She deftly eluded all contact except for the absolutely necessary or the completely unavoidable. The titillating game drove Case to the point that he could look at the picnic table when he drove down the highway and get stiff. *It's just a stupid picnic table!*

Case felt his inclination for pushing people's limits rising strong and restless. He needed to knock down her wall, test her. He considered grabbing her and kissing her, just as a test. Should he? How far would she let him go? Could he touch those breasts he stared at as often as he could?

He saw Catarina appear at the edge of the park. He made a decision. They would watch this magnificent sunset together and tonight would be the night.

Case watched as she shook her damp hair and finger combed it into wild waves. I could do that for her, he thought.

"You're late." Case rose from the table to greet her.

"I know, I'm sorry." She offered no explanation.

"I have a lantern, but it's almost time for you to be home."

"I can't stay, but I came to bring you something." She dug in her bag for a small binder.

"Yeah?"

"Look, it's a special picture dictionary. I made it for you."

Case lit the lantern. He made sure their hands touched when she handed him the notebook. He made sure they brushed shoulders as they sat down at the table. That was two contacts for tonight. He checked; she acted as if the touches were the most normal, inconsequential events. Irritation washed over him. *Patience, patience.* He talked himself down.

He examined the notebook's cover. Catarina had created a pen and ink mural of Mayan gods and stories, much like the ones in the field shack school. It was intricate and painstakingly detailed, a work of art wasted on a cheap notebook.

When he didn't open it, she reached and turned to the inside for him. Each page had three columns. The first column was a list of words in Catarina's precise printing. Beside each word was a drawing of what the word was. The third column was a replica of what Case showed her the word looked like to him. There were pages and pages with hundreds and hundreds of words.

"Catarina, when did you do this?"

"Oh, a little at a time, over the last three weeks. Can you tell what the pictures are?"

"This is incredible!" The hug he gave her was spontaneous, but the kiss was calculated. She wore a gardenia in her hair like she wanted him to think of her differently; he thought she was ready. He slipped his hand around her neck touching skin he never touched before. He brushed her lips and pressed to get inside her mouth. Catarina shoved him away and she was rough about it.

"Gringo! Stop it. Stop it!" Case released her immediately and Catarina touched her mouth with the back of her hand. "What are you doing? You are breaking the rules!"

"What rules? We don't have rules."

"Yes, we do. I am the teacher. You are the student. This is professional."

"Student? I thought we were friends!" Case was embarrassed by his misjudgment and crushed at the tag of "student." He backed off a whole yard.....a mile away from where he wanted to be. Catarina glared accusations.

"That's easy. I won't be your student. I quit." He reached for her more gently.

"Gringo, we are not even friends! You don't know me. Why learn to be friends when you are going to be gone soon anyway?"

"Where am I going?"

Catarina searched for words. "Wherever gringos go, away!"

"Nah. I'm going to hang out here, maybe start a little business down on South Padre."

"You're going to be a beach bum! I want to go to college more than anything, but I can't. You could go to college. You could do anything.....anything you want!"

"I went to college. I flunked. You are the only one who has ever helped me." Case thought she would say something nice, but she didn't. Catarina's silence usually preceded a stand off. Case decided to go easy. "OK, so now I know something about you. You are serious about going to college. What else do I need to know to be your friend? When's your birthday?" He reached for her.

"Shut up! And don't touch me!" She slapped at his hand.

She was actually screaming at him. This was not the controlled Catarina he thought he knew. This

57

female was nuts! Case wondered if he should stand his ground or run for his life. He felt completely helpless.

"It was the kiss," she said. I've been wondering when you would try that and I thought I was prepared. I wasn't!"

"Catarina, that was no kiss. That was an attempted kiss. It's like attempted murder. It didn't happen."

"This is not what I want."

"I just wanted a kiss. Where are you going with this?"

"You know it wasn't just a kiss! It changes everything. We have no future!"

"How do you know?"

"Our lives are as different as lives can be and besides, for me, there is someone else."

Case's spirits dipped before a feeling of relief confused him. What would he do with her if he got her anyway? Catarina wasn't a woman to be toyed with. She was too special. What was he thinking? He screwed up. Friendship was best for the moment and he knew he had better act fast. Catarina was suffering and looked as though she was ready to run. Friends it would be. He had never been "just friends" with a female. Guess there was a first time for everything.

He extended his hand and said the word out loud. "Friends?" Case stooped down to look under the heavy hair that fell over her face. Catarina met his eyes and accepted his handshake.

Case just couldn't help himself; he had to push things. With his eyes on her mouth, he pulled her toward him. Yes, he saw the panic on her face that he desired. The test was over. She wanted him. At the last fraction of a second, he changed directions and kissed her on the forehead. Her skin burned his lips like the sun.

"Catarina de la Alvarado, my friend," he pronounced, like a minister declaring a couple man and wife. But he knew for certain, she was not immune to him. There was just someone else, for now.

Chapter 6

The Florist

Dellicious Designs bought most all of Abuelita's flowers. The owner, Jan, paid generously for the blossoms Abuelita loved and tended. They were cut early in the mornings before the dew could evaporate from the petals.

Abuelita's arthritis was bothering her today, so Catarina was making the Saturday delivery. As soon as she finished, she would head for Ito's farm and another day of picking, earning ten cents a pound. Her hands would be busy, but her mind would not.....dangerous.

The plastic pails of water and flowers banged her shins with every step; she didn't notice. Even the wire handles cutting through her fingers couldn't distract her from her obsessive thoughts about El Gringo.

Catarina played the scene of last night's attempted kiss over and over in her head. She toyed with each moment, inserting different events at each turning point. What if she had let him kiss her? Where would it have taken them last night, next week, next year? Could she sample just a little of him and stop? What if there was no friendship rule? She had the power to abolish it. What if Case were a Mexican man, more accessible, more appropriate?

What if she could eliminate her body's need for sex altogether? Just stop feeling. Is this what she really wanted? Then she could concentrate on her future, learning, teaching, making a difference in the world. She silently damned the biology that made her a woman driven by such powerful desires. She damned the manipulative liar who awakened her needs. She knew she did not love him. She certainly didn't like him. The man was too easily replaced in Catarina's bed time fantasies.

El Gringo didn't know it, but he made love to Catarina almost every night. She kissed her pillow and pretended she could feel his lips. She ran her fingers through her long hair and closed her eyes to see his face. It was a temporary indulgence. If her worst fears were true, if she was pregnant, no man would want her. That would make giving up desires for Case Becker easier somehow.

The door chime at Dellicious Designs blared. Catarina propped the door open with one foot and slid the pails inside. She could hear Jan talking to a customer in the back room where the glass refrigeration unit kept the blooms fresh.

"Be right with you!" Jan's cheerfulness was dependable.

Catarina scooted her flowers closer to the wall. Her eyes wandered to the gifts and trinkets for sale in the shop. She wondered what kind of people had money for such pretty, useless amusements.

61

Her attention fell to a new display. It was a life-sized cutout of a couple in elegant formal wear. The stunning male model was escorting a movie star who seemed to enjoy posing for the camera. She had straight blonde hair and a long slender body. The white gown she wore was too sexy to be a wedding dress. Her arm draped through her escort's elbow possessively, and her fragile hand with beautifully manicured nails rested on the man's forearm. Catarina compared her own strong hands. There was little resemblance. The display was an advertisement for tuxedo rental. Catarina studied the cardboard man's blue eyes and knew. That was Case!

"Abuelita? Ah, Catarina." Jan appeared around the corner. "This customer doesn't like our orchids today. Did you bring gardenias?"

"Yes, I did." Catarina turned from the blue eyes on the display to encounter the real thing. El Gringo was leaning on the counter ordering a corsage.

"Here, Case, these are as fresh as you can get. They are always flawless. Look at these."

Case's face lit up in pleasure. He started to say Catarina's name. She imperceptibly shook her head no. She did not want to acknowledge that they knew each other. Case raised an eyebrow but honored her request. He picked up the heavy pails before Catarina could lift them to the counter. Sweet scents disturbed the air making Catarina feel the presence of the attempted kiss. She touched her hair where the gardenia rested the night before.

Case gave Jan a wicked grin. "No, I don't think I'll take the gardenias. Sharon wouldn't like me thinking about another girl while I am with her." Jan shamed him playfully by shaking her forefinger in his face.

Heat rushed through Catarina. She looked out the window, for she knew El Gringo was referring to her.

"I'll take these roses." Case selected some of the American Beauty Reds and walked over to the cutout. He held the cluster of flowers up to the wrist of the movie star. "These will look great."

"That display of you and Sharon gets more business for my dad's formal wear shop than anything we have ever tried. You two look like you belong together. Thanks for letting us use the picture."

"Don't count on any more of them. If I have my way, tonight's occasion is the last tuxedo event of my life." He laughed. "A damned fund raiser for an art museum! I'll be the only guy there in flip flops!"

El Gringo liked to laugh a lot, but Catarina had not paid attention to his laugh before. It was a good sound. Deep, relaxed, sincere. Her eyes got glassy. It never occurred to her that he had other women in his life. She was embarrassed at her lack of awareness. Cutout Sharon was very real and very beautiful. Real and unreal at the same time. At this moment, Catarina regretted the lie she told Case when she claimed there was someone else in her life. She felt a twinge of guilt about lying to a good man. But, unavailability gave her safety. She forgave herself.

Catarina saw Jan's hands tremble as she took the roses back from Case. "Catarina, would you put these in the back for me while I write up this sale?" When Catarina stepped closer, she noticed Jan wore heavy makeup covering a discoloration on her neck and there was a bandage on her left wrist. White gauze was slipping out from under the cover of a long sleeved blouse. As soon as Catarina reached the refrigerator in the back room, she heard whispers.

"Jan, you've got to report this."

"I'll be fine; it was nothing."

"It's not fine. You deserve better."

"Not every woman is going to get someone as good as you, Case." Jan's whisper held a note of tenderness and regret.

"Next time, call me. I'll find a way to take care of it."

Catarina pressed herself into the wall between the two rooms. She craned her neck just enough to get one eye past the doorframe. El Gringo and Jan embraced. When Case released her from the gentle hug, he kissed her forehead.....just like he kissed Catarina's last night. Jan was married! El Gringo cared for this woman.

Jealousy rolled through Catarina like a wave of nausea. She didn't know whether she was more jealous of the intimacy she just observed or of the beautiful cutout woman in the display. She did know she had no rights. This man was not hers.

As soon as the doorbell chimed and Catarina was certain Case was gone, she joined Jan in the front of the shop. "Señora, the cost is ten dollars today."

"Thanks for delivering the flowers. Is Abuelita all right?"

"Sí, but her hands are hurting with arthritis."

"I'm sorry. I just enjoy visiting with her. I miss her when I don't see her."

Catarina couldn't help herself. "You know Señor Becker?" El Gringo's name felt strange on Catarina's tongue. She never referred to him by his name, for it was too intimate an act.

"Yes, since high school. Do you know him?"

"Only a little. He got some supplies for our school."

"Oh, yes, Case is wonderful that way. Always doing things for other people. Always rushing in to save the day. You are lucky to know him." Jan opened the cash register and took out two fives. She hesitated and took another. "Here is some extra. Can you buy some more school supplies with this?" She winced when she closed the cash drawer with her left hand.

Catarina touched the bandage on Jan's wrist. "Are you all right?" She looked into Jan's eyes for a truthful answer.

"I don't know," she admitted.

Catarina took the money. "You love Señor Becker?"

"Doesn't every woman who meets him? Our local knight in shining armor! He loves to rescue us and we love him for it."

The bell sounded when Catarina walked out of the shop. Her uncontrollable thoughts about El Gringo assailed her mind, swirling in the new unexpected information. Someone named Sharon wanted Case, someone who was everything Catarina was not.....tall, sophisticated, rich.....a blue-eyed Anglo. And, Case loved another, a married woman whose husband beat her. Surely God had good reasons to forgive Jan if she cheated on a husband like Logan Dell.

Chapter 7

Logan's Taunt

Sometimes, when choices are taken away from you in life, things are easier. Sad, but easier. Abuelita said that. Now, Catarina understood what she meant. She had clarity in her thinking that wasn't present before. Yesterday, Catarina was struggling with the impact of an almost kiss. Today she knew it was nothing. El Gringo had many women in his life, certainly more than the two she found out about yesterday at the flower shop. Jan said as much. "Our local knight in shining armor. He loves to rescue us and we love him for it."

Catarina visualized the living, breathing El Gringo married to the queenly cut-out Sharon. That was the way it would be. Now that she knew he was taken, Catarina was liberated.

There was little reason to meet El Gringo this evening, but she was going anyway. He now understood what he needed to do to conquer his eye-brain disconnection. Most important of all, he figured out that there was nothing wrong with his basic

66

intelligence. Over the last weeks, Catarina watched him make the same journey of discovery that every child makes when he masters an important piece of the world. It was sheer joy for both teacher and student. The only thing he needed from her now was more pictures in the expanding dictionary.

The new friendship rule between them was good. It would give Catarina the freedom to enjoy his playfulness. He did make her laugh; María was right about that. Seeing him in a different way would allow her to let him go. Her soul wriggled in its prison of self-control. A whiff of fresh air came in. She hurried her step so she could see him sooner.

She thought of the moment this morning when she hugged Alberto and made the decision to keep her baby and raise it on her own. When the baby started to show, there would be little happiness. Abuelita would be so disappointed in her. It wasn't wrong to look forward to this little moment with a friend this evening, was it?

But, the woman in Catarina couldn't step away from El Gringo without one small female satisfaction, one moment of torture for the man who was everybody's hero. She wore a multicolored skirt and a gathered blouse that fell provocatively off her shoulders. She was dressed for flirting.

By the time she reached the edge of the park, there was a noticeable skip in her walk. El Gringo was waiting. He was smiling too. He had snow cones, raspas!

"I could have bought coconut, but that flavor was blue. I've already seen you with blue teeth; I decided not to take the risk. Your choice, strawberry or strawberry?" He offered them both to her.

Catarina selected strawberry and savored the warmth of the shared memory that was so funny and delightful. When Case reached into his back pocket to produce two plastic spoons with a magician's flourish, she laughed her special music. She wondered if he would sit beside her today instead of across from her. He took the bench on the opposite side of the table. A little dip of disappointment expressed itself on her bottom lip.

The sweet cold of shaved ice trickled down her throat and she moaned in pleasure. She paid too much attention to his lips closing over the mound of ice heaped in his spoon. *Stop it, Catarina!* She scolded herself. *Just take another bite.*

"How was the banquet last night?"

"The banquet was boring."

".....and Sharon?"

"Sharon is never boring."

Catarina planned on torturing El Gringo! Was it his plan to torture her as well?

Case changed the subject. "Why did you not want Jan Dell to know we knew each other?"

Catarina took another bite of her raspa. She stumbled. "I, uh, thought you didn't want people to know I was tutoring you....." She saw Case direct his gaze over her shoulder. His eyes narrowed and his face went stern. "What are you looking at?"

"Nothing good." Case's frown deepened.

She turned her head to look behind her. Her physical reaction was violent. Catarina waited for morning sickness to assail her every day when she woke. It never happened; but the sight of Border Patrol Officer Logan Dell brought the waves of nausea she feared. Her head whipped around; she fixed her stare on the snow cone while she listened to his heavy steps come across the grass and stop behind her.

Case spoke first to deflect attention from Catarina. "Hello, Logan. What can I do for you this evening?"

Her spine straightened and her eyes lifted to a steady focus somewhere over the water. Maybe Logan would let her alone. He was unpredictable. She had seen him arrest illegal workers regardless of the mordida they paid him. She had seen him let others go for no reason at all. Maybe he was in a good mood tonight.

Logan responded. "Case, I see you are entertaining Miss de la Alvarado tonight.....Cat-uh-rih-nah, aren't you going to say hello?" He mispronounced and drug out the syllables of her name in a slur that robbed it of all its grace and beauty.

"Are you having a nice evening, Officer?" Catarina addressed him without looking at him.

"Officer? You always call me Logan. What's wrong, Catarina?" Logan showed his teeth like a predator enjoying a hunt. "I'm just out doing a little shopping for myself. I see you are open for business." The sneer he directed at Case made Catarina's stomach heave.

Case rose to his feet and Logan moved his right hand to rest casually on the gun at his waist.

Logan looked at Case as he spoke to Catarina. "Just kidding, Catarina." He looked back at Catarina when he addressed Case. "She does have a special sauce, don't you think?" Logan licked his lips while he fondled the handle of his gun with his thumb.

"Well, Catarina, when you are in the mood, you know how to reach me."

"You think something happened between us, Bastardo?"

"Don't get huffy Chiquita. I did you the courtesy of wooing you. I didn't have to." He leaned in to touch a curl of her hair.

Catarina jumped up to meet his face so close she could smell the tobacco on his breath. Her explosive fury made Logan back up. "It didn't happen, Logan!"

Her snow cone dropped to the ground and splatted dark strawberry stains on Logan's shiny boots. He stepped back and casually shook the ice off of each foot. "I guess you owe me a shoe shine. I'll bring them round when I'm ready."

Case took control. "If this goes any further, I don't think you're going to like the headlines."

Logan looked quizzically at Case.

"Renegade Border Patrol Officer threatens Case Becker? Investigation reveals....." Case shrugged his shoulders. "What would it reveal, Logan?"

"Is that a threat?"

"At least I did you the courtesy of.....warning you." Case mimicked the tone Logan used in insulting Catarina.

Logan's thin, lazy lips curled into a smile. He gave a knowing wink and tipped his hat to Catarina. "I guess my work here is done. Ya'll stay out of trouble now." He did not look back as he walked away, but his hand never left his gun. A cloud of dust followed the patrol unit out of the parking lot.

Case's voice sounded far away. "Catarina? Catarina, look at me. He's nothing. Everybody knows what an ass he is. He just saw us having a nice time and wanted to ruin it."

Pain and humiliation filled Catarina's eyes. She whirled to leave but her skirt caught on the corner of the table and tore. She fought to free herself. Case put his knee on the picnic table bench to lower himself to her height. He freed her skirt, took her hands and pressed them down on the table. He bent his head to touch hers. She struggled to escape. All she wanted was to disappear.

"Stop. Stop!" His voice was kind and tender.

Catarina wished she could feel the warmth of his hands touching hers. She couldn't. If she had been this close to him five minutes ago, she would have given in, turned her head into his face for a kiss. If she didn't get away from him, she still might. He pressed his head and hands into her. Five seconds became ten seconds, long enough to decide she wouldn't kiss Case and let Logan be right. She wasn't selling anything. She lifted her head and turned away.

"Catarina, I've got a business decision to make. Let me tell you about it; I need you to help me. You've changed my life, made me see what I can do. Now you have to follow through. I want to talk to you." His voice was slow and calm like he was reasoning with someone about to jump off a bridge.

Catarina managed to spit out, "Do it yourself! It's gringo business; it has nothing to do with me." She raised her eyes to Case's face. "We're done." She said it like she meant it.

Case reluctantly lifted his weight from her hands and let her go.

Chapter 8

Kiss in the Rain

C̶ase cruised the highway in his wrecker while he listened to the radio's dire prediction of the coming storm. He watched the trees bend as gale force winds blew in. This kind of weather was good business for Becker Rescue Services. He could have waited at the office for distress calls to start coming in, but he usually trolled for accidents in these conditions. The first wrecker on the scene got the business.

The real reason he was outside in the weather was that Case loved storms. He loved to feel the presence of Mother Nature's forces. The smell of ozone reminded him of the power she had over man; the taste of it heightened his excitement.

As he drove, Case's mind wandered to Catarina. He was committed to trying his best to banish her from his thoughts. He accepted the common advice among young stags trying to break away from an unwanted attraction. The answer to forgetting a woman was simply to sample more women. The goal was to distract yourself with women you did not want, women who would give more, leaving you no time to think about the woman you did want. Since the philosophy appeared to be so successful for other men, Case was hard at work proving the theory valid.

This past week, he sampled the lips of the winner of the Queen of Cotton pageant. She wasn't jail bait, but she was too young, still under the watchful eyes of her parents. Her innocence probably wouldn't last much longer for the girl had thrown herself at Case in the game room of her own home during a reception celebrating her coronation. She was ripe.

He flirted shamelessly with the cashier at the Bar-B-Q Barn. Everyone assumed he went home with her because most every other man did at one time or another. Case never had and didn't this time either.

He allowed the pretty young widow who attended church where his family worshipped to straighten his collar and remove an imaginary thread from his jacket.

Then, of course, there was Sharon. Sharon, who liked to dress him up and take him to fund-raising dinners. She came back to town after a nasty divorce, leaving her doctor husband in Dallas with his girlfriend and a fraction of his fortune. Sharon's daddy was a good lawyer. She treated Case well, like he was special. She even forgave him for not marrying her the first time around. She told him so, then added, "We both had a lot to learn."

Case believed it was acceptable to leave them all hopeful even though none of them held the same allure they had possessed before he met Catarina de la Alvarado.

The last time he saw Catarina, she didn't even say goodbye. She ran away without allowing him a chance to show her that Logan's insults were irrelevant. Somehow, he still believed he could fix the hurt.

He looked for her in the park and along the routes he knew she took to work and home. He stopped by the flower shop on Saturday morning. Because he wanted a meeting to appear accidental, going to the one place he knew he would find her was out of the question. Case stayed away from the school on Ito's farm.

Maybe he would find some peace in the storm. He parked at the intersection of the highway and the resaca, across the street from the park. He settled himself against the interior door of the cab to watch the lightening show.

Through the sheeting water on his windshield, he saw someone caught in the rain. The poor soul was fighting the wind with a huge piñata fashioned in the shape of a bull. The papier maché figure was collapsing and the colorful trails of paper ribbon drug in the mud. Case honked his horn and flashed his headlights signaling an invitation to come to safety. No response. He waited until the person got a little closer and repeated the signal.

The wind picked up and began to howl through the trees. It snatched the piñata from the person's grasp and blew it into the side of Case's truck. Case heard the thunk. There was Catarina standing in the downpour holding one leg of the paper bull.

The rain was driving hard drops, loud enough that Case could not hear her steps as she approached the truck. She disappeared from sight when she stooped to gather the remains of the piñata. The door to the passenger's side opened and the wind blew in carrying sheets of water, pieces of a paper bull and Catarina.

She squealed a curse in Spanish and her dramatic whoop filled the interior of the cab. She was drenched. Her dark, pretty hair was plastered in wild designs around her eyes and neck. Her blouse needed to be wrung out. The head of the bull began to list to one side in excruciating slow motion and came to rest on the dashboard. Case and Catarina looked at each other and started laughing.

Case saw she was shivering and reached for a beach towel behind his seat. He threw it over her head like he would a dog's and began to dry her hair. When he moved the towel to dry her shoulders, they quieted. Case and Catarina had never been completely alone before. There were always family members or school children. Even when they studied by themselves in the park, there was always the chance someone would see them. This new intimacy was crushing. The sky darkened and thunder began to roll. Case watched lightening flicker on her face.

All the things he ever thought of saying to her fled his mind. Since he had no words, he wrapped her body in the towel. He pulled her forward and they rested forehead to forehead. Imprisoned energy roused to course freely back and forth between them, communicating a cosmic attraction they would never again be able to deny existed.

Case's record for holding his breath under water was four minutes. So, he knew it was four minutes later when he gasped and a low moan broke from his chest. He gathered Catarina's face in his hands and devoured her mouth.   Even in his semi-consciousness, he was aware that he was exposing a depth of physical passion he feared would frighten her.   He kissed her harder.   She kissed him back giving more of herself than he expected.   She accepted his tongue and melted into him.   Her arms encircled his neck and he shifted in his seat so he could gather her full against his body.   He wanted her to feel his hard penis against her clothes. He ground it into her until it found its place against the barrier of cloth between her legs.

The battering wind swayed the heavy vehicle. The rain beat furiously, making the cab echo with vibration.   Lightening struck a tree across the street. Case and Catarina entered a primal place where secret urges and demanding desires can not hide.

Neither Case nor Catarina could stop the kiss.   It was as if the universe in the form of a storm was in control.   Only when outside sounds abated did the kisses start to slow, matching the pace of the heavenly rain.

"One more."   Case was demanding, begging. Catarina put her hand on his chest to force distance between them. Lips parted. Tongues teased. It was a different kiss, more relaxed.   They were careful, for each knew what lay beyond the thrill of touching each other.

As Case released her and straightened the terry cloth towel on her shoulders, he ventured to let his knuckles brush the front of her wet blouse where he knew her nipples would be.   Her chest rose at the delicate pressure.   They were hard and he lingered as long as he dared.   He closed his eyes and thanked God she did not push him away.

This was the woman he could never love and leave. He knew she understood him on a level no one ever had or could. With her, he could be exactly who he was and exactly what he wanted to be. All their differences didn't matter. Her family would accept him; they already had. His family would be surprised, but happy for him. He would cherish her until the end of time.

"God! Jesus! Catarina. You know what this means?"

"Nothing. It means nothing." Her voice was flat.

"You can't say that. I've let you know how I feel!"

"Men feel this way all the time."

It was as if she slapped him in the face. He ignored the pain and pressed her hands between his. "No, they don't. You felt what I felt!"

"Did I?" Catarina lied to calm herself. Emotional survival meant she had to think of this incident in a certain way. This was not the beginning of something new. It was the end. El Gringo didn't know this was a goodbye kiss. It was just an instant she allowed herself. She took the kiss as a memento of a feeling she would never know again. Somehow it made her feel powerful, taking what she wanted.

Quickly she started visualizing, placing Case back in the compartment where she tried to keep him in her mind. She saw his blue eyes vanish behind the lid of an imaginary black box. She wouldn't open it again for a long time, only when it was safe for her to remember. She took a deep breath.

"Catarina. Don't do this."

She pulled her hands away from his. She rested them on the place where her baby would grow. She would need to go back to Mexico soon. There were no words in Spanish or English that could tell him how she felt, so she said nothing. She just sat, very, very still.

"I'm driving you home." Case opened his door and stepped to the front of the truck to toss away some limbs blown against the bumper by the storm. He heaved the branches to the side of the road, then stood for a second with his arms dangling at his sides like a gunslinger. Some invisible trigger released his rage and frustration. He exploded and pounded the hood of the wrecker with his granite fists until the metal caved in and tears streamed down Catarina's face.

When he spent himself, Case jerked opened the door and threw himself in the driver's seat. He had enough frustration left to slam the door with alarming power.

The truck's CB crackled. "Case, where the hell are you? We got enough accidents to keep us busy 'til tomorrow. Case! Come in. Come in, Case."

He picked up the receiver. "Yeah, where do you want me?"

"Get the Cadillac at Highway 77 and Sonora Drive. There is a minor injury there. You may need to help out."

Case fired the diesel engine. "I'm close. ETA three minutes." The wrecker jerked onto the pavement.

"I'll walk." Catarina said.

"No." The truck was already moving, so Catarina sat. She was physically drained from the emotional roller coaster she was riding. All she had energy to do was stare out the window. The world was starting to stir and people were coming outside after the fury of the storm.

She noticed another wrecker drive by with the red Becker Rescue Services logo on it. Its yellow lights on the roof were revolving. At the stoplight at Harrison Street, there were four more Becker Rescue Services trucks lined up waiting to go south. A fifth one pulled up beside them. The driver tipped his John Deer cap. Case raised his hand to acknowledge the man. Catarina looked over at El Gringo. There was clearly a question on her face. He ignored her.

All the houses on Camino Ratama were floating in a shallow lake of mud. It happened every time there was too much rain. The houses all rested on blocks or posts of some sort, so no one's home was flooded, this time. Case slowed down to travel safely through the water. The wake from the tires sloshed against trees and fences. Catarina could see him moving into his crisis management mode.

When they stopped in front of the pink house, they found Sixto helping a neighbor retrieve his corrugated plastic carport roof from Abuelita's front yard. Sixto walked to Case's truck window and motioned for him to roll down the glass. "Did Catarina invite you to our fiesta? We want you to come."

"No, she didn't. What fiesta?" Case's jaw muscle flexed. Catarina almost fell trying to get out of the cab.

Sixto ignored the snarling look Catarina gave him. "El Cinco de Mayo, Saturday. We have all our friends over. There will be Mariachis, cervesa, dancing." Sixto pointed to the melted pile of papier maché Catarina left on the passenger's seat. "But no piñata."

"Maybe next year." Case was in a hurry to get to the wrecked Cadillac and away from Catarina. He shifted the transmission into first gear and moved forward about fifty feet. He stopped, ground into reverse and drove backwards to Sixto.

"Aye, you change your mind?" Sixto asked.

"Not changing my mind.....just not giving up." Case looked directly at Catarina. "What time?"

"We party all day. Come any time; but the music starts at seven."

It all happened so fast Catarina had no chance to argue. There was no reason El Gringo shouldn't come to the celebration other than that she didn't want him to.

"Damnit, Sixto!" She watched the big vehicle pull onto the highway as another Becker Rescue Services truck honked a greeting. This one was hauling a black pickup with a smashed front end.

Catarina stomped up the steps and went to the corner of the living room where the phone sat. She didn't see what she was looking for. *Does Abuelita even have a phone book?* She got down on her knees and looked into the dark under the chair. There.....The Rio Grande Valley Yellow Pages. She fumbled through the listings to the "t's" for towing. Nothing. She found the "w's" for wrecking. No. She tried the "r's" for rescue services.

She found more than she expected, a full page display ad featuring a map of the state of Texas. A star rested next to the name of almost every town in The Valley and every major city in the southern half of Texas. The stars started in San Antonio, included

Houston and all of the Gulf Coast. Becker Rescue Services was an empire of land and marine operations. El Gringo wasn't just a truck driver, he was obviously a very rich business man. But, Catarina still didn't want him at the fiesta. She threw the phone book against the wall and prayed he had the sense not to come.

Chapter 9

El Cinco de Mayo

Case returned to the very pink house on Camino Ratama just as cheerful strains of Mariachi music began luring revelers from all over the neighborhood into the yard. Abuelita's house was already bursting with people.

Case hoped he brought enough gifts and food to distract Catarina from the tension he anticipated between them. He carried a watermelon under his arm and crispy pecan pralines his mother made. He had firecrackers for the kids, a bottle of José Cuervo for the grown-ups and in his teeth he held a string attached to a huge piñata made in the shape of a cow. It was the closest thing he could find to the bull that drowned in the storm. He was covered with offerings, yet he was still recognizable. No one else was that big.

Sixto met him at the garden gate. He took the piñata string out of Case's teeth. "Hola, Gringo, aquí está!" Christmas lights were strung along the chain link fence and through the bushes. The ferocious

Chihuahua attacked like a raider from across the border. He grabbed Case's pants leg in his teeth and shook it as though he could tear it off.

María Sanchez came to defend the obnoxious dog's behavior. "This is Pancho Villa."

"Is he the real one, back from the grave?" Case tried to shake the dog off.

"Pobrecito, es El Gringo un hombre peligroso?" María cooed.

"That means dangerous. I'm dangerous? Case lifted his leg into the air with the dog attached.

"Pancho, come to me. Let go." María entreated the dog with baby talk. Pancho's little lips raised in a low growl revealing teeth firmly embedded in a tear in Case's favorite jeans. Sixto passed off the piñata and took the melon and the tequila.

"I think Pancho wants to spend the evening with me," said Case. Pancho glared with bulging, defiant eyes. "Let's go for a ride. Let's go find Catarina." Case dragged his leg, dog attached, gently around the side of the house into the fiesta in progress. There were even more people than had been at Abuelita's birthday party. Those who recognized him welcomed him, and each introduced him to another family member. With every greeting, his eyes searched for Catarina.

Sixto introduced him to the leader of the band. "This is my cousin, Baldemar. He's just back from Louisiana. He named himself Freddy Fender, after his guitar, so he could be famous."

"Buenas noches." Case tried to be polite while he still searched.

Baldemar hoisted his drink. "It worked; didn't it?"

María arrived with a rubber ball to entice the dog off Case's leg. She threw it and Pancho Villa raced across the yard beyond the lights to retrieve his favorite toy. "Now that I have done something for you, I want you to do something for me," María announced.

"Really." Case examined the tear in his jeans.

"First, you are going to learn to dance."

"I don't think so." Case's protest was insignificant against María's determination. Freddy Fender and his band broke into conjunto norteño music. It sounded like a polka, happy. María pushed Case into the crowd and forced him through the steps and twirls in an exhilarating physical ritual. María was a good dancer and a directive teacher. It didn't take long. Once Case understood the rhythm, she relinquished control and let him lead. He felt good about that. She flirted with him openly. He did not feel good about that. María was pretty, but he could only worry about what Catarina would think.

Case found Catarina dancing with Alberto. Her party dress was trimmed in creamy lace. The skirt swirled around her ankles and her blouse dipped in a vee neck to display a delicate silver crucifix resting exactly where her cleavage started. Her black eyes already followed Case. The defiance he saw there told him she didn't expect him to stay long.

When the band took a break, Alberto drug Catarina to the place vacated by the musicians. He called to the crowd. "Mira, mira! See what I can do! Catarina and I have a song."

"Not now, Alberto." Catarina turned to walk up the steps to the kitchen.

"But we practiced and practiced." Alberto picked up a guitar and began to pick out notes. His fingers, grubby from little boy's games, danced over the strings as he followed Catarina until she relented. She whirled to face him and stomped an imaginary cockroach, grinding it into the ground. Alberto strummed the melody and Catarina sang the lyrics of "La Cucaracha." They started slowly, building speed with each short verse.

When Catarina could no longer keep up with him, she stepped behind him, reached over his shoulder and strummed the strings while he fingered the frets of the instrument. They both played the same guitar. When the crowd started hooting and cheering, Catarina and Alberto switched. She took over fingering the chords and he strummed. They played faster and faster. Both musicians were breathless at the final "Olé!"

María and Case clapped their hands and headed for the ice chests. They grabbed beers.

"Are you taking Catarina to the fireworks tonight?" María sounded mysterious.

"What fireworks?"

"At Cantina Los Indios by the low water crossing."

"I hadn't planned on it. Why?"

"I want to go meet someone there. Maybe, someone I shouldn't." María whispered in his ear.

"So, in exchange for getting rid of Pancho Villa, you make me polka, dull my senses with alcohol and trick me into covering for you with Catarina?"

"Sí," María drew the word out long and fluttered her eyelashes.

"Does Catarina know what you are up to?

"She will when I tell her. Can I?"

"I don't think Catarina will agree to this. I'm not sure we are friends any more."

"Don't be stupid. She likes you, trust me. If she says yes, you will take us, sí?"

Case thought he was safe. Catarina would say no. He shrugged his shoulders to indicate he would let it happen. María left to approach her cousin. Case watched them talk from across the crowd. He tried to interpret Catarina's reaction as María laid out her plan. María's hands were placed in a position of prayer. Catarina looked directly at him; he held her eyes until María's face lit up with delight. *Shit, what am I doing?*

María twirled partnerless through the dancers to come back to him. "Vamanos a las nueve! For gringos, that means we are leaving at nine o'clock." She measured his skepticism. "It is time for you to dance with Catarina now. Go ask her."

Instead, Case found Abuelita at the dessert table. He took her cake away from her and whirled her onto the dance floor. Throughout the evening, he danced with every female from the ages of five to ninety five. He was the life of the fiesta.

As the evening progressed, Catarina spent more and more time dancing with a man in his mid thirties. The man was very clean and his white linen clothes were impeccably pressed. He had a good haircut, a moustache and an air of ownership. A diamond winked on his pinky finger. Sixto liked him too, for he laughed and slapped the man on the back.

It was hard for Case to keep his eyes from straying to Catarina and impossible to keep his eyes from shooting daggers at the man in white. The other man in Catarina's life could be a threat after all.

While Catarina danced with one of her neighbors, the handsome man courted Abuelita. Case watched him present her with a gift. It must be jewelry, judging by the shape of the box. In the middle of Abuelita's demure delight, he presented her with another box. She listened to the man while he explained. Both Abuelita and the man turned their heads to look at Catarina. The man in white was smiling with plans. Abuelita was not.

Case didn't want to see any more, and when the piñata was hoisted into the air, he took the opportunity to do something he'd wanted to do all night.

Alberto was blindfolded first. Los Lobos turned him around so many times he was too motion drunk to stand up. When he tumbled into the grass, the guests exploded with laughter. They were full of alcohol, music and friendship. No one noticed the gringo slide into the shadows of the evening.

Case circled from the back yard to the front. He saw an entourage of shiny black cars peopled with slick gentlemen, well dressed thugs and a military escort. There was no doubt as to whom they belonged. Case paused by the front door, hoping to overhear something that would give him a clue as to who the man in white could be. Hot gardenia smells assaulted him while he waited. He reached to stroke a petal, creamy with light from the moon. He couldn't resist; he picked one.

Not hearing anything of interest in the men's conversation, Case entered the screen door and took another two steps into the kitchen. He looked for Abuelita's cow cookie jar. It sat on the counter. It was empty; all the money collected on her birthday was gone, probably used for corn flour, beans and milk. The fists full of change he had been saving for a month made a disturbing clang every time the coins dropped into the jar. Case looked over his shoulder to see if anyone from outside noticed. If he was in luck, they didn't. Mission accomplished. Case strolled through the back screen door into the perturbed face of Catarina de la Alvarado.

"What were you doing in there?" Her eyes flashed challenge. His gaze was steady as he presented her the fragrant gardenia he had been compelled to pick. "You want to give me a flower you stole from la planta de mi Abuelita?"

She rejected him again. Case raised the blossom to place it behind his own ear instead of hers. He slid sideways past her, down the wooden steps and into the party. He spied Pancho Villa at the buffet table. He picked the little dog up and together, they went through the food line. They selected the things they liked best. They dined sitting Indian style in the grass. Pancho sat in the space between Case's knees and looked longingly at his drink.

Case understood. "OK, you can have some; but we have to watch our livers, right?" They drank together until nine o'clock, time to leave with María and Catarina. Case liked mojitos. Pancho liked cervesa.

Chapter 10

Fireworks

Catarina knew when she agreed to María's plans for the evening that she put herself in danger. She hoped.....what? That she could re-establish the friendship rule with El Gringo? No kissing; no rescuing? Or did she hope that María would evaporate into thin air and he would then grab her, ravage her with kisses until she was seduced into losing control? Which?

What she had not considered was how unpleasant El Gringo would be. Sexual frustration and rejection mixed with mojitos did not become him. When María pushed Catarina into the seat of the truck first, Catarina and Case were forced to sit thigh to thigh for the ride to the fireworks. María pressed herself close so that Catarina was mashed against El Gringo's leg. She felt every vibration of flesh, every stretch of sinew and movement of muscle as he angrily ground the gears with every curve. Catarina felt as tortured as the transmission.

Cantina Los Indios was a seamy bar where many a boy lost his virginity on a dare. It was the kind of place where adventure could be found if you wanted, and no one asked your name. It was a locally famous place without being openly talked about at all.

A motley collection of indoor and outdoor furniture spilled from the front porch of a ramshackle, two room structure and onto bare dirt under some mesquite trees. There was no real boundary as to where the establishment began or ended. Plastic tables mixed with utility cable spools, abandoned sofas and a Naugahyde recliner. All were in various stages of weather rot. Light inside was supplied by one exposed bulb; the moon provided the outdoor light. Five men played a poker game in front of the headlights of a rusty Ford.

As soon as Case turned the motor off, María jumped from the truck and slammed the heavy door before Catarina could get out of the cab. Catarina had to snatch her hand out of the way to keep it from being crushed. María thrust her head through the open window to give Case instructions. She was as explicit as she had been on the dance floor.

"The fireworks start at 10:00. Don't come for me until midnight, no earlier."

"What are you doing?" Catarina exclaimed. "We are here to watch the fireworks too."

"No, you're not. You are here to drop me off. Go somewhere else." She tossed a coy look over her shoulder. "Have fun until medianoche. Adios." She broke into a skipping run toward the moonlit figures milling around and celebrating outside.

Case scanned the assortment of suspected drug dealers, smugglers and murderers. "I know this place. We can't leave her here."

"Everyone knows this place." Catarina wondered what María was really up to.

"Who is putting on these fireworks anyway?"

"La gente. The people. I see some I know."

Case noticed three uniformed men drinking at one of the spool tables. "What's the Border Patrol doing here?"

"Celebrating." Catarina flashed an irritated look at Case before she realized he was concerned about María's citizenship. "Don't worry, María was born on the U.S. side. She has a birth certificate."

"Well, you don't."

Catarina watched María disappear into the bar. "We can't go back to the house without her."

"Great, we can slap mosquitoes, sweat and not talk to each other here in the dirt for the next three hours." Case reached into the dash board compartment for bug repellant. He sprayed far beyond necessity, filling the air with toxic mist. Catarina started to choke. When he finished, the cap wouldn't snap back on. After a couple of tries, he threw the can hard against the dash.

"Are you always unpleasant when you don't get your way?"

"Yes." He fumed and the silence festered. Sounds of people having a good time drifted into the cab. Someone won a poker hand. The bartender arrived with a round of drinks for one of the tables. An old man told a dirty joke.

Case said, "Let's go to Padre."

"La Isla? Tonight?"

The diesel engine rattled in response to a twist of the key in the ignition and they traced their way back out of the brush, down the farm to market road and onto State Highway 100.

"Have you been to the island before?" Case asked.

"Not in a long time; it's too far without a car. What's out there?"

"Do you like constellations?"

"What?"

"Stars, you know."

"Stars are beautiful."

"Some have stories that go with them."

Silence followed. Catarina knew it was her turn to speak. "You know these stories?"

"Some of them."

Case's words were the last. That was all the conversation she could manage. They drove past a dozen private little Cinco de Mayo fiestas. Squatters living in colonias of tiny shacks dotted the salt flats. If they had electricity, the yards were lit up in celebration like Abuelita's house. If not, they had bon fires burning. Once, they passed some children re-enacting the revolution by throwing firecrackers at passing vehicles. They screamed "Libertad! Viva Juárez!"

Otherwise the ride was too quiet. They did not talk. The road was straight as an arrow, no twists or turns. Every rapid mile brought Catarina closer to being completely alone with El Gringo. This was different than the spontaneous encounter during the storm at Resaca Park. Forces of nature had thrown them together that day.

Tonight, Catarina could have controlled the turn of events many times. She still could. The string of tension drew tighter with every moment, stretching as if a piano tuner was looking for high C. She glanced away from the road to look at him. He seemed as miserable as she was.

Case slowed for the series of speed traps through Port Isabel. He turned right at the old light house just as they approached the water. They passed the bait shops, motels and shrimp boats. When they got to the swing bridge, there was no wait.

Catarina felt as though she was leaving behind everything that grounded her. She could smell the ocean now. Its exotic scent excited her level of awareness. She listened to the tires clack over the metal grates, and noticed when the bumping sounds turned into a steady rhythm as they gathered speed going across the bridge to the island. The rhythm was hypnotic and she let the sounds do their work.

As soon as they reached the island, El Gringo turned north into the dark towards the uninhabited dunes where stars would shine brightest.

Catarina began to squirm uncomfortably in her seat. While still driving, Case reached into a compartment in the driver's side door, then handed her a heavy-duty flash-light he kept there. "Just in case you need to hit me," he teased.

Catarina took it. She couldn't believe she was allowing this to happen. They left the lights of hotels and restaurants behind them. Catarina's skin tingled with anticipation and dread. Her breasts felt full and she could feel a certain craving begin between her navel and her knees.

Case drove until they reached the end of the blacktop road that ran the length of the island. Then, he turned into the sand dunes that separated the road from the surf. The tow truck had four-wheel drive. It could go anywhere. Catarina could hear the waves crashing on the shore over the grinding and whining of the gears as they strained to handle the soft sand. She didn't ask where he was taking her.

El Gringo spit out the word, "Shit!" He swerved to avoid hitting something. The truck's bouncing headlights flashed off a man waving a can of Budweiser in the air and begging them to stop. His gait was unsteady and his other hand held a line dangling a huge redfish. He wore a pair of fisherman's wading pants.....one leg in and one leg dragging behind him in the sand. A second man, wearing a tight Speedo swimsuit walked into the light beams. Case circled the wrecker, shining its lights on their pickup.

There was a third man inside the vehicle at the steering wheel. The mass of fishing lures studding his hat jingled each time he gunned the motor. With each effort, the tires threw sand high into the air. It rained back down over his companions in clumps. Catarina couldn't decide which of the men was the most ridiculous.

"Great. Drunks." Case looked at Catarina. A change came over him. "Are you OK if I stop?"

"Sí. I'm fine. I have weapons." She flicked the flashlight on and off with one hand and squirted bug spray from the can with the other. She smiled, confident El Gringo could handle any situation. If these men had bad intentions, she was certain they would be sorry. Besides, maybe this distraction was good luck after all. Now she had a chance to consider the events she was about to allow to unfold.

When he kissed her, would she say no? Would he stop if she did say no? More important than either of those questions was this one. Could she allow herself the pleasure of having El Gringo and let it mean nothing?

She watched El Gringo confidently approach the men. His arms were relaxed, hiding the power she'd seen when he dented his hood. He was ready for anything unexpected.

His big voice sounded over the waves. "That fish over the legal limit?"

"We're sthuck!" the man with the fish slurred.

"Well, yes, you are. How long you been out here?"

"Since about seven o'clock. Nobody could help us."

"That might be because you've dug yourself a hole so deep your axle is resting on the sand." Case leaned over to see how he was going to get his towing equipment hooked up.

When the man holding the fish bent over to assist in the inspection, he lost his balance falling into Case fish first, beer second and body third. Case cushioned their fall with his elbows and Catarina began to giggle. When the drunk threw up on the middle of Case's back, Catarina pulled a beach towel to her mouth and sank below the dashboard and out of sight. She could hear more sounds of retching and liquid hitting the sand. Finally, the man delivered his only explanation. "We had a few beers."

With her laughter almost under control, Catarina popped her head up to look out the window. Case cussed, stepped out of his sandals, stripped off his violated shirt and stomped into the surf. When El Gringo was waist deep, he took off his pants. Catarina's breath caught in her throat at the sight of him standing in the moonlight, swishing his clothes through the surf. How many times had she wondered about the body under those clothes, wondered if his skin was as taut over his muscles as it seemed each time she could not avoid touching him.

He grabbed a piece of floating seaweed to scrub a stubborn spot and then, tossed it aside. When a swell sucked the water level low enough to expose his backside down to his knees, Catarina turned her eyes away from his naked body, even though she didn't have to. It was just that such unadorned beauty was agonizing to watch. Suddenly, she was acutely aware of a soft offshore breeze caressing her skin.

When she looked back, Case was still in the water pulling his pants up over his hips. The muscles in his back rippled across his V-shaped torso. When he turned around, his hair was wet and slicked back from his chiseled face. María was right when she said he had the body of a warrior. Catarina was glad El Gringo couldn't see her cheeks burning in the dark.

Case came back and looped his wet T-shirt on the CB antenna. Catarina handed him a towel. "Can you get these guys out of the sand?"

"It's more of a question of should I get them out. These idiots don't belong on the highway. One is passed out hugging a fish. The guy at the wheel can't tell me his name. If this last one can't walk a straight line, I'm leaving them." He finished drying himself.

"Hey, buddy!" Case called. The third man looked up from the hole in the sand. "Come over here, I want to see if you can walk. Put your finger on your nose and close your eyes." The man passed Case's version of a field sobriety test. "What's your name?" Case asked.

"Bob. That's Joe driving there."

"Bob, you got some more cervesa? I think I'm going to need one," Case said.

"I think we got a little left." Bob proudly grinned as he went to the bed of the pickup truck and opened a fifty gallon ice chest to display three cases of beer still floating in water and ice.

"Bob, how bad do you want to go home tonight?"

Bob's grin faded as he realized there would be conditions to his rescue.

"Here, let me help you." Together, Case and Bob lifted the ice chest out of the pickup and they began to pop the top of each can of beer and pour it into the sand. The man behind the wheel watched in drooling disbelief. The first man cuddled his redfish and slept.

Once the tow harness was hooked up, it only took seconds for Case to pull the pickup out of the sand. Case got out to disengage the chains and harness. "You stay on harder sand, closer to the surf and you'll be OK," Case said. He helped Bob scoop up the sleeping man with his red fish. They dumped him in the bed of their truck.

They pried Joe's fingers off the steering wheel and shoved him over to the passenger's side. Joe mumbled, "You taking the little lady down the beach for a kiss?" The words were barely intelligible.

"No, that's my sister. We are meeting my four brothers up at the cut for some early fishing in the morning."

"Really, a girl that likes to fish?" Sarcasm dripped and Catarina understood why El Gringo lied.

"Yeah." Case ended the conversation. He declined to take payment and shook Bob's hand while the embarrassed man apologized for his friend's comments.

When Case got back into the truck, he waited while the fishermen's headlights crept down the beach and turned off the sand onto the highway. He checked his diver's watch for the time and turned the truck north again along the surf line.

The level of tension between Case and Catarina was better now. Catarina took her sandals off and propped her feet up on the dash. Her cotton skirt hung between her knees and she held it close to her thighs so the wind couldn't blow it up. Case's shirt still hung on the CB antenna and flapped in the wind. He saw her eyes on his bare chest and grinned.

"No fair!" he said just before he reached over and loosened the fabric of her skirt from her fist. The skirt blew away from her legs just as he intended. Catarina knew he could see exactly what he wanted.

She observed him as he divided his attention between her fluttering skirt and his driving. Catarina's eyes wandered to his lap. The button to his pants gaped undone, and the zipper strained against the push of his erection.

"Can't help that," he said. "Want to go back?"

Catarina turned her face away from him, breathed in the wind and closed her eyes. She wanted him. She wanted more than just a goodbye kiss. She wanted to know what it was like to die and go to heaven in the arms of Case Becker. When she considered everything she had been through and all she was about to face in life, she decided she would give herself this one gift.

"You didn't ask me to dance tonight," she said.

"You didn't want to dance with me."

"How would you know?" She was actually flirting with him. She leaned toward him and sniffed. "You don't smell as bad as I thought you would."

He shook his head. "Can you believe that guy?" Case and Catarina laughed together as if they were relaxed and happy.

When there was no glow on the horizon from the lights of Port Isabel, Case turned and parked between the dunes and the surf. The only light shone from the Milky Way and the only noise came from the surf rolling towards the island. Case got out and rummaged around under the seat. He came out with an old patchwork quilt and a can of baby powder. He stood beside the open door and doused himself with powder. He brushed his hands over his skin in motions like he was enjoying a shower.

"What are you doing?" Catarina watched his tan turn to eerie alabaster in the moonlight.

"The powder dries your skin so you can knock the sand off. Makes you feel like you have had a shower. Can't live without it down here." Case spread the quilt and sat down on it. "Here, want me to do your feet?"

Catarina climbed down from the seat of the truck and joined Case on the quilt. She left her feet in the sand and pulled her skirt up just past her knees. He dusted the powder over her toes, smoothed it around her ankles and tenderly brushed the sand away. She watched him as he began to struggle with his breathing. Catarina stayed still and his strokes roamed imperceptibly further and further up under her skirt.

His touch became firm on her thighs and when his hands and her skirt rose to her hips, she put her arms around his neck. Case slid one hand to gather her to his groin and the other to the quilt to ease their bodies to rest next to each other.

His lips hovered above hers. They breathed the air, warm from each other's mouths before he began the tender kiss. It was like their first kiss should have been - sweet, sensuous, lingering. It was an extension of the gentle strokes he had given her legs as he washed them with powder; but it was just a formality. They both wanted more than tenderness.

Case ground his hips into her skirt. Easy at first, building until they both gasped and fought for air. His hard body was exactly where it needed to be and Catarina matched his moans and writhing pressure. She sensed that Case was about to orgasm when she broke away and lurched to a sitting position.

He grasped at her like he was afraid she was going to run. Instead, she moved her hands through her hair, back down her neck to caress her own breasts and smoothed her skirt. Her voice was small when it interrupted the sound of the waves rocking the sand. "Is this a sin?" she asked.

"No, it's what God created us for."

"I'm not so sure."

"I spend a lot of time with God, out here, in nature. I know in my heart it is absolutely true."

"God didn't tell you anything."

He touched her arm and said, "Sure he did. Remember what you told me at our first lesson? Why do I have blue eyes and you have brown ones? God made it so."

She pulled her windy hair out of her eyes so she could see his face. She looked into his eyes until she believed what he said and lay back down on the quilt to be with him.

"I want to feel your skin." Case gently lifted her blouse over her head. As he suspected, she had no bra on. It thrilled him. He allowed himself to look at her as he never had before. He had always tried to look at her eyes, so he wouldn't see her body. Now it was impossible to see anything else. All the sights he had denied himself flooded into his brain. The line of her collar bone extending to her shoulder, the moistness of her lips, the curve of the beginning of her breasts, the slope that filled to firm roundness topped with a dark nipple, the skin covering muscles that gave her shoulders and arms such a beautiful shape. *Oh, God, Catarina, you don't know what you look like, do you?*

Catarina let him look at her as long as he wanted. His fingers trailed the length of her neck, across her breasts and back to gather her in his arms. When he pressed her chest against his, the heavens created a cocoon around them. Nothing else existed in the universe.

His lips strayed from her mouth down her neck to her shoulder. Eventually, of its own accord, his mouth found her nipples and they were hard and waiting for him. Catarina arched to meet him. As his teeth teased one of them, he felt Catarina fumble with his zipper and slide her hand into his pants. His penis leaped to meet her touch.

Now, he felt confident about touching her between her legs. The fingers of his hand found the edge of her panties. He lifted the seam and slowly searched her soft curls, going as deep into her as he could. She was ready for him there too. She responded beyond his expectations. Back and forth, he loved her. She flinched and tightened with each stroke as she came closer and closer to being as hard as he was.

His fears of being too physical with her were swept away by fears of not being physical enough. He thought she was starting to come, but he wasn't certain, so he didn't stop. His hand slid the length of her from her core back out, over and over, as many times as he could bear. When he reached the ragged edge of his own limits, he put himself inside of her.

She graced his body with a new storm of passion that defied all modesty, excited him beyond his experience and surely disturbed the sleeping rabbits and coyotes in the dunes. He prayed to God that no one was close enough to hear her for he feared he would be arrested.

After his first orgasm swept over him, there was only a pause before he began to move inside her again. He stirred her delicious and compliant body, deep and sweet, until her cries brought him to the peak of mind destroying pleasure again. Then he lost consciousness.

Case fluttered his eyelids; he must have slept for a moment. Catarina was lying on her back with her head turned toward him, just looking, studying him. She looked so sad when he wanted her to look happy. She raised her chest to his touch when he reached to run his hands over her breasts. Was Catarina wondering if he would hold her after sex? He gathered her into his arms and they counted shooting stars. He held her until the moon set, until the waves from the rising tide threatened their quilt and until they were an hour late picking up María.

Chapter 11

María's Secret

The truck door slammed and Case had no chance to get out before Catarina and María tiptoed into the home of their friend, Selena Ganza. Selena lived in town with her American husband and would cover for their late night by claiming they were with her. Case felt good. Very, very good, but not happy. He had both dreamed of and dreaded this night, for now his life with Catarina would either be something more, or be over. Unlike most women would have, Catarina did not talk of love. They didn't even discuss seeing each other again. Case longed to whisk her away from the hard life of labor she led, protect her from the likes of men such as Logan Dell and give her everything she wanted, including a real school for the migrant children.

He pictured keeping the family business, building it and building his own family with Catarina by his side. And, yes, marriage would solve all these problems. *What a joke! I can't marry her; she still calls me El Gringo! Does she even know my name? He watched the front door to Selena's house softly close.*

With their study sessions over, he needed a way to insert himself into her life, a way to be with her for a while every day. She might not love him, yet; but she loved the kids at that shack she called a school. That was his ticket in. Better yet, maybe he should do something bigger, help Catarina with her own dream of becoming a teacher.

He was riddled with doubt, uncertain that she was ready to accept what he felt for her and he needed her so much that he hated himself for taking the risk he took tonight. *What is to become of Case Becker? The first woman I can't live without might be the one woman who doesn't want me!*

* * * * *

Catarina and María crept into a guest bedroom. As soon as the door was shut, María broke the silence. "That was a strange ride home. Where did you go? I was worried that you were so late." She took off her dress and admired her luscious figure in Selena's full length mirror. "I wish I had a mirror like this."

"We helped some fishermen stuck in the sand." Catarina stripped out of her skirt. She folded it and caressed the spot where Case's manly body had rubbed and left a scent.

"Sand? Where did you go?"

"To the island, down on the beach. They were stuck. We had to help."

"Catarina?"

"I'm fine. I'm fine."

"Catarina! You did it. You kissed those poet lips! You did! Turn around. Let me look at you." María took Catarina by the shoulders and whirled her around. "You look like a woman who has been loved and loved well. Tell me! Tell me all of it. I want to feel what you feel!"

Catarina wasn't about to spill all the intimate details of her evening; and María's sensuous suggestion made Catarina uncomfortable. She knew that María wanted to enjoy thoughts of sex with El Gringo for herself. But more, Catarina could barely stand the memory of what happened whirling in her own mind. Making love with Case Becker was beyond what she expected. She had never experienced such pleasure and such fear. The thrill of connecting with his body would never be matched. She was haunted by lingering physical sensations. She unwillingly closed her eyes and it happened again. Her abdomen contracted and the intensity increased.

It was the spiritual connection that disturbed her most. Case repeated her own words to her. "God made it so." She shuddered at the power of it. She would never give voice to what took place this night. The story could not come out of her mouth and into the reality of sound with anyone, not even María.

"Shut up, María. Nothing happened."

María folded her arms around Catarina. Her voice changed from taunting to gentle kindness. "Yes, it did. Something big happened. Why do you want to deny it? You are an amazing woman. He is enough man for you. Others have not been. Take him. Let him love you. Love him back!"

"I have no intention of loving him!"

"Catarina, this is so important, I am going to tell you a secret." María sat on the bed and pulled Catarina to sit with her. She lay back on the pillows and drew Catarina to lie beside her face to face. They squirmed down into the softness. "It is a secret no one.....no one knows." María whispered into her ear, then paused for effect. "I do know who Alberto's father is."

Catarina's eyes widened then softened as she saw a tear slide from María's eye into the pillow. She waited for the confession that was about to come.

"It's true. I did have two men in my life when I got pregnant with Alberto. I thought the father of my son was the one that did not love me, so I rejected the one who did love me. It took years and Alberto's first grade picture to tell me the truth." María reached into her purse to retrieve a worn snapshot of a child and a newer one of Alberto. She held them out side by side for Catarina to see. "He looks just like Sixto. Don't you think?"

Catarina looked at the photos; there was no mistake. No one else on earth could be Alberto's father. "Why are you telling me this? You should be telling Sixto. He will be so happy! He loves Alberto."

"I can't tell him."

"Why not?"

"For the same reason I am telling you my secret. My moment with Sixto is gone. I have lied to him for years. I believed the other man was going to leave his wife and we would be married. But, I'm not the first fool to fall for that story."

"María....."

"Beware of Logan Dell. I see him after you. I hear he has not changed his ways. He still preys on young women who are innocent enough to believe he will love them, marry them. He is very, very good at making a girl believe.....I had known him about three months when I fell in love with Sixto." María looked thoughtful, wistful. "What I am saying to you is that if this gringo makes your heart lurch into him, if he makes you laugh, if you trust him, take him! Never, never let go. Nothing in the past matters; your differences don't matter. Only being together in the future matters." She patted Catarina's still flat tummy.

Catarina was stiff as a corpse. The man who taught Catarina to hate her own desires, to reject the idea of trust, and killed the hope that loving someone was possible for her was the same man who ruined María's life ten years ago.

Catarina parted her lips to say something, then, changed her mind. What she had to share was not going to make María feel better. She would save her side of the secret for another day.....if ever, for María's advice about staying away from Logan Dell was too late.

Chapter 12

Money for School

The pain roused Catarina that night, but not enough to fully wake her. She thought it was part of a dream where she vaguely remembered dancing with María and needing to change her clothes. When she woke and got out of bed, she discovered she had started her period. The stain on her nightgown was an answer to an abandoned prayer. Everything was going to be all right.

The dark decision whether to visit María's mysterious friend in Matamoros or not evaporated. The nightmare of having to raise a child with no money, no job, no education and no husband disappeared. Her lungs swelled with gratitude. She closed her eyes and buried her face in her forearm.

Catarina's life was back to where she wanted it to be. She vowed to fill out the paperwork on the student visa today and get it in the hands of Delores García. She vowed Logan Dell would never touch her again and she vowed not to fall in love with El Gringo.

Catarina went to the bathroom mirror and

discovered a happy smirk on her face. It blossomed into a full fledged, beaming smile as she called out, "María!"

* * * * *

Catarina and María left Selena's house and walked towards Camino Ratama in the cool predawn. Everything was wet this time of day. The trees dripped condensation, flowers looked like sparkling picture post cards and green foot prints darkened the grass where the girls stepped. The edge of the sky was pink and promised a beautiful morning. This was an exquisite time of day. The promise would last until mid morning. Then the dew would burn off into the heavy atmosphere and the sun would bake cracks into the earth.

"Are you going to see him again?" María's encouraging tone sounded intimate in their solitude.

"I'm thinking about it." Catarina was going to be forced to redefine her relationship options. The "goodbye to El Gringo memory" she created for herself last night was suddenly not so final. It was possible he would not pursue her, but not probable. She needed to be prepared for either event. She knew he was not married; but there were too many other women. In the daylight, Catarina considered the possibility that she was just one more notch on El Gringo's gun.

The worst thing that could happen would be for him to expect her to be his. For some reason, men wanted ownership. The things they traded for it included trinkets, safety or fear. Some women bartered themselves for marriage, not that this was a possibility with El Gringo. He was.....gringo.....a rich gringo; and he didn't have what Catarina wanted.

That intangible thing was rooted deep in her soul and it wasn't something any man could give her. She wanted to make a difference for people like herself; she wanted to be a teacher; she wanted to prove she could do it against all odds. To make this happen, no man could own her. She must own herself.

"The first thing I am going to do is finish that student visa application. Mrs. García is going to help me pass the entrance exams. If I can do it, I will be in school this fall. I'll have to study hard; I've never taken a test before."

"Catarina, if you ignore a man like Case, he will look elsewhere," María warned.

"Who?"

"Case Becker. El Gringo! Don't be stupid!"

"I don't want to think about him now. I'm thinking about getting into school."

"Fine. Have you thought about how to pay for it? It's not free."

"Mrs. García's looking for some kind of aid for me, a loan maybe."

"You still have to pay a loan back. You barely make enough to feed yourself."

"Thanks for the encouragement, María."

This was the moment María was looking for. "You can do me a favor, for money." She watched Catarina's curiosity peak. "You want to know how I pay my rent?"

Alarm crossed Catarina's face. "No! I don't want to know!"

"I work at Cantina Los Indios."

"María! With men?" Catarina stopped dead in her dewy footsteps.

"I knew you would think that. That's why I didn't tell anybody. I just serve drinks, talk to the lonely ones, wash dishes. It's nothing; but the money is great! The owner doesn't pay anything, but he lets me keep everything extra a customer gives me."

Catarina's first feeling was relief that María was working instead of sneaking off to the cantina to meet someone. Then she thought of the hot field where she, herself would spend this day. She knew how her back would ache, her fingers would bleed and how little she would take home to Abuelita when it was over. Working in the cool night on the low-water crossing at the cantina didn't seem so bad.

María continued, "I've saved enough money to take Alberto to Guanajuato to see our family. But, if I leave my job for two weeks, it won't be there for me when I get back. I want you to do it for me.....please? If you want to kill yourself, you can work for Ito in the daytime too."

Catarina started walking again. María positioned herself directly in front of her cousin and walked backwards while she continued her plea. "You know José Fanco, that old man that stays with the Garza family? He's there 'til closing every night, playing poker. He'll walk home with you.....All you have to do is smile, be nice, and the men will pay you more. Look at this dress." María fanned her skirt and twirled. "You might have to slap a few hands; just be playful. It's only for two weeks."

That dress didn't come from the Catholic church's basement. No wonder María had pretty clothes.

Catarina stopped again to think. She knew today was her day to start anew. It was her day to strike out and make things happen for herself. María asked her for a favor at the right moment and applied the right motivation. Catarina said, "I'll do it."

* * * * *

Delores García's Chevy was already at the shack when Catarina arrived at the end of her day in the fields. She was hot, weary and happy. She had the student visa application completed. She couldn't see exactly how she was going to make her dream come true; but she knew she was taking the first steps.

"Here it is! I finished. Now what do I do"

"Delores took the papers. "Oh, Catarina, I thought you were too afraid."

"I am afraid.....of the tests. My English is good, but my vocabulary is not and I don't know math."

"I'll help you every day. I promise; you can do it."

Children came rushing in. There were hugs for everyone. Love and learning go hand in hand and the children were learning more and becoming more excited every day.

"Look what's coming." Delores' gaze was fixed on a Becker Rescue Services truck surrounded by a cloud of dust. It was pulling off the road next to the shack. "Catarina, be nice," she warned.

Here it was, Catarina's first encounter with El Gringo; and it was coming much sooner than she thought it would. She wasn't ready. He actually bounded out of the truck and in through the door. He seemed jaunty, more energized than ever.

"Hey, some of you big boys, come help me." Four of the oldest boys rushed outside to see what surprises were in store. Case judged each child and filled his arms with what he could carry. The boxes the children brought in were laden with more school supplies. One boy carried a real chalk board. Case carried a box marked with the words "Level I Reading Workbooks." He set it on the ground.

When Catarina peered inside, she choked. Lying on top was a bouquet of flowers, store bought ones from Dellicious Designs by Jan. This was horrible! Catarina didn't want El Gringo bringing her flowers. Everyone would know!

Case grabbed the flowers and presented them to Catarina with a flourish. She was preparing a rejection in her head when he whipped out a matching bouquet and presented it to Mrs. García. The woman preened and gushed with delight. No woman was immune to this charming man.

"Ah, one more thing." Case returned to the truck. The last box carried an unmistakable aroma with it. "Hamburgers for everyone!" The kids didn't quite get it, so Case took a chance with his Spanish, "Hamburguesas?" The scramble to the box almost knocked the big man down.

Case stayed the afternoon with the kids. Not much school work was done. He mounted the chalk board on the wall. He gave rides on his shoulders for the ones who wanted to see what it was like to be so tall. A little girl who had never uttered a word to anyone crawled into his lap and whispered "Gracias" into his ear.

Catarina's feelings were torn. Her body had not recovered from the cravings of last night. The feeling of his hands was still on her. She knew he was here at the school because of her. Was it just a sideways move to make her indebted to him? His whole performance left her feeling strangely unbalanced.

Mrs. García dismissed the children. "Tomorrow, we will work harder. We will use the new workbooks." She touched each child as they left the shack and tucked the last hamburger in the pocket of the little girl who needed it the most. Case helped the women close up. He removed the braces that supported the wooden windows and locked the door.

While Case and Catarina unsuccessfully tried to avoid eye contact, Mrs. García thanked him over and over for the school supplies. She chattered about having to hurry; there was a PTA meeting at her school that night and papers to grade.

The more likely it seemed Catarina and Case would be left alone, the more pent up Catarina became. The gravity of his presence pulled her toward his arms. The consequences of being consumed by a passion that could come to nothing but heartache pushed her to look for something, anything that could break her from this slowly shrinking orbit around him.

"Will you let me take you home?"

"No."

"OK. Let's talk, under our tree here."

Catarina walked ahead of him to the lone tree.

It was thriving because of the water Catarina poured on it every time she washed the wall. She touched the trunk. "I'll have to keep watering it even though we have a chalk board and eraser now."

Case walked toward her and she examined him. She could feel the relaxed rhythm of his muscles. She noted his one-eyed squint in the setting sun. She felt the orbit tightening. Her only weapon was to turn her back to him. There was an instant when she felt the air stir behind her before he embraced her. She couldn't help but lean her head back into his chest and he read it as a sign that he could let his hands roam over the front of her body.

He breathed hot breath into her hair and turned her to face him for a deep tongue-sharing kiss. Re-experiencing the languor and satisfaction from the night before was delicious, but it didn't last long. When he hardened against her, they both increased the urgency of the kiss.

El Gringo broke the embrace just before it would have been too late. "Not here." His voice was rough and sweet.

Catarina shook her hair and wondered where her willpower disappeared to.

Case began. "I don't know where this will lead.....this thing between us."

Catarina was surprised. Men weren't usually this concerned about the future or this honest about feelings. She let him continue.

"I think.....I think you don't know if you want me or not; but I know you do want to go to school and I want to help you. I want to pay for it."

"What?" Catarina thought, surely she

misunderstood.

"I mean, I have money. I can help you....."

The color faded from Catarina's vision. She could not see through the intense white covering the world outside her mind. "You give me money for last night? You make me a puta?" Her voice was disbelieving, quiet and accusing all at once.

"No, it's not like....." Before he could finish the sentence, her thundering slap slammed his mouth.

Now Catarina's raised her voice. "You take my body and give me money? What do you think that makes me, Gringo? It makes me a whore, Gringo, a whore."

Case grabbed her as she tried to run. She screamed in rage as she struggled to get away from him. She raged at her own naivety, her powerlessness and the fact that men were physically stronger than women.

Case held her in a straight jacket grip, very different from the embrace of the kiss. She only stopped kicking him when she realized that no amount of punishment she could inflict would enable her to get away. He was even stronger and harder than he looked.

Case whispered into her hair. "Catarina, Catarina, I have been with a whore. It was nothing like last night, nothing at all." Catarina began to sob big heaving sobs that left her gulping in enough air only to fuel the next expression of rage. He held her, held her until she shuddered in exhaustion.

"So, what do you want? You want to get married?" He hesitated only a fraction of a second. "You don't love me. For God's sake, Catarina, you call me El Gringo. Do you know my name?"

Case. Case. Case. Catarina knew his name, she just couldn't say it. To say his name would symbolize the opening of the gates to her heart. To hope for love, trust and all joys of life that went with it. She didn't believe in that kind of love.

He rocked her in the vise of his tight embrace. Catarina's vision slowly cleared from white to thick fog and then to haze. When she could breathe normally, she knew she had her reason to destroy the bond she felt with this man. He provided the perfect way. A whore was a whore, regardless of how payment was paid.

Case Becker was just a kinder, subtler, more insidious version of Logan Dell. At first, the price Logan paid was love lies. When that didn't work any more, he paid in safety from deportation for her and Sixto.

Catarina stood still in Case's arms while she looked for the cold, familiar place deep inside herself where she could be safe. All she had to do was wait a little longer for El Gringo to release her body. Then, she could go home to let her anger heal her.

Chapter 13

Driving on the Levee

Case sat with his back to the sun while he waited at the abandoned gas station. This place served as a pick-up and drop-off point for los migrantes. It was here that farmers selected the strongest and fastest workers available to pick for them. He straightened his shoulders and twisted his arm behind his torso to peel his shirt away before it scorched into his skin. It was only May. A thermometer screwed to a rusty metal post read one hundred thirteen degrees. No breeze.

He stood to take a drink from the community dipper attached with twine to a galvanized tub full of water. In it floated the remains of a ten pound block of ice. This kind of heat was deadly. A burro and a bicycle were tethered in the shade of a dusty olive tree. Case noticed that the burro's water dish was empty. He found a hose. The water was hot, muddy and smelled like canal water, but the burro didn't care.

A cloud of dust announced the arrival of the tractors long before they rounded the corner of the field. They pulled cotton trailers fitted with chicken wire sides, eight feet high. Sweating brown men and women hung chest to chest, hip to hip, their fingers entwined in the heavy wire for balance. It was standing room only. The tractors stopped in front of Case.

One older man had collapsed from the heat some time during the day. He had to be handed down from the trailer bed into waiting arms. His friends walked him carefully to the galvanized tub of water. They had to coax him to drink.

Sixto jumped down from the trailer after the old man. "Hola Gringo. Looking for Catarina?"

"No, Catarina's not talking to me right now."

The look on Sixto's face explained he already knew that. Case waited while Sixto walked to the tub and drank from the dipper, long and slow.

"I bought a chicken. Come help me eat it."

Sixto did not answer and started walking towards home.

"I got cold beer, and mangos," Case tempted.

Sixto stopped to reconsider. His eyes wandered to Case's wrecker. "You gonna' teach me to drive that big truck?"

"Sure, first lesson, right now!" Case let Sixto climb into the driver's seat. "You know how to drive with the gears on the shaft or on the floor?"

"Never driven before."

Shit. Why am I so impulsive? This was the newest wrecker in Case's fleet. An illegal guy with no driver's license who didn't know a gear from a tailpipe driving off on a joy ride? "I changed my mind. I better drive us down to the river. Then we can start with the basics." Both men got out and switched seats.

They drove down the highway with Sixto hanging his head out of the window enjoying the air like a dog. He measured the speed of the vehicle by holding his arm into the wind. "How much does a truck like this cost?"

"You want to buy one?"

"You teach me to drive, maybe I buy this one!"

Case parked the truck on a straight of dirt road that ran along side the levee. After he reinstalled Sixto in the driver's seat, he began by explaining the function of a clutch. Sixto's mistakes were predictable and the ride wasn't easy. The vehicle lurched and jerked violently up and down the dirt road while he learned to feel the balance between the transmission and the accelerator.

By dusk, he was through with the rabbit-hopping stage and on to learning to use four wheel drive in reverse. Sixto was having a lot more fun than Case was. Still, Case couldn't help but experience moments of pleasure between Sixto's joy and his own moments of terror.

Backing up went quite well. Then, Sixto manipulated the gears to move forward again. He was being very careful, giving the engine lots of gas and slowly releasing the clutch. The wrecker bucked like a prize bull and charged up the side of the levy, tipping over the edge before the engine choked and died. Case grabbed for the steering wheel.

"No! I can do it! I can do it!" Sixto insisted. He restarted the wrecker, found reverse and floored the accelerator. As the wrecker lifted itself into the air and landed in a horizontal position back on the dirt road, Sixto let out a gaucho's cry of delight,

"Yeeeehaaaaaaah!" He sat listening to the music of the diesel engine, smiling and shaking his head. "This is a good truck."

Case relaxed his white knuckled grip on the door post. "Yeah, a good truck. I think that will do it for today. That chicken is not getting any fresher."

They ate their dinner in the companionable silence of men who have bonded through adversity of their own making. The chicken was moist with wood smoke, the mangos sweet and the beer cold enough to make them forget the heat of the day. They watched the sunset, all gold and blue and purple when it died over a field of cucumbers.

Sixto began, "Our mother is in California."

"What's she doing in California?"

"We lived close to Houston when Catarina was born. Her papa got killed when she was a baby," he explained between bites. "Un accidente. Fell under a tractor. Our mother had to work very hard to feed us. She even picked cotton. That's the worst work there is. But it wasn't enough. She was beautiful, like Catarina. So, after a while, she entertained men."

"Oh." Case's stomach started to shrink.

"Later, she married a man who had loved her a long time. She left us with Abuelita and never came back. They went to California. In the north part, I think; it is not so hot there."

Case began to understand where some of Catarina's anger came from.

"She was lucky, my mother."

"How was she lucky?"

"She still believed in love."

"Don't you?" Case asked.

"Sí, but mi amor does not love me back. I don't know why. I try to be a good man, do what is right. Mostly I believe in family, not getting into trouble. I do my work, love my people."

"Family is good." Case agreed.

"You asked me one time if Alberto was my son. I want a son like Alberto. There was a time I wished he was mine so bad, I thought he was. I knew he was. It took me a long time to believe the truth. He is a good boy. That day, looking for him in the water, I was so scared."

"Me too," Case said. "We didn't let anybody know it, did we?" The night got cooler and the chant of the locust slowed. Dark descended while they finished their dinner.

"Does your beautiful sister believe in love?"

"Ah, finally you ask. Catarina. She knows someone will always want her. Many men, maybe. But, Catarina? I feel sorry for the man who loves Catarina."

That startled Case. He jerked his head to meet Sixto's grimace.

"Catarina loves only school. She wants to need no one. It's hard to understand her sometimes."

"Did she tell you I want to help her go to school?"

"She told me you wanted to give her money."

"What else did she tell you?"

"That she said no. I told her she did the right thing."

"Sixto, its just money. It's not even mine. My grandmother left it to me. Catarina taught me to read. She should have some of it."

"No, it's not just money. If we didn't earn it, it has power over us. It obligates us."

"What if I gave it to you and you gave it to her?"

"No."

"What if I lend it to you?"

"I can't pay it back. No. You want to help? Give us the power instead. Change things. Look." Sixto pointed at headlights bouncing in the dark about a half mile away. "Border Patrol, looking for people like me." Sixto reached for their beer cans and paper napkins. The chicken bones they would leave for the wild creatures that would come for them in the night. "Vamanos; let's go."

Sixto tossed Case the keys and they sneaked through the fields and levies with the headlights off. There was no need to attract unwanted attention.

"Drop me off at the barracks at Ito's. I'll stay there tonight." Sixto was through talking about Catarina.

Chapter 14

Finding Catarina

Case slapped at his alarm clock, that noisy squawking bastard. He tossed and turned so late last night that he was afraid to trust his internal clock, afraid he would oversleep his meeting this morning. The attorneys from Houston were on the move, pressuring for the sale of Becker Rescue Services. They showed up often, brought more stacks of paperwork and complained constantly.

The reason negotiations were bogging down was Case's indecision. There was a time he doubted his ability to head the business. Now, he was feeling more self-assured. Catarina planted the seed of confidence in the one area of his life where he always had misgivings. His natural fearlessness was taking hold. He was feeling more powerful and an idea was starting to hatch in the back of his mind. The men around the bargaining table sensed the change in him, like animals. They wanted to close this deal while they still had the upper hand; but that wouldn't happen today.

Sharing his idea with Catarina would be so much fun. He wondered if she would be proud of him. Case stretched like he did every morning. He thought it ironic that Catarina de la Alvarado had turned his world entirely upside down. Here he was, considering going to intellectual war with men who had superior educations and far more experience than he did. Somehow, Case believed he was going to come out on top.

His certainty regarding his proven prowess with women, however, was in serious doubt. He couldn't do anything right. Basically, last night, Sixto told him no one had ever found the key to Catarina. Case had never failed to rescue a damsel in distress yet; and this feeling of incompetent helplessness with a woman was entirely new.

After his business meeting, Case would be free for the day. The weather was going to be fine so there wouldn't be much rescue work to do. It wasn't like Case to moon around over a woman and listen to sad Country Western songs, but now he understood why people do those things.

He wanted to talk to Catarina. The last time he wanted to find her, he had to wait for an act of the Mayan Thunder God, Chac, to deliver her to his truck in the rain. He hadn't been very proactive. This time, after the business meeting was over, he would go to the school again, maybe just do some reconnaissance, see how she was doing.

* * * * *

When the children saw El Gringo, they dropped their pencils and stormed his legs and arms. It reminded Case of the kind of affection shown to him by his Chihuahua friend, Pancho Villa. Mrs. García scowled.

"I'm sorry. I didn't know I'd be such a disruption."

"Case, we're always glad to see you." She started trying to recapture the children's attention. "Siéntese; sit down!" She looked back to Case. "I don't ever have enough time with them."

"Catarina's not here today." Case stated the obvious.

"No, she is working extra hours. She said she won't be here all week."

Case let out a sigh.

"You like her, no?" Mrs. García smiled. Case blushed under his tan and shuffled his feet. "Is she being difficult?"

"Delores, you have no idea." The body language of frustration swept over him.

Mrs. García handed him a workbook. "You're obviously not doing anything else; I could use some help. Here. Lola needs to know how to hold a pencil."

"I don't know what to do."

"Yes, you do." Mrs. García pointed to Lola and turned her attention to another child.

Case walked over to the little girl who had thanked him for the hamburger. She was squatting, resting her workbook on the dirt floor. She held the pencil with both hands and stabbed at the page trying to make an "A."

"Lola, that's your name?" Case didn't know he could talk baby talk. Her round brown eyes traveled up his long legs, all the way to his face. She nodded. Case lowered himself to the floor. There was so little room that two boys had to move to the other wall so Case could sit. "Here let me show you; use one hand." Case took the pencil and positioned it in the miniature fingers of her right hand.

Lola said something in Spanish. Case thought she said, "These fingers don't like my pencil."

Bemused, Case fumbled for the Spanish words to ask her, "Do any of your fingers like this pencil?" Lola moved the pencil into her left fist and held it forward. Case took the pencil out of her hand. He positioned it between her thumb and forefinger. Together they placed her left hand on the workbook and Lola made an "A" by herself.

"You do one." She held out the pencil. Case took it and made an "A" of his own next to Lola's.

She squinted her eyes and put her nose closer to the workbook. "Yours looks funny," she said. She took the pencil back and fixed it to match her own. She smiled the smile of success. "We are better together."

Case kissed the top of her head. If only he could convince Catarina to see things this way.

* * * * *

In the next few days, Case realized how few places existed for his path to cross Catarina's. He began to think that perhaps she moved up The Valley to work for someone else or went back to Mexico. They truly did live in different worlds. He began to lose hope that he would ever have an opportunity to explain that he never meant to hurt her, that he understood why she was so sensitive and got so mad. He was even ready to ask for the friendship rule back, anything to keep her in his life at some level.

During the last three days, he took to visiting the picnic table where they used to study at Resaca Park. He would arrive just before sunset, half expecting to see her walking across the park toward him. She had to forgive him. Even if she didn't want to be with him, he couldn't live with the memory of Catarina looking at him the same way he saw her look at Logan Dell. The thought made his eyes sting in a very unmanly way.

He wanted to thank her for making such a difference in his life. He wanted to tell her what a gift she had given him in making him the dictionary. That's why he had the notebook with him. He had picked out pictures of new words in hopes she would help him put them in.....sorry, forgive, college, kiss, feel, maybe even love.

He'd hoped that night they made love on the beach would be a beginning. It felt like she was just looking for some reason to hate him, while he was just trying to love her in the only way he knew how. He watched the sun's golds, purples and blues spread across the horizon. She didn't come. He wouldn't be watching the sunsets with Catarina anymore.

Case's frustration churned and boiled in his guts. A growl of rage ruptured into his throat and exploded into a blood curdling demand that the universe recognize and deal with his pain. He hurled the dictionary into the muddy waters to drown. It didn't sink fast enough, so he used his foot to stomp it down in the water.

Across the resaca, a dog responded to Case's bellows with aggressive barking. Case barked back. The ensuing exchange of threats roused the entire neighborhood of dogs, those that were penned and those that roamed free. A big German Shepherd jumped his back yard fence and came to dance a challenge on the bank across the water while a stern male voice called "Mack. Come."

Laughter started to creep into Case's roars. He caught his breath and shook his head at the absurdity of his situation.

The screaming release worked its magic. He could think again. He would go to Abuelita's one more time. If Catarina wasn't there, he would go to Padre Island, steal one of Skipper's boats and not come back until he wanted to.

* * * * *

Abuelita's little house was quiet tonight, no twinkling lights, no guests. Case paused with his fist in the air before knocking on the screen door. He had no idea what he was going to say. When he did knock, the screen door squeaked a little under the pressure of his fist. "Abuelita?" He called before he heard shuffling in the hall.

"Case, hola. Como está? How are you?"

"I'm good, thanks." Case's lying eyes looked to the floor. "Hola, Pancho Villa! How's the big bad bandido?" Pancho growled, bared his teeth and wagged his tail all at the same time. "Is Catarina here?"

"No, no está aquí. You still haven't talked to her?"

"Not yet."

"Do you want to give her another message?"

"No. Where is she tonight?"

"Oh, she is with her friend Selena Ganza. She is staying all night."

A new feeling surged into Case's body. It seemed to enter through his lungs and flash-spread over his skin. Selena was Catarina's alibi friend. Catarina would be up to no good tonight.

"Is María around?"

"No, María went to México to visit family, Guanajuato. Would you like to come in?" Abuelita's invitation was delivered to Case's back.

"No, thanks." He was already through the gate.

Just how quickly could he get away from here? What an idiot he was. He was spending his nights moping around a picnic table while Catarina was out partying! He was dreaming of a life with her and she was running in the other direction. The conversation in his head was turning into a tantrum. His tantrum morphed into an obsession.....finding Catarina.

He drove to Selena's house. No one was home. There was only one place he could think of where she might be. The best place for her to get into trouble was Cantina Los Indios.

* * * * *

Friday was cash payday in the fields, so the cantina was packed. Case heard the juke box long before he saw the building. There was no room to park close to the shack; he had to park alongside the road. From the higher vantage point of the wrecker, he could see over the cars to the tables sprawled over the grass and even through the open door to the inside. He decided to wait, to see what he could see.

This was not spying. This was a public place. He had the right to go in and have a beer just like anyone else, a small comfort considering his state of mind. What played out before him next was surreal. He felt completely detached. It was like he was watching a screen play unfold before him.

Catarina appeared in the doorway. She was wearing a white sundress that bared her shoulders. Her hair was arranged on top of her head so that tendrils fell down to kiss the skin of her neck, just as he longed to kiss it.

The light behind her glowed yellow and Case was so immersed in her beauty that he forgot to wonder why she might be here. As she entered the yard, a man followed her, the same man who paid so much attention to Catarina at Abuelita's Cinco de Mayo celebration.

Smooth and pressed again in all white casual clothing, he looked far too elegant to be among the riffraff of Cantina Los Indios. Case scanned the parking lot for the entourage of black cars and found it waiting in the tree shadows next to the river.

The man chose a rickety table for two. The owner of the bar followed them out of the door and set two drinks before them. *Catarina has a date!* The man in white reached for his wallet, but the owner held up the palm of his hand indicating that the drinks were on the house. This stranger with Catarina was being treated with the same deference Case had seen at Abuelita's house. *Who is this guy?*

One piece of music ended after another, as Case watched the man openly appraise Catarina and flirt with her relentlessly. His every motion communicated confidence in his intent. Case felt an escalation of a strange feeling he had no name for. Seeing Catarina with Logan had not made him feel like this, and he even believed that Catarina had been with Logan in a most intimate way. But, in this unknown man, this cool, important, dangerous man, Case sensed a true threat.

Catarina did not touch her drink. Her date had another. The man reached to take Catarina's hand in both of his and lifted it to his lips. At that moment, when the man's lips touched Catarina's skin, Case identified his unknown emotion. For the first time in his life he was jealous.

Catarina did not shrink away from the kiss although she did lean back in her chair when it seemed the man asked her a question. Without a pause, she shook her head no. The man let go of her hand but not her eyes. He leaned back to relax in his chair; he smiled. A few minutes later, he rose and bowed slightly as he softly blew her a kiss farewell. He is not done, Case thought. But, the man did leave. Case watched him walk to where a driver waited in a dark sedan. Catarina went back into the bar.

Minutes later she returned to the yard with a tray full of drinks. She started serving customers and taking cash. Catarina was working! She didn't look like a barmaid. The white sundress she wore made her look like an angel. The message she sent with every glance was, "You can look, but not touch." She served with grace and returned the smiles of the hapless, beauty struck, common men.

Case's emotional chemistry cooled as he watched. Catarina should not be here even if she did need money for school. What was he going to do about it? He had an hour until the bar would shut down to figure it out. He wasn't hopeful. So far, he had not been able to get Catarina to accept anything from him, even a ride home.

Closing time came and the owner left Catarina to clean up. How could the man do that? There were three customers still drinking. They were from The Upper Valley and by the mortarboards and tassels they wore, they were at the cantina celebrating their recent graduation from college. Cars their daddies bought them waited in the parking lot while they had been tanking up on cube libres all night.

Case recognized one, a lineman from the University of Texas Longhorns who had just been named an All American. His father owned an automobile dealership and was a customer of Becker Rescue Services. All three men were big, full of disrespect, booze and testosterone. One made his move on Catarina.

"Hey, pretty baby, I haven't seen you here before."

Catarina pretended she did not understand. "No Inglés."

"No English doesn't mean you don't understand. You know what I need. I know you do. I'll be nice, please?" He patted his knee. The others laughed at the pretend begging. The strap of Catarina's sundress fell on her arm as she twisted her shoulder to dodge a hand.

Case got out of his truck and walked purposefully toward the cantina. As the second man put his hands on Catarina's hips and pulled her into his lap, a big voice spoke out of the shadows.

"Catarina, are you ready to go home?"

Four faces reacted as Case materialized before them. Catarina's expression was one of recognition and relief. The hoodlums looked disappointed and Catarina whirled away from her captor.

Case continued. "Time for you boys to get on home. Need any help with that?" Without the adrenaline of the chase, the men fell into the drunken state awaiting them. Case thought it comic as the three of them looked up at him and made silent but unanimous decisions to leave.

"Don't bother to come back. I'll be here tomorrow night too," Case promised. The high performance engines of a blue Ford Mustang and a red Corvette convertible whined against the brakes getting ready for a whoop-it-up road race back up The Valley to wherever home was. Case could hear their noisy banter all the way to the highway.

"Gracias." Catarina began clearing the last table.

"How are you getting home?"

"I walk. It's not far."

"Hell, it's over five miles, Catarina!"

"I walk as the crow flies. I'm not afraid of the dark." She carried the glasses inside.

Case waited for her in the yard. He hated this.

Surely there was some way for him to help her that she could accept. The cold calm he had needed to confront the drunks slipped as the minutes ticked by. He did not like what eased into him instead. He knew the fierce jealousy and possessiveness building inside him was not what was needed to deal with Catarina, but he could not stop it. As she locked the door, he expressed his feelings out of tight, bitter lips.

"Catarina, what do you think you are doing here? This is dangerous!"

"I'm here shopping for men to give me money." She flaunted the angry lie into Case's indignant face.

"What?" Case had been on an emotional roller coaster for days. It topped a peak and hurled him into a face forward drop. He lost his stomach, teetered to one side and no longer possessed sensation in his legs. When he reached the bottom of the ride, he saw before him a proud, trembling woman, lashing out to protect what dignity she had.

Softer, he said, "I've wanted to see you all week." Case didn't have to look down to search for her eyes. Catarina was still standing on the porch. It made her eyes level with his. "I want to tell you I'm sorry."

"Sorry? For showing me the truth? That was the best thing you could have done, Gringo. I thank you. I slipped, let you distract me. I needed to get back to reality."

Case could see Catarina would not be reached tonight. "I am driving you home."

"I'm fine."

"I am driving you home." Case firmly took her elbow and guided her down the steps. He led her toward the truck relaxing only as he felt her resistance wane. If she wouldn't give in to him, at least she would give in to common sense. When he reached into his pocket for his keys, she took advantage. She darted into the underbrush and was quickly out of sight.

"Damnit, Catarina!" Case went after her. He crashed through the mesquite thicket, whipping limbs aside and dodging columns of yucca plants. Their huge white blossoms towered over him in the pale moonlight. When he barreled into a prickly pear cactus, he yelped and decided he needed to slow down in the dark.

He stopped to pull the wooden spines from his flesh. He sucked the back of his forearm and tasted blood. He used the time to listen, determine Catarina's direction of flight. He calculated a point of intersection and when he appeared in front of her, she gasped. He sidestepped her kick to his groin and folded his arms around her in a struggle that sent them lurching to the ground. His weight collapsed on top of her leaving her powerless. He grunted; she moaned; they lay still.

The smell of her, the feel of her, the thudding of her heart as she tried to catch her breath drove him to do what men do.....act. Case found her lips and took them. Catarina made a sound of protest. Case was lost in her and truly did not notice.

Catarina ceased to struggle and the kiss became deeper and more loving. He entered her mouth. She relaxed and let him in. He released her wrists to pull her hips into him and willed her to fold her arms around his neck. Case knew that Catarina was what he needed to be the man he wanted to be. Right now, at this moment he had to let her know he did not want to live without her. She had to forgive him.

His breath shot from his lungs as the force of a cowboy boot collided with his ribs. He rolled off Catarina to stare into the three leering faces of the men he had just run off.

"Thought we might find you two, doin' the dirty dance."

"We started to just watch, but it was getting too good! We've decided we're going first." Drunken laughter communicated their intent. They gave each other congratulatory looks, making the mistake of giving Case time to get to his feet.

"You stupid jackasses," Case pronounced. He was superior in every way to all three put together. It only took the power of one punch each for them to be lying on the ground. While they were down, Case lifted each of their heads delivering a knockout blow just as if he were a commando making sure his enemy was dead. One he grabbed by his hair, one by his shirt and the last by his arm. They would not be following anyone else tonight.

"Come on, let's go," Case whispered to Catarina. She followed him through the dark, back to the truck. When they were safely inside, he reached for her again. She shrank back and shook her head no. The temptation to kiss her anyway was almost more than he could bear. He needed restraint, one step at a time. At least he knew she was safe.

Case drove her to Selena's house and parked. Catarina looked at him with the question of how he knew to go here, but she did not ask it.

"Abuelita said you were staying here.....Who is that man in the white suit?"

"None of your business!"

"I'm sorry," Case exhaled, shook his head and leaned back in his seat.

"I know." Catarina hesitated a moment. "I don't want to see you any more. That kiss tonight, what happened between us at the island, it's not what I want."

"You don't understand....."

"I don't want it explained to me. I mean it. Don't come around, Gringo."

Chapter 15

Regrets

Abuelita was sick. She fought a nagging cough for weeks that finally turned into a lung-rattling assault on her otherwise robust health. Her energetic liveliness slipped a little with each passing day. The neighbor's homemade cough syrup only worked because the recipe called for a cup of whiskey. Any kind would do.

Catarina's days stretched longer and longer. In addition to working for Ito and covering María's job at Cantina Los Indios, she took over caring for the flower garden, cooking the meals and doing the laundry. Now, Abuelita was in bed all day, every day. The sun wasn't up this morning when Catarina cut the flowers to deliver to Dellicious Designs.

Before she left, she had to make sure her grandmother had food and water at her bedside. After making the delivery to Jan, she would work all day getting Ito's spinach picked before the locusts ate it. She hoped to arrive for work at the cantina by six. The bar stayed open until 2:00 am. She would have only four hours to sleep tonight unless Abuelita was worse. Then she would have none.

Catarina arrived at the flower shop before it opened, but she didn't have to wait long before Jan's bright smile appeared behind the glass door. The keys jingled as they turned in the lock. Jan exuded such warmth and acceptance that Catarina cringed at her own unwitting betrayal of such a nice person. When Catarina discovered that Logan Dell was married to Jan, she was physically sick. Each time she saw Jan, the memory of that moment flooded her head again.

"What did you bring me today?" Jan practically sang the words, a mark of her sunny outlook on life.

Catarina set her buckets of flowers on the floor. The bell chimed as the door closed and immediately chimed again as Case Becker walked in behind her. He looked very different from the last time she saw him. He wasn't angry. While he seemed perfectly relaxed, Catarina was alarmed by the closeness of his solid male body. The smell of soap from his morning shower teased her nostrils. Clean male skin, she could taste it on the air.

He stood right beside her, ignoring her completely, treating her like an invisible, flower delivery girl. It hurt. There existed a silent echo between them, "I mean it, don't come around, Gringo."

"Morning, Jan. You doing OK?" He was upbeat, doing fine without Catarina.

"Hey, Case. Tell me you need something lavish and expensive." There was laughter in Jan's request.

He solemnly said, "I do." When he saw the quizzical look she gave him, he said, "Not that kind of 'I do'."

"I keep expecting Sharon to call me any day....."

"Well, you can quit waiting. These flowers are for Sharon, but she's not going to like them."

"All girls like flowers. That's why I'm in business."

"Not this time. These have to ease the bounce when I tell her I'm going to be gone for a year."

"A year! Where are you going?"

"Around the world! My buddy Skipper, you know, the one with the boat business on Padre Island? He referred me to an older couple wanting to sail the seven seas before they die. They've got a nice new boat and just need some extra muscle and someone with enough water savvy to keep them from killing themselves on the trip. That's me.....I'm sailing off on a boat named *The Merry Maker*."

"I've always admired you, Case. You just see something you want and take it. Think of something wild and do it. When are you leaving?"

"Don't have a date yet, There's a lot of preparation for a trip like this."

"What about your business?"

"I think I'm going to sell it if the offer is good enough. That's why I'm wearing a real shirt today. Makes me look smarter." He pointed to the buttoned-down collar scratching his neck.

"Case Becker, what will we do without you?" Jan's smile wasn't quite as bright.

"I'll worry about you, Jan." Case took her hand and drilled a message into her eyes.

"I'll be fine. Actually, things have been great recently." She patted his big fist. "Now, you tell me how much money you need to spend to get yourself out of hot water this time."

Catarina heard the words in her head as if she were saying them aloud again. "I mean it. Don't come around, Gringo." She'd told Case to stay away, and he was doing better than that. He wouldn't even be on the continent.

This was probably good; it made things easier. Their lives were not meant to be lived together and she could forget about him quicker. Catarina congratulated herself on her good luck.

Still, she felt another sting when he walked out of the shop without speaking to her at all. Sharon was getting a goodbye bouquet and Case hadn't planned to tell Catarina he was leaving at all. A lead weight settled in her chest. This was what she wanted; wasn't it?

* * * * *

Catarina had two more nights to work at the cantina. The owner noticed how much longer customers lingered and how much more money they spent with Catarina around. He was greedy and suggested she might replace María on a permanent basis. Loyalty to her cousin wasn't the only reason Catarina declined. She was learning to defend herself against the harmless drunks. Lewd comments slid right by her now. The money she was saving for school was worth the hassle. The real reason she needed to leave was that Logan Dell discovered her whereabouts and pursued her with renewed vigor. She had to stay out of his sights.

Catarina needed her student visa approved for more reasons than just attending college. It would allow her to stay in the United States without being afraid of Logan. She was functioning on the ragged edge of her emotional and physical limits, praying she could make it two more days.

Catarina drug herself into the house on Camino Ratama at 2:30 am. She was depleted of her last ounce of strength and she could hear Abuelita coughing and gagging in the back bedroom. Catarina opened the bedroom door to check on her. She took one look at her grandmother and ran to the phone. She fumbled through the directory and dialed the number wrong, having to start over twice.

"Mrs. García?"

A groggy voice said, "Yes?"

"This is Catarina de la Alvarado, I'm sorry, I know it's late, but I don't have anyone else to call." All the words tumbled out in a single sentence.

"Catarina, what's the matter? Are you all right?"

"No, no, I'm fine. It's Abuelita. She's so sick; she is coughing so much her lips are turning blue. I can't fix it. I think she needs to go to the hospital and I'm alone. We don't have a car."

"I'll be right there."

Catarina hung up the phone and rushed back to hold her grandmother through another violent spell that left the old woman spent and helpless. It occurred to Catarina that her rock, her anchor, her sweet, vivacious Abuelita could die. The word "No!" screamed in her mind. She lay Abuelita's head down on the pillow.

"Mrs. García is coming. I'm taking you to the hospital."

"No money," Abuelita whispered.

"Shhhh, don't talk. I have money; don't worry." Catarina went to the other bedroom and reached into her underwear drawer. She found the brown paper sack containing the tips from almost two weeks of working at Cantina Los Indios. She reached into her pocket for tonight's money. She hurriedly separated the bills, first into stacks of pesos and stacks of dollars; then she organized them into denominations, smoothing out the wrinkles with the care given all precious possessions. She added tonight's earnings to the stacks, rolled them up and secured them with rubber bands. She knew exactly how much was there, one hundred sixty-nine dollars and seventy-three cents. It was more money than she ever dreamed of having at one time. She put the money in her string purse and gathered some things for Abuelita to take to the hospital.

There was a soft knock at the door; it was Delores García. The two women half carried, half walked Abuelita down the steps and eased her into the back seat of the Chevy. This exertion initiated a new strangling spell and Catarina's fear sharpened.

The county hospital was not far. They pulled directly under the awning covering the emergency entrance. Mrs. García ran inside to get help and Catarina tried to rouse Abuelita. She couldn't.

"Dios! Oh, mi Dios, no! Abuelita!"

An attendant appeared with a gurney. He eased Abuelita onto the starched white sheets and rolled her through the automatic double doors. A lady came around the admissions desk and prevented Catarina from following the gurney down the hall of shiny linoleum floors. Every memory of childhood happiness she possessed disappeared as Abuelita was wheeled around a sharp corner in the mint green walls.

Hospital sounds and smells assaulted Catarina's senses and she allowed herself to be coaxed into taking a seat at the admissions desk. The questions began. Catarina provided a robotic answer to each of them. Patient's full name? Age? Your relationship to the patient? How long has she been sick? Are there any other health issues? What medications does she take? Do you have health insurance?

That question brought Catarina into the moment. She focused her eyes on the clerk. "No, no insurance," she said.

The clerk stopped writing. She took note of Catarina's worn appearance while she tapped her ball point pen on the plastic laminate desk. "How will you pay for treatment?"

"How much will it cost?" Catarina's gaze was steady. The woman raised her eyebrow as she lifted her phone from the cradle. She punched an inter-office extension. Catarina gently put her finger on the phone button that disconnected the call. "I have cash."

"I'm not sure what the total cost will be.....she'll definitely need to stay the night. How much do you have?"

Catarina placed all of her money in front of the woman. "I have one hundred sixty-nine dollars and seventy-three cents."

The clerk selected the roll of dollars and pushed the pesos back across the desk. "I'll start with this."

Catarina found Mrs. García in the emergency waiting room. "Thank you for coming. You don't have to stay; I'm not going home. They are going to keep her overnight and I can't leave her here alone."

Mrs. García touched her shoulder. "I'll stay just a little while, until the doctor comes to tell us how she is." The two women embraced and sat down. No one else was there. The uncomfortable chairs, the scrambled newspapers, the vending machines were theirs alone. They fell into anxious silence.

"I miss the kids at school." Catarina said.

"They miss you too. I was going to have to tell them not to come for a few days until you got back. I just can't do it all."

"I'll be back next week."

"Once Case Becker started coming, we worked out a schedule. He's really very good with those kids." Mrs. García sneaked a look at Catarina from the side. "He's not exactly a traditional teacher." Laughter hid between her words. "One day, he took them exploring; he called it going on safari. Now we have to store a box of rocks and bones. There is a jar full of dead bugs too; bugs I never knew existed! The tarantula is still alive and well. Ugh, his eating habits are hard to take. How long do tarantulas live? I swear, those kids learn more from him than they do from the both of us."

Catarina felt a bristle of indignation before full fury hit. She closed her eyes to hide it. Her lips made a straight line. How dare he step in and take over the thing she created! That impossible man was supposed to stay away. This school was her dream, the path to her redemption for every bad thing that ever happened to her, for every bad decision she ever made.

The sum of the events of the day slammed her. It seemed she couldn't miss a step in life without getting overrun by something. Abuelita was sick. Her money was gone and there wouldn't be much more, for María was coming home in two days. Logan was on the prowl and this news about El Gringo might topple every belief about him that kept her safe from loving him.

Her back hurt. Her feet hurt. A vice squeezed her temples and little flashes of light accompanied the slightest noise. None of these pains kept her mind from whirling. Doubting herself was something Catarina did not spend a lot of time on; but tonight, she doubted all her plans, the school, college and her choices about Case Becker. She even suspected the iron will that kept her going every day was failing her. Maybe she could go on if she could just rest for a while.

She didn't know why her search for peace turned her thoughts tender at this moment, but it did. In spite of how angry she was at El Gringo, she longed to lean into his massive chest. She wanted to be held and protected, just for a little while; and Case Becker was the secret place where she wanted to be.

"Miss de la Alvarado?" The doctor came into the waiting room. Catarina practically jumped into his arms. "Your grandmother is going to be fine. She's developed pneumonia, not uncommon if you don't take care of a cold at her age."

"But she's going to live." Catarina sounded as flat as she felt.

"Yes, we'll keep her over night, give her oxygen, fluids and antibiotics. You can take her home tomorrow."

"Can I see her?"

"As soon as we get her in a room."

"Gracias, muchas gracias."

"You're welcome. Looks like you need to take care of yourself too. Get some rest." A voice called the doctor's name on the intercom and he excused himself.

"Thank God." Mrs. García reached to hold Catarina.

"Thank you. I don't know what I would have done if you hadn't come." Catarina accepted her friend's embrace.

"I'm just glad she's going to get well. I am going to try to get some sleep before school starts. You're sure you don't want to go home?"

"No, I'm staying."

Mrs. García headed for her car. "Oh, I almost forgot. I checked to make sure your visa application was received and in process. It seems they've lost it. You're going to have to start over on the paperwork."

This news was the last blow for Catarina. She nodded her head indicating she understood and waved goodbye. As soon as her friend was out the door, Catarina found the far corner of the waiting room. She leaned against the wall just before her knees buckled under the weight of her obligations and ambitions. She was trying so hard! Her face contorted; she slid down the wall and cried herself into shallow slumber.

Chapter 16

The Money

Abuelita's illness kept Catarina out of the fields for two days. It was a blessing, for it allowed Catarina to sleep. She arranged for a neighbor to stay with Abuelita while she worked nights at Cantina Los Indios. That money she had to have.

Tonight was her last night. At closing time she washed the last of the glasses and dumped the empty liquor and beer bottles in the metal cans just outside the door. Now she had to lock up. She learned to check the bathroom for anyone passed out next to the nasty toilet. Once, she had to roll a man from the bathroom, between the tables and onto the porch. She felt a little bad, leaving him outside for the night; but this job had its limits.

As María promised, old José Franco was there to walk Catarina home most nights; but tonight, the cantina's most dependable customer was sick or drunk or otherwise missing in action again. He had no phone, but neither did the cantina.

Catarina got the baseball bat from behind the bar. The beat up old thing had hit more heads and walls

151

than balls. The owner made a habit of carving names
into the wood, the names of men he used it on. It was
flecked with stains and scarred with a long history of
violence. He affectionately called his bat Zorro. It was
the weapon of enforcement and the symbol of law and
order at the cantina. Since José was not around, Zorro
would serve as moral support and protection on her way
home.

Since the frightening incident with the drunken
men, Catarina felt vulnerable in a way she never had
before. She was more watchful, more prepared. She
practiced swinging the bat a few times and made
vicious sounds to get psyched up for the trip.

All that was left to do was to turn out the light
on the rickety front porch, lock the front door, do the
sign of the cross and head for home. "In the name of
the Father, the Son and the Holy Ghost." Done.

She would travel straight, as the crow flies to
minimize exposure to danger. Taking the road was
longer, more visible with more chances to run into
trouble.

Catarina calmed her apprehension with a slow
deep breath. She clenched her fist around the tips in her
pocket with one hand and shouldered the bat with the
other. She talked to Zorro so any stalker would not
think she was alone. "I hope you ordered enough
tequila for the weekend." She walked along the edge of
the grass.

"Are you ready?" Two shadows whispered to
each other just outside the pool of moonlight. Their
low voices were muffled by the sounds of night frogs
and the rhythm of cicada songs.

"All I have to do is run past her, shove this bag into her and keep running. Right?" A fog smelling of alcohol and tooth decay accompanied the man's every word. He was dirty, as if he had been on the road for years.

"Right. Run until you come to where the railroad tracks switch and head north. I'll be chasing you. Don't stop. If she recognizes me the deal is off."

"One hundred dollars?"

"One hundred dollars."

"What's in the bag?"

"What do you care?"

"If it's pot, I want some." The derelict started unzipping the bag to check the contents. The bigger man cuffed him on the side of the head as he grabbed the bag and zipped it back up.

"Here she comes. It's just old stuff she left at my house. She dumped me. I just want to scare her. Nothing rough. OK. Go. Go!" The whisper became a hiss.

Catarina heard the steps pounding the gravel behind her. *Oh, God. No!* It was her last night. This couldn't be happening! She was determined to keep her head and knew that surprise was her best chance to prevail against any assailant. She grabbed the bat with both hands, planned her timing to the cadence of running feet and swung with the full force of her body as she turned to face her attacker. Zorro hit him in the chest, hard enough for her to hear air rush out of his lungs, hard enough to make him drop the canvas bag he carried. A dirty stranger looked at her with crazy, disbelieving eyes before he stumbled forward into the darkness. She had never seen his face before.

Her heart only beat twice before she heard the second runner. A form darted across the corner where mesquite trees made night shadows behind her. He was so close Catarina felt the movement of air around him as he passed, chasing the first man into the brush. Frozen, she listened until the grunts and gasps and then the footsteps faded away.

She stood ready to swing the bat at either man who returned for the bag. No one came. All her senses cringed on high alert. She would have heard the faintest sound, caught the slightest movement. Nothing. She didn't know if it was safer to go back into the flimsy cantina or try to make it home.

Catarina looked at the bag lying at her feet and curiosity overcame common sense. Slowly she bent down and unzipped the bag. She saw money. Lots of drug money! Grocery money. College money. Freedom.

Another surge of adrenaline flooded her body. *Check the trees to the left; look for headlights on the dirt road; listen for rustling behind the cantina.* Since there was no one to fight, she fled, taking the bag with her. It was much heavier than she thought it would be. Her breath came in shallow gasps. She adjusted the bag's long strap over her shoulder so that the load hung from her neck to her hips. She hoped that if anyone shot her in the back, the money would absorb the bullet.

A half mile away, whispers were no longer necessary. "Shit! You didn't tell me she would be armed. She could'uv killed me! Damn! I think my ribs are broken." The derelict winced and doubled over in pain.

"Here, let me check you." Case pressed his hands firmly into the man's chest in several places and instructed him to take deep breaths. "No sharp pains?"

"No, but I'm pissed!"

"You're OK. Here's two hundred. You're gone, right?"

The man held his ribs and glared sideways. Case opened his wallet to reveal two last twenty dollar bills. The man snatched them. "I'm gone. Chicago's a lot cooler than Texas anyway."

The whistle from the train they were expecting moaned in the distance and the clack of rail against wheels sounded slower and slower as the train came closer to the intersection. Together they looked for a car with an open door. When they spotted one, they ran ahead of it until Case could boost his accomplice into the slowly moving car. Hopefully, the man would make it to Chicago and would never be seen again. It was a risk Case could live with. He may have done something wrong. He had done nothing illegal.

Case watched the train gather speed. When he was certain it was going too fast for the man to safely jump off, he turned to catch up with Catarina. He would secretly see her safely home as he had every night since he found her working at the cantina.

Tonight she must have flown instead of walked. With such a head start, Case could not catch up. He arrived across the street from the pink house just in time to see Catarina standing at the front door. She was still carrying both the bat and the bag, desperately searching the street to see if she had been followed. She looked so scared, so vulnerable. Case watched her drop her key, retrieve it and slink inside.

He felt fine about his deed, in a grim way. He didn't understand the struggle of power and pride that had developed between them. Catarina had a soft place in her heart for everyone in the world except herself and him. She needed taking care of even if she was capable and determined. So did he. That was a funny thought. It never entered his mind before. He needed to be taken care of too, just in a different way.

He'd won the battle and lost the war. The money would take care of Catarina even though Case would be thousands of miles away on *The Merry Maker*. This was the biggest lie Case ever told. It was the only one he ever told of any importance. The money meant nothing to Case, but the lie did.....and it was worth it.

Now, Catarina could figure out things for herself. She could go back to Mexico and live like a queen. She could build her own school if she wanted to. She could pay off the gangster in the white suit and leave him in the dirt. She didn't have to be any man's mistress or wife.

Chapter 17

Sixto's Truck

Catarina woke clutching at the sheet tangled around her neck. It was damp with her sweat; she unwrapped herself again. She struggled to count the number of awakenings she suffered that night. Too many. Some were alarming disturbances that sent her racing through the house to hunt for intruders and check on Abuelita. Others were just enough to let her know she wasn't truly sleeping. Eventually, she must have slept; she missed the sunrise and now a shard of dusty light pierced her right eyelid.

A car door slammed; it sounded close. Catarina raised her elbows to look out the open window. Alarm bells clanged through her head. She grasped under the bed for the canvas bag. *There it is.* How could Logan have found out about the money so soon? Yet, there he was, right across the street. Catarina counted on the bushes in front of the windows to conceal her desperation and her lack of clothing when she yanked the paper shade down.

She couldn't decide whether to put on clothes or hide the money. This was a tiny room, barely big enough for a bed and a dresser. *There is no place to hide the money!* She had no story, no explanation, no time. Logan headed for her front door. Catarina threw the bag on the floor of the closet and grabbed the first article of clothing her hands touched. It was crawling with winged insects, termites. She looked at the wall that separated the closet from the bathroom. A termite disappeared into a crack in a wrinkled piece of wood.

Logan pounded the doorframe harder than he needed to. Catarina jerked the rotten boards away from the wall and stuffed the bag behind it. She pressed the wood back against the hole and tossed some dirty clothing against it. Logan pounded again and called her name.

"Catarina! Get yourself out here."

She stepped into a pair of pants.

"Catarina, I'm coming in!"

She pulled a shirt over her head at the same time she opened the front door.

"It's about time. You going to invite me in?"

"No." Catarina pulled her tangled hair out of the back of the neck of her shirt and stepped onto the porch. She avoided his eyes and prayed he would not smell the fear on her. Logan was talented that way. He could always tell. She flattened her back against the door in an attempt to put as much distance between them as possible.

"How's my girl?" He ducked his head to give her a kiss. Catarina sidestepped and he put his arm against the wall to block her escape. "You still mad at me? Hmmm?" Catarina turned her face away from the baby talk. "No kisses?

Logan stepped back. "How about some questions then." He flashed her that quick wink, the one you almost had to know was coming in order to see it. He shook a Camel cigarette out of the pack from his pocket. He struck a match on the door frame, leaving a mark in the paint. He took his time, drawing a long breath.

"There was some trouble early last week out at Cantina Los Indios. You know anything about that?"

Trouble last week? Logan wasn't here about last night! He didn't know. "I don't remember anything," she hedged.

Logan flicked an ash. "That surprises me. Three hot-shots from up The Valley got cheated on the tab by a waitress."

"Really." Catarina marveled at how stories got so mangled.

"Yeah. Some big vaquero took sides. Busted 'em up pretty good. You know anything about that?"

"I don't remember any special fight. Drunks take swings at each other every night."

"You'd remember this one. Put one guy in the hospital with a broken jaw."

"Ask them who did it," challenged Catarina.

"I did; they aren't saying."

"What do you care about something like this anyway? You are Border Patrol, not police."

"Catarina, you know me. I've got to keep tabs on my people. Can't have them straying too far off the reservation. There's danger out there for people like you." He took a long drag on the cigarette. "Those hell-raisin' labor organizers starting wars, throwing around promises of a better life. There's all sorts of people who think they know what's good for you. You need to be careful, stay closer to me."

A different kind of alarm went off in Catarina's stomach. "I don't know anything about a fight," she calmly declared.

Logan twisted his boot on the porch and ground the cigarette butt into the paint. "When's the last time you saw Case Becker?"

Catarina's heart rate picked up speed. "No lo creo; maybe Cinco de Mayo. Abuelita had a party; lots of people were here."

"Lots of people, huh. If you think of anything I need to know, you get in touch. I always repay favors people do for me." Logan tenderly pushed a strand of hair behind her ear. "I miss you, Catarina. I hope nothing bad happens to you. Tell that brother of yours 'Hello' for me too." He stepped down from the porch, adjusted his trooper's hat, and walked to his car. His fingers touched the brim in a mocking salute as he drove away.

He doesn't know. He doesn't know about the money!

Catarina opened the door with trembling hands. She checked to see if Abuelita was awakened by Logan's visit. She was sleeping peacefully; the medicine was working and she was getting better.

Spending any of this money would not be wise. What better way to come under suspicion if it was reported missing. But Logan scared her. She was not going to renew her relationship with him and that put her whole family in danger. Threats of deportation were starting to sound like threats of physical harm.

She remembered how helpless she felt when she was alone and needed to take Abuelita to the hospital. What if she and Sixto needed to run? She fretted a little before she began to feel powerful. The best way to protect her loved ones was for her family to have their own transportation. Catarina decided to buy one thing; she decided to buy a car.

* * * * *

The smell of burned coffee saluted Logan's senses; the Border Patrol station just wouldn't be home without that odor. He stopped to pour himself a cup on the way to his desk. The grimace he made when he sipped said, "Hot and nasty." Logan didn't care so much. He lived with a taste in his mouth so bitter he didn't mind the coffee's stale touch on his tongue.

"Hey! Get away from my desk!" That brat, Junior Officer Ripps was closing one of Logan's side drawers.

"Just looking for a pen that writes." Ripps backed off with his hands held in the air like a suspect. While Logan straightened the top of his desk and looked to see what was missing, Ripps turned his back and pinned an antique Texas Ranger's badge to the crotch of his uniform. He strutted down the aisle between the desks, making sure every officer in the room saw what he was doing.

Satisfied that everything on his desk was in place, Logan unfolded his newspaper. Every day he looked for crime like there wasn't enough Border Patrol work laid on his doorstep. He even liked to fabricate a little crime from time to time. It helped him instill fear in the people he needed to control. Newspaper reporters came up with handy information for all kinds of schemes.

When Ripps believed he had sufficient attention, he returned to Logan's desk and started reading the paper over Logan's shoulder. There was a caption under a picture which Ripps read aloud, "Texas Rangers Disrupt Labor Ralley. Look at that outfit, big white hat, pearl-handled gun, five hundred dollar cowboy boots.....that what you want to be when you grow up, Dell? A Texas Ranger, like your granddaddy?"

Logan didn't notice the insult bouncing in front of his nose. Ripps stepped closer, threw his hips forward and asked, "Has Jan ever seen your granddaddy's equipment?"

Logan flicked the edge of his paper and saw his grandfather's badge pinned on the bulge of Ripps' pants. There was a tightly wound coil that lived inside Logan Dell. He nurtured the anger that allowed it to thrive and kept it taut at all times. This was a perfect moment to unleash it.

He lunged from his chair, grabbing Ripps at the knees. Coffee flew into the air, dropping like rain on the government reports and official memos. Ripps twisted away and managed to get a chair between him and Logan before Captain Kennedy stuck his head out of his office to check out the ruckus.

Logan wanted to draw his gun. He wanted to stick it in Ripps' face and pull the trigger. An incident like this on Logan's record would tank his Texas

Ranger's application for the last time. Junior Officer Ripps was one lucky s.o.b.

Captain Kennedy was a quick study; one look at the two men and no one needed to tell him what happened. "Ripps! Only one asshole allowed per unit. Dell's got seniority, understand?" Kennedy paused to emphasize his authority. "Give me that badge."

There was no warm relationship between Logan Dell and Captain Kennedy. Dell accepted Kennedy's authority as a condition of meeting certain personal goals, and Kennedy couldn't ignore the stats. Logan Dell was his unit's top performing officer with the most productive personal network, had the most arrests and held three marksmanship records in the State of Texas. He also had the thickest personnel file, not necessarily a good thing.

Kennedy handed the badge to its rightful owner. "Ripps, what were you thinking?"

"I was thinking you weren't here, sir." The men in the room suppressed their snickers. The captain stabbed his junior officer with a look of total disgust. The line of tension that stretched between Ripps and Dell shifted to Ripps and Kennedy. Kennedy intensified his stare until Ripps looked at the floor.

"Uh, I apologize, sir." Ripps spoke over his captain's shoulder. "Dell, I apologize; I was just fooling around.....Captain, sir.....uh, are you going to write this up?"

Kennedy looked back and forth between the two men. "I only write up things that are worth the paperwork.....Is this worth the paperwork, Logan?"

Logan let Ripps suffer a few seconds before he answered, "I hate paperwork."

Captain Kennedy surveyed the room. "Don't you men have things to do? Get out of here."

Scuffles of activity accompanied the men out the door. Logan's phone rang; he put the Texas Ranger's badge in his pocket. "Dell here."

"I got rid of it."

"How?"

"Sold it."

"What?" Logan hissed into the phone.

"I sold it; easy money. It's gone; you don't have to worry about a thing."

"I was thinking about a fire!" Logan rubbed his forehead. Criminals just weren't all that smart. "Who'd you sell it to?"

"I don't know; I didn't ask for I.D. She had money; I had a truck; I gave her a steal of a deal."

"You don't get it, do you?" Logan closed his eyes and sighed. "What did she look like?"

"That was the good part; she was hot." Lips smacked like kisses in the receiver. "Wavy hair, brown with some red in it. Real ripe, if you know what I mean."

"Are you jerking off?"

"I put the word out I had a truck for sale cheap, and she came by with her wetback brother. They were definitely under the radar types. They won't cause any problems."

"You're an idiot." Logan slammed the phone down. He was mad as hell, but this mess just proved that sometimes opportunities crossed your path in the strangest ways.

Chapter 18

Swimming Lessons

The little house on Camino Ratama rattled on its cinderblock foundation. Catarina could sleep no more. Alberto and his wild pack, Los Lobos, were here. *When are those boys going to learn the difference between indoor and outdoor behavior?* She could hear at least three different voices. Carlos and Javier taunted Pancho Villa until rabid barking escalated to top the mix of sounds. There were more boy voices, too many to count. The house shook again. *What are they doing out there?* Catarina wrapped her pillow around her head, but the effort was useless.

She had not reported for work at Ito's farm in three days. No one would miss her. That was the way of migrant workers; they showed up when they could. Catarina used these days to sleep; and when her body started recovering, so did her mind. She had taken to languishing in bed, mulling over her new situation.

She did feel safer now that Sixto had his own truck. It was a twenty-year-old, rusty Ford. The odometer had probably turned over more than once, but

165

Sixto said that the motor ran good. He asked no questions about how she saved enough to buy such a luxury.

The mere presence of the money was changing Catarina. There were so many decisions she never faced before. When there is no money, you don't ask for things. The answer is always no. The money hidden in the closet wall brought swirling thoughts into Catarina's head, thoughts she had never dealt with. They weren't trivial decisions about buying new clothes, going on a trip or living a worry free life.

She thought perhaps she should consider the purchase of documentation that would allow her to enroll in school. Why wait on a student visa that might never come? Everyone knew of a "friend of a friend," someone available to provide black market birth certificates, green cards and driver's licenses for a price. Now she could pay the price.

Catarina longed to confide in someone. She couldn't. The secret of the money hung on her tongue, waiting for her to drop her guard so it could spill out. It burned on her lips, too dangerous to share. Someone like herself had no rights on this side of the border. If one wrong person knew, she would lose everything - the money, her dreams, possibly even her freedom. She was in danger from both law enforcement and the criminals who abandoned the money. Even if she told someone she loved, a slip in judgment might put her behind bars or get her killed. There were many opportunities for error; and Catarina felt more alone than she ever had in her life.

It made her sad to know what the future held for her. Secret would pile upon secret; it would never stop.

Sixto's truck was just the first lie. Should she pay Abuelita's hospital bills? How would she explain having the money to do that, or to enroll in college? She would have to create lies to cover that too. Maybe, with the identification papers she bought, she could get a good job and earn money. Catarina expected to work, not live off cash that could build a school when she was ready. All the turmoil made her sick, but not sick enough to give the money up.

The only relief from her stress was the sweet oblivion she allowed herself in fantasies about Case Becker. If she looked at her situation just right, she could ignore the logic that always stopped her from exploring her feelings about the gringo. Now that she had the money, she didn't need any man. That was the real problem, wasn't it? She didn't want to need any man. Money changed this too. Perhaps, now, she could let herself want just one man.

Her body burned hotter for Case with each passing day. It was a mistake letting him out of that box where she kept him in her mind. But, he was the only person who made her feel safe, even if that safety was just a fantasy. Warm illusions developed into very real yearning to see him.

When she closed her eyes, she saw his naked back-side revealed by undulating waves in the moonlight. She watched him bathe his arms, stomach and buttocks. She thought about what hung in the front of his body, washed by warm caressing waters.

Her body reacted as if Case were actually with her. Her breathing changed, her breasts filled and her hips moved. She couldn't help teasing her teeth over her bottom lip. *Stop it. Stop it. Stop!* Catarina was angry with herself.

Los Lobos fell against the wall outside the bedroom so hard the latch bounced out of place and the door eased open. Catarina was compelled to get up and check the security of the boards in the closet. She still didn't have a safe place to keep the money, so it lay there behind the termite-eaten wall, making a noise like a thudding heart.

The smell of rich coffee wafted into her room. She yelled above the din of wrestling, shrieking boys. "Abuelita! Café, dámelo pronto!" She listened to her own voice and knew she sounded cross, irritable. When she stumbled into the kitchen, it was her brother who extended a steaming cup of coffee to her.

"Buenas días, Princesa."

"Shut up, Sixto."

"Qué pasa? Did you not sleep well?"

"Why do we have all these boys here? Did you bring them?"

"Sí, and I have more to pick up."

"Is that what you are doing with our precious gasoline? Collecting boys to torture me?"

"Boys! Outside, ándele!" As Sixto herded them out the kitchen door, one of them tried to get back inside. Sixto hooked the latch. "Gas is cheap, lives are not. El Gringo has been giving swimming lessons for the last two weeks. I told him if he wanted to help, he would change lives. Today is graduation day.....and a race! He is changing things."

Sixto's joyful attitude intensified Catarina's black mood. "Gringo, Gringo, Gringo! What is this? How has he become so important to everybody?" Catarina folded her arms on the Formica table and dropped her face into them. "I'll be glad when he's gone."

Sixto assessed his sister's little tantrum. He put two spoons of sugar into Catarina's cup. He stirred thoughtfully and tapped the spoon on the chipped rim. "No, you won't."

Catarina's silence agreed.

"What's happened, baby sister? Qué pasa? You are not smiling any more. I've never seen you smile like you smiled at him. I could tell you didn't want to, but you did."

"He's leaving. Es un asno and he's a gringo."

"Well he can't help being a gringo. That won't change. Sometimes women do change their minds about jackasses and maybe he would stay if he had something to stay for."

Catarina fought the tears she did not want Sixto to see. A gulp of coffee helped her swallow the lump in her throat so she could speak. "I don't know what he is to me. I don't want him to be anything."

"I know you don't believe in true love, Catarina, but I do. And, I am the one who is right." Sixto touched her shoulder with a brother's affection. She covered his hand with hers.

"I love *you*, Sixto." She looked up at him, her eyes only slightly watery.

"Come to Resaca Park today," Sixto invited. Look at him as he really is. Watch the boys race. There is a swimming lesson for adults afterwards. You don't swim so good; you should take a lesson. He is a good teacher."

The thought of seeing Case made Catarina's fingers tighten around her cup. She took a gulp of coffee. "Maybe. Don't wait for me. I am not riding in that truck with Los Lobos."

Catarina watched Sixto leave in the truck overloaded with boys. Arms waved out the windows, feet hung off the tailgate. It was a clear violation of their plans to keep a low profile on the new purchase. Oh, well, the park wasn't far. Maybe no one would notice.

Catarina wandered outside to finish her coffee and check the garden. Everything looked fine. She could see evidence that Abuelita was feeling much better. There was a pile of freshly pulled weeds by the steps. A damp hole in the dirt awaited planting of a new rose bush.

Catarina considered Sixto's invitation. She walked back in the house to wash the dishes and brush her teeth. When she looked in the bathroom mirror, the image reflected in it said, "Take a swimming lesson."

* * * * *

Catarina wore a black, one-piece swimsuit she had borrowed from María and never returned. Although it was very plain, it was not modest. It was cut high on the thighs. The plunging back dipped low, past the small of her waist, inviting imagination to take over where the cloth ended. Catarina tried to imagine Case's face when she took off Sixto's shirt that she wore as a cover-up. She felt warm inside and wondered if she was a cruel person, wanting to send Case off on a trip around the world on *The Merry Maker* with a magnificent hard on.

She walked into the park unnoticed. That was good for she wanted to watch. She strolled to the edge of the water, well away from the delighted screams of the children and cheering onlookers.

Case was completely uninhibited as he hooted for the strongest and encouraged the weakest. No child completed the swimming test without feeling he had done his best. When the last swimmer climbed onto the bank, Case lined them up and called the name of each one. They graduated from swim class and each received a homemade certificate congratulating the accomplishment. Case was a good instructor and all the children were doing well.

Then Case held up three aluminum foil medals dangling from strings and shouted, "Who's up for the race?" They jumped up and down in excitement. All wanted to race. As Case and Sixto tried to position the boys into starting places along the bank, Catarina decided to venture closer. She had to watch her step so close to the boggy water.

Looking down, her eye caught something floating between the leaves of the cattails and hyacinths. It was a book with a familiar cover.

It was Case's dictionary. Her ink art on the cover was ruined. The central figure of Ix Chel, the Mayan goddess of the moon was all but gone. All the glue in the binding was dissolved and water swollen pages popped open as she pulled the book out of the water. Liquid streamed from the pages back into the resaca and Catarina felt a sharp pang of betrayal. They worked so hard on this together. *How could he do this?*

Catarina blotted the exterior with her shirt. She opened the cover, expecting to see all the words and pictures dissolved. A few were faded; but most had been entered in cheap ball point ink, the kind that never comes off your clothes. The majority of the work was still there.

Just inside the cover were some loose pictures, waiting for their words to be entered into the dictionary - a heart, a graduation cap, a couple kissing, and a cutout from a children's Sunday school pamphlet, depicting the return of the prodigal son. Was that for forgiveness?

Catarina's heart turned over inside her chest. She wasn't sure which of them needed forgiveness the most. Catarina was beginning to suspect it was her. She wiped some mud off the book in the grass and put it in her bag. She took a deep breath and raised her eyes, searching the cheering people until she found Case. She began walking toward the finish line.

The race was coming down to the wire. Alberto touched the bank first followed by Carlos and then Javier. When every swimmer finished, Case awarded the medals and then pronounced all the children winners. There was ice cream on a stick for everyone.

Catarina waited her turn at the end of the ice cream line. When Case looked up from the ice chest to hand out the last bar, he looked into Catarina's face. His surprise flashed into a scowl.

"I came to watch Alberto," she explained. "And maybe take a lesson.....in your next class."

Case turned his back to her and started tossing empty drink cans into the ice chest. "Anybody is welcome. We'll start in about ten minutes." He spoke to her as if she was a stranger. He picked up the ice chest and headed for his truck.

That was cold. Talking to El Gringo was going to be harder than she thought. Had Case already moved on? Or moved back.....to Sharon? It was possible, for he was a man who seemed to be easily aroused, a man of urgent needs. Maybe María was right about men and Catarina had waited too long. Why was he staying at the truck instead of coming back?

She told him to get lost, told him he was not what she wanted. She thought of the pictures loose in the dictionary. They were pictures for her; she knew they were. How long ago did he throw them away? It had to have been at least two weeks. Case sat in his truck staring at the highway. All of her certainty about what she would do was dissolving. He was giving her plenty of time to get confused, scared.

Case left his vehicle and started back towards the water. Embarrassment at the bold move Catarina was about to make washed through her. She clutched the front of Sixto's shirt. *I can't do it.* She looked down at her feet and watched them move towards home.

Case's step quickened when he saw her leaving. He called, "Catarina, don't go! I'm sorry; I was rude." He caught up with her and firmly grabbed her elbow.

She could have pulled loose but she didn't. Even that simple touch electrified her. She looked from where he held her arm up into his face. Then, he let go.

"I won't bite. I promise. Please stay."

Catarina said nothing as she turned to take her place with three others for a swimming lesson. She desperately wished she had not come. Now, she didn't want Case to see her in the slinky black swimsuit. She didn't want to telegraph her attraction to him, especially

173

not so blatantly. She wished she had worn her old, faded red suit until she tossed the shirt to the ground and saw Case's reaction. It was everything she hoped for. His jaw dropped. His eyes froze on her legs. He stuttered and never completed a sentence. He avoided her eyes and shook his head in dismay.

When he found his voice, he spoke to his students, "Let's get in the water. Go out to about waist deep." Case needed to get in deeper water fast, fast enough to conceal his reaction to Catarina's swimsuit. He cleared his throat and began the lesson.

"I am El Gringo. Cómo se llama?" He pointed to the man on his left.

"Me llama Manolo."

"Me llama Rita."

"Me llama Yolanda." Yolanda was very short and had to bob up and down to keep her mouth above the water line. As Catarina introduced herself, Case maneuvered the group to allow Yolanda a more comfortable spot.

"Learning to relax in the water is very important. It is the difference between floating and sinking, flotante o hundimiento. Everybody wants to float, right?" The mix of English, Spanish and sign language was working fine. "Today we are going to float on our faces and on our backs. Then we are going to go a little deeper and learn to tread water."

The scene was a slapstick comedy at its funniest. Wails of delight and fear mixed with splashing and gasping. Manolo sunk like a rock. Yolanda flailed and repeatedly slapped Case in the face as she struggled. Rita wouldn't let go of his neck. The group made as much noise as Los Lobos.

Case assisted each person in relaxing and proper positioning for a dead man's float and a face up float. It was difficult to float when you had the giggles.

When Case came to help Catarina, she noticed he did his best not to touch her anywhere he shouldn't. When she relaxed enough, the dead man's float was easy. Floating on her back was a little trickier. His arms supported her until she was in the right position. Then they hovered gently just under her body without touching her. Still, he was close enough she could feel the heat of his hands through the water where there was no bathing suit to separate them. She focused on that intoxicating sensation.

Water filled her ears and sound receded to some distant place. She continued to relax. *Ah!* He released her. She was floating on her own! She lost her focus and started to sink. As her face went under and her arms started to flail, Case was there. He held her firmly until she caught her balance and could stand on her own. He just didn't let go soon enough. Their bodies entwined and Catarina gasped at the huge hardness she felt between his legs. He stared into her eyes with intensity no one in the swimming class could miss. Anyone could see the fire that leaped from Case to burn over Catarina's skin. It arrested them all.

"Gringo? Are we finished?" Manolo waited nervously for an answer. The two embarrassed women were already climbing up the slippery banks.

"Yes, we're done today. Everybody did fine."

Manolo called after his wife and sister, "Rita, Yolanda, es todo para hoy. Vámanos." Manolo smiled over the back of his shoulder to see if Case and Catarina would kiss. They didn't.

Case released Catarina and stepped away from her. It was good that he did, for she could not move. The jolt of energy from his touch left her paralyzed. Every part of her wanted him. She didn't have to wonder what his hands felt like on her breasts. She knew. She knew what his mouth tasted like and how it felt to have his weight on her. She told him to get out of her life and he was doing just that.....walking away.

Every step took him into more shallow water. It was now down to his knees. What was she going to do about it? This was happening now. She only had seconds; it was now or never. A breeze blew Sixto's words into her ear, "He might stay if he had something to stay for."

Catarina, urged to action, ducked under the water, grabbed a double hand full of slimy resaca mud and threw it at Case's back. Her arm was strong and her aim was true. The fat splat hit him directly between the shoulder blades. Black sludge trickled down his arched back before the big glob fell into the water.

He slowly turned to confront Catarina. Another glob hit him square in the forehead. A little minnow jumped out of the goo back to the safety of the fish world. If someone carved a statue of a man frozen in disbelief, it would look like Case did now.

The mud gumbo slid down to cover his eyes and nose. He made great ceremony of wiping it away and slinging the muck. He grabbed water to rinse his face. Once, twice, three times. A blue-eyed gleam of revenge sent Catarina racing for the opposite bank, knowing there was no way she was going to escape.

The inevitable happened and her shriek drowned under the water when Case dunked her. When he let her up for air, he took advantage of her struggles to touch and grab as he pleased. He held her powerless while he gathered his own fist full of mud to rub on the bare of her back. He slipped his finger inside the fabric and dropped another fist full down the front of the slinky suit.

She twisted free. That's when they each laughed. With a moment's eye contact, they both lunged for the mucky bottom. The furious fight of screaming and mudslinging left them both covered in resaca ick. It was a strange seduction.

Catarina slipped; Case caught her. He dunked her more gently this time and moved his hand over her face and neck to swish away the grime. Their legs entangled again and Catarina discovered that the fight dissolved the tension between them, but not the violent attraction. He was still hard and not shy about letting her feel it.

In the full light of Saturday afternoon, they splashed and washed each other until they were as clean as resaca water could get them. There were people watching, but Case and Catarina didn't know it. Their awareness was limited to each other.

Case helped her to the bank and caught her again when she slid back on the slippery slope. He pointed to where her swimsuit was slightly askew revealing a tempting swell of breast next to her arm. Catarina scolded him with her eyes. He answered her with a raised eyebrow and a look that said, "Don't blame me; I'm just the messenger." He wrapped her in a towel. They sat side by side on the grass, close together, not touching. They caught their breaths and enjoyed that special feeling that resulted from playing in the sun and water.

Case stared into the sky to check the time. "What next?"

"Have we ever been on a date?" Catarina asked.

"No."

"I want to go on a date."

"Damnit, Catarina what for? Why would I go out on a date with someone who won't even take a flower from me?" Case threw his wet towel hard on the grass and looked down between his knees.

Catarina leaned forward, turning her head to find his face. She flirted, "Sometimes, things change. I don't know if I can explain it. Maybe actions speak louder than words. I didn't take the flower, but I did take a swimming lesson." Catarina delivered the statement as if it were a question.

Case waited a full sixty seconds before he took her hand. "You know I'm leaving in a few days."

"Sí, I know." She looked at him from under her lashes. "So you better not wait too long to say yes."

He smiled. "Is tonight at six too soon?"

"Gringo!" Los Lobos dashed across the park toward Case and Catarina. They all spoke at once. "Gringo, will you take us frogging tonight? We have batteries for the flashlight and rice and butter and peppers to cook with." Carlos stabbed the earth with his carved, stick gig, perfecting his aim. Alberto folded his hands in prayer pleading, "Por favor?"

Case laughed at his favorite pile of boys. "No, not tonight. Ask Sixto, he'll take you."

"We already asked him; he can't. He has to use his truck to help Tío Ray move his furniture." They continued to exhibit the uncontrolled behavior that earned them the name Los Lobos.

"We are going to shine the light in their frog eyes and kill 'em and cook 'em ourselves." Alberto shined the light in Javier's eyes while Carlos stabbed the air with his gig.

Case resorted to managing them like dogs. "Hey! Down. Stay." It worked. "Maybe some other time."

"Nooooo, tonight. It's a good moon," Alberto whined.

"Not, tonight. Catarina and I have plans," Case announced.

"A date?" Alberto made a disgusted face.

Case smiled at Catarina. "Yes, a real date."

"Are you going to kiss her, like you did Lucy?"

"Maybe."

The chorus of "ick, gross, oooh and smacking lips followed the boys through the grass and out of the park.

Case touched Catarina's cheek and trailed his finger tips over her lips. "Maybe I'll kiss her better than I kissed Lucy."

Chapter 19

Dancing at Padre

Memorial Day was the beginning of summer at the beach. In The Rio Grande Valley, summer wasn't marked by the arrival of heat. It was marked by this specific date and anticipation of hotter heat. Case loved it. Summer. The steaks tasted better; the water temperature was perfect for swimming. Even the fish were easier to catch. Sunsets were more brilliant and island breezes more precious.

What would a date with Catarina on a summer night like this bring? Even though she made the first move, Case clearly let her know he would be paying for dinner. He wanted to take her to one of his favorite places, a dilapidated shack on the bay side of the island that had been converted into a restaurant. He wasn't trying to impress her with nice things; he wanted her to have a good time.

A groaning, dripping air conditioner spit ice from its perch in the window when it froze up. If a piece landed in a customer's plate, dessert was free. There were only eight scratched wooden tables, and

180

each was always occupied. The restaurant didn't have a
name or a liquor license; but it did serve the best steak
on South Padre Island.

Fare was simple.....steak, potato, salad, bread,
lots of butter. After a day playing in the sun, nothing
tasted better. Attire was "come as you are." Neckties
cut off of overdressed customers hung from the ceiling.
Case was so tall the low hanging ties brushed his hair as
he crossed the room. A group of fishermen talked of
their day on the jetties and smelled of their fresh catch.

The warmth of the afternoon sun glowed on
Catarina's skin. Case knew the feeling, something just
short of a sunburn that made cool hands irresistible.

"Hey man!" Case heard a hearty laugh and
looked beyond Catarina to see Bob, one of the men he
pulled out of the sand the night of Cinco de Mayo.
Tonight Bob sported a Speedo and a Hawaiian shirt of
clashing orange and blue. He was clearly over fifty and
so was his bikini-clad date.

Case shook the hand extended in friendship.
"Case Becker. I see you made it safely home."

"I knew you were lying about her being your
sister." Bob turned to Catarina. "You, my dear, look
precious.....this is Mavis. Would you like to join us?"

Catarina glanced at Case; she was willing.
Without consulting her, he replied, "No, we are going
to sit as far away from you as possible.....no offense."

Bob pretended a tragic face and placed his hand
over his heart. "I'm crushed. It's good to see you
though. Thanks again for your help the other night."

"You're welcome." Case waved and said,
"Goodbye, Bob." Good natured Bob returned his
attention to Mavis.

Catarina smiled across the table at Case as if she liked him. They had never been so relaxed with each other. It was strange and wonderful. She didn't tense with every brush of his body. She reached out to touch his shoulder once and she let him sit close enough to rest his bare knee next to hers. His initial thrill settled into nice. It felt right.

Case watched her intently perusing the menu. He wondered what made the difference in her attitude about him. What was going on in that willful mind of hers? Was it the money she found? He was certain they would not be here together if she knew what he'd done. Case caressed her with his eyes and renewed his vow to make certain she never found out.

She was everything that intrigued him. Unaffected by superficiality, brave and smart. She managed to melt both his self-doubt and his heart. Yes, melt was the right word; she was hot in so many ways. There was something happening between them. He liked it; he liked it a lot.

Dinner did not disappoint. The moment their plates arrived, the air conditioner belched and tossed a chunk of ice into the sour cream topping of Catarina's baked potato. Her startled squeal alerted the waiter.

"Free dessert!" Case retrieved the ice and held it up for the waiter to see. The prize acknowledged, Case couldn't find a suitable place to put it on the table, so he popped it in his mouth to melt and swallow. Catarina rewarded him with musical laughter.

Laughter came easy tonight. It bubbled up over the least little things. Case picked up the naked T-bone from his steak and sucked the tender pieces left clinging; Catarina did the same. These morsels were the best part. When it came time for their free dessert, they ordered an apple pie a la mode. The crust was flaky hot; the filling was tart with hints of lemon and the melting iced cream swirled in the plate with cinnamon and butter. How could hovering over shared food be so intimate?

They lingered over extra glasses of iced tea until the lone waiter came by. He pointed to the check waiting on their table and asked if they wouldn't like to pay now, then he glanced toward the people waiting in line for a table.

"I don't guess they are going to let us stay any longer." Case reached for his wallet.

"This was really nice, Case, thank you."

It was the first time! She said his name as though she had called him Case forever. It rolled off her tongue as naturally as the more distant El Gringo. The sound induced a quick intake of shallow breath and Case felt another shift of energy between them; a barrier collapsed. He was uncertain if he should acknowledge it, so he rose and held her chair for her to get up.

Case opened the door. It was easy for Catarina to walk under his raised arm to exit the shack. They stood in a moment of indecision in the parking lot for they had no specific plans for the evening. Sounds of a band drifted from behind the dunes. The annual Memorial Day dance was starting at the open air pavilion.

"What's next?" Case figured this question had worked this afternoon, so why not try it again? The answer was better than he expected.

"Could I have a kiss?"

His reaction was immediate. He pulled her to the side of the building away from the light. He pinned her against the unpainted boards. His hands pressed against the wood on both sides of her; his chest crushed her body. His own urgency surprised him. He moved on her mouth, entering her body in search of answers. He found the edge of what he was looking for and she had to put her arms around him. She arched the length of her body into his. The intensity grew into rhythmic movement that Case sensed began to make her uncomfortable. He retreated to gentle brushes of his lips that allowed them to talk.

Catarina's eyes were still closed. "We're in public."

"I want more."

"I'm scared!"

"Of me?"

"Of you.....and me."

Case squeezed her as tightly as he dared. He growled an utterance of self-control and rocked her side to side in his arms. Someone turned up the speakers and music from the pavilion got louder.

"Let's go dance. You want to?"

Catarina nodded yes. He touched her hair; her lips and then gently tapped her nose with his forefinger.

"Then, tonight, we dance."

They walked across Padre Boulevard and around the dunes that hid the pavilion. It was a design of two intersecting circles raised on pylons above the sand. Its canopy-shaped roofs made silhouettes like open air circus tents against the dusk. By the time they reached the entrance, the sound was deafening. Case paid the cover charge and they entered the throng.

The music was for high energy, no-touch dancing, the kind where everybody "did his own thing." The floor was packed with a crowd of seventeen to thirty year olds from all over The Valley. A breeze off the surf spread smells of coconut oil and suntan lotion through the cigarette smoke. Case's hand pressured the middle of Catarina's back, guiding her across the space to an area where there was room to breathe. Case felt a blow to his back.

"Case! I've been waiting on you! We're going to use you for girl bait. Where've you been?" It was Scott Spears; he was stumbling. *Great.* There was no alcohol served at the pavilion, but that didn't keep beer and shots from being hidden in the trunks of cars in the parking lot.

"Scott, you're not going to pick up a girl if you can't stand up. Have you kissed the floor yet?"

"Nooooo!" he dragged the word slowly out into three syllables. "I'm saving myself for the right woman.....and this is the right woman right here." Scott leered at Catarina. He reached for her; his lips were loose and searching for a kiss. Case intercepted Scott's hand as though it was extended for a hand shake. Case used his famous strength to grind Scott's knuckles with a message of ownership. "Hey, take it easy, if she is yours, just say so!"

"Just did. Nice to see you, Scott." Case turned his back on the man and led Catarina to the edge of the dance floor where they could work off some of the energy that plagued them.

They danced every dance. There was no way Case was willing to sit out a number and create an opportunity for someone to step in as Catarina's partner. Each man in the stag line watched her every move and Scott couldn't take his bleary eyes off her. Case was jealous just knowing that Scott was having the same carnal thoughts about Catarina that he himself was having.

It was the band's custom to play a slow dance before they took a break. It gave couples a chance to hold each other and enjoy all the visual enticements in which they had been indulging. The music soothed and Case drew Catarina into his arms. He folded her into his chest, lowered his head to hers and moved body to body with her. Their difference in height barely allowed her toes to touch the floor. They swayed to the music, but covered very little ground. As the song came to an end, he kissed her face right where the damp hair clung to the side of her closed eyes. He lingered as long as he dared when the music stopped.

"Let's get something to drink." He led her to the concession area. Case was well known on the island and many people greeted him. The crowd was not completely Anglo. There were a few brown faces, but Catarina did not seem to know any of them. People looked at her and she smiled back, but Case noticed she spoke to no one. *I'll have to fix this next time. Tonight I want her for myself.*

"I'll have two Cokes." He handed the cashier the money.

"Es Benito!" Catarina beamed at a man charging through the crowd towards them. "Benito!" She hopped on her tiptoes to see him.

"Catarina!" Benito picked up Catarina and swung her around in a big welcome bear hug.

Their embrace looked much too familiar to

186

make Case happy. Just how many old boyfriends was he going to have to get rid of? A moment ago he felt sorry for her not knowing anyone here. Now he was unhappy that she recognized a face. What was the matter with him?

"You look beautiful.....happy. What are you doing here at this gringo party?" Benito asked.

"I'm here with a gringo." Catarina took Benito by the hand and turned to Case. "Case Becker, Benito de la Alvarado, my cousin."

Case could now sincerely extend his hand to a man with the same last name as Catarina's. "Cousin? That's good. Nice to meet you." Both men grinned.

"I understand, mi amigo. I curse fate my whole life that she was born to my father's brother." Benito shook his head sadly and shrugged his shoulders in long accepted resignation of his bad luck.

"Benito, are you working?" Catarina asked.

"Yes, I started helping this band with their lighting and sound a few weeks ago. Sometimes they let me sit in and play bass. Who knows, eventually they might make me an official member. Meantime, I meet people in the music world. That's what I wanted to tell you. I pointed you out to the bandleader. See that guy with the bandana? Wave. Smile. I told him what a good singer you are. He said you could do a number. Will you?"

"Now? Tonight? What number?" Catarina looked back at the musician in the bandana. He didn't look too crazy, but still.

"Anything you like. They know everything. Maybe that one you sang at Graciella's party?"

"That's not a dance number."

"People will like it. Will you do it? It's just for fun."

Catarina glanced up at Case for his opinion. He held up the palms of his hands and shook his head indicating he wanted no part of this decision. She looked back at the guitarist who was motioning her to come up on the stage. He picked a series of notes to let people know the break was over. He grabbed the microphone and made an announcement to the crowd.

"We have someone special with us tonight.....it's my friend Benito's cousin Catarina. If you want Cousin Catarina to sing for you, you have to convince her to come up here. She is feeling shy tonight. Come on, people. She's pret-ty!" The band leader's eyebrows raised; the musicians on stage started clapping. Benito let out a wolf whistle that told the audience this was going to be worth it. The clapping was contagious and the noise swelled to the point that Catarina had no choice. Her hand slipped out of Case's and Benito led her toward the stage.

Left with nothing else to do with his hands, Case clapped too, just slower than the crowd around him. He was losing his intimate evening alone with Catarina.

There were no steps to the stage. The band leader leaned down. "My name is Jake; this is Jerry. Give us your hands." The two men effortlessly pulled her above the crowd and onto the stage. The three of them conferred a moment while catcalls, comments on her voluptuous figure and a marriage proposal came from the audience. Jake returned to the microphone while Jerry instructed the other musicians.

Jake made the announcement. "Ladies and you

not-so-gentlemanly   gentlemen,   Catarina   de   la Alvarado."

Sweet notes of the lead guitar floated a Latin rhythm in the air. Case looked around to assess the reaction of the crowd, then crossed his arms to protect himself from whatever unknown emotion he was about to experience. This didn't feel at all like the other time he watched Catarina sing. At the Cinco de Mayo party, she played with Alberto. She flirted with every man, woman and child there, while her eyes challenged Case to object. Tonight, the new closeness between them he experienced at dinner was reinforced. She looked only at him. His arms dropped from his chest.

The crowd quieted. The sweetness and purity of her voice hovered over the audience like the sound of an angel. She sang a ballad that told the story of star-crossed lovers. She shared an emotional side of herself that Case had not seen before. She touched and enthralled each person. Even the musicians were captivated; all eyes were on Catarina standing in the light of the stage. A girl standing next to Case wiped a tear off her cheek. Scott looked more besotted than before.

Case saw all of their reactions but he knew Catarina was singing about him.....about them.....telling him their story could have a sad ending. When she finished, the crowd was silent, pausing as if asking permission to applaud. When Catarina lowered her head, the noise came. Loud. Sincere. Emotional. They asked for more, but Catarina demurred. She sat on the edge of the stage and hopped to the ground. She rushed straight for Case. Everyone there now knew who she sang to. The hug she gave him told them so.

Case whispered, "The minute this calms down, we're leaving."

It took a lot longer for the attention to Catarina to die than Case wanted. It was impossible for them to dance again. Finally, he found a moment to ask her, "Would you like to take a midnight sail?"

"You have a boat?" Catarina was surprised.

"I know a guy who has a boat. It's the same thing." His blue eyes twinkled; it was a necessity to flirt with her now. Too many men had noticed her.

"I'm going to the ladies room first."

Case whispered. "I'll meet you at the truck." He let her leave and waited a few minutes before he headed for the parking lot. They arrived at the same time. The moment the doors slammed, they fell into each other's arms laughing, kissing little fun kisses. The conspiracy of escape made them feel closer.

Case started the big engine and cringed at the noise it made. *No sneaking away in this monster.* He headed for Skipper's Watercraft Rentals.

Chapter 20

Alberto's Adventure

".....fourteen, fifteen, sixteen. Sixteen frogs!" Alberto, Carlos and Javier danced over their catch and threw their arms up in victory.

"That is five for each of you and six for me!" Alberto laid claim to the extra portion.

"No fair! Carlos killed the most frogs," Javier defended. "He killed eight."

"Just because he wouldn't give me my turn with the gig! Besides, frogging tonight was my idea."

"Alberto, you always think you are the boss."

"I am the boss. You two should start calling me El Jefe. I always have the ideas." He looked from one defiant friend to the other. ".....OK, we split the last frog's legs and draw straws for who gets them. Es mejor?" Carlos and Javier agreed this was a better solution.

It took a while for their little fire to get hot enough to cook. Javier made the mistake of putting green wood on the blaze. Alberto and Carlos claimed the upwind side of the fire and forced Javier to sit in the path of the dense smoke to teach him a lesson.

When the fire did get hot enough, it was too hot. The rice stuck to the bottom of the stew pan, the frog legs were crispy black and the boys forgot to put the peppers in with the rice, so they ate those raw. The meal was delicious.

"This is fun! Sixto and El Gringo are going to wish they came." Javier stuck the head of the flashlight inside his mouth. His cheeks were stretched to maximum capacity and the light showed through his flesh making a red, ghoulish sight.

"You look like a dead person." Carlos grabbed the flash light to try it on himself.

"Have you ever known a dead person?" Javier asked. "I mean, known a person who died?"

"I know about some people that died. But, I didn't really know them." Alberto took his turn at the flashlight and stuffed it in his mouth.

"My grandmother lived in Tijuana; she died Tuesday." Javier got quiet. "I'm not so sad, but mi madre, she cries a lot."

Alberto tossed a stick into the fire. "I think my father is dead. I'm not sure. It's what my mama says."

"Tu madre wouldn't lie about something like that.....would she?" Carlos asked.

"I don't know. She acts funny when I ask her about him, especially when I ask her how he died. It's strange. I don't ask any more."

"My grandmother used to say, 'Javier, every living thing has a purpose in life and every death has a higher purpose.' I don't know what that means, but she said it a lot." Javier stared into the embers. The mood was getting much too somber.

Alberto glanced at the frog carcasses. "Well, the purpose of those frogs' death was to be our supper. And the purpose of their lives was to have baby frogs so we can gig 'em and have supper again."

Carlos laughed and threw a dirt clod at Alberto. "We only ate the legs. What about the brains, the guts, the bones, the blood, and their squinty eyeballs? They should have a higher purpose too."

"Shut up! I'm trying to remember my grandmother!" Javier wasn't impressed with Carlos' attempt to lighten the mood. The fire collapsed into itself and began to go out. Sparks flew on the updraft into the dark of the night.

Javier offered a possible tribute to his departed grandmother. "We should bury the bodies so that they can rot and plants can use them and grow stuff for their baby frogs to eat. That would make them have a purpose."

"Alberto's eyes sparkled with mischief and mystery. "I know a much higher purpose than that. Come with me."

Chapter 21

Starry Nights

Skipper rubbed his bald pate when he saw Case through the window of his shop door. "What the hell do you want? I live here, you know. It's almost midnight; I gotta close sometime." He strained to see who Case beckoned to follow him. The old sailor witnessed an angel float out of a Becker Rescue Services tow truck. He looked back at Case and said, "Oh, man, are you in trouble now."

"I want to borrow the thirty footer."

"Tonight?"

"Tonight."

"For how long?"

"Until....." Case could not hide his hunger for the woman beside him. "Skipper, this is Catarina de la Alvarado. I've promised her a midnight sail. Catarina, this is Skipper, the best sailor on the island."

"Buenas noches, Señorita." Skipper enunciated each word respectfully as he took Catarina's hand and brushed a kiss on it, European style. Then he folded his other hand on top of their clasped ones. He smiled and tilted his head.

"Mucho gusto," Catarina replied.

"That's enough, Skipper," Case said. "Catarina, go over there and pick out a suit from the rack. We might want to take a swim."

Skipper's shop not only served his rental business, it had an apartment upstairs where he lived. The retail area on the first floor carried beach accessories and supplies for those who rented boat slips from him. You could buy anything from a life jacket to a bottle of fine wine.

Catarina looked for Skipper to give his permission to shop the swimwear. After a quick glance at the choices, she protested. "These are all bikinis! I don't wear bikinis."

Skipper walked to the rack. "Darlin', that's a sin against mankind. Here, try this one." He handed her a tiny orange string of a thing.

"I don't think so." She scolded him with her eyes. "Maybe this." She selected a turquoise one that looked like it would cover most of her bottom. The top was a halter that tied at the back of the neck. It was the suit with the most fabric in the store, but she still looked doubtful.

Case reached for a soft, sheer cotton sarong. It was swirling with powerful moving colors and shapes. He liked it because it looked like he felt inside.

"Take this too. You might get cool."

"Can I have this hairbrush?" Catarina held it up.

"Sure you can, Honey. You kids hungry? Here let me fix you up with something." Skipper filled two grocery bags with cheese, bread, pickles, fruit, chocolate and two bottles of wine. When Case came over to inspect the bag, he discreetly dropped the orange bikini in the bag too. Skipper grinned a dirty old man grin while he checked to see if Catarina noticed.

"When does the boat go out for rental again?" Case asked.

"Tuesday."

They carried their supplies to the docks just outside the shop and stopped next to the fanciest sailboat in the marina, *Everlovin'*. It was big enough to take them anywhere, even into the Caribbean.

Catarina's jaw dropped. "I was looking for a little boat. Es grande! Señor Skipper, are you going with us?"

"No, I'm going back to bed! Case can handle it. You might need to help him with some of the line."

"Line? Is that the ropes?"

"Yes ma'am, the ropes. This is your first sail, huh." Skipper showed her where to stow the food in the galley below deck while Case went through the captain's check and readied the mainsail.

Case knew just where he would take her. They wouldn't go south through the jetties towards Mexico. The open Gulf was too exciting a ride for tonight. This trip needed to be slow and easy. Less sailing and more stargazing was what Case had in mind. That meant staying in the majestic Laguna Madre that ran north up the coast of Texas between the island and the mainland. Plenty of room for lovers to get lost, not that Case ever got lost on the water.

They used the silent electric motor to quietly putter past sleeping pelicans and boats moored for the night. Lazy snoring came from the bowels of one of the cabin cruisers where someone slept on board. In the open bay, just when the breeze was right, Case hoisted the sails and the craft strained into the wind.

Catarina felt the touch of the thick night air on her skin. She licked her lips and tasted salt. Every bit of her felt alive; she prickled with anticipation. She turned away from Case and leaned into the breeze so her hair would blow away from her face because she knew Case was watching. She ran both hands through her wavy tresses, threw up her arms, shook her head and turned towards him. She rewarded his worshipful look with a smile.

Catarina could pretend this wasn't happening or she could let herself enjoy every moment of the evening. What would Abuelita think.....dessert first? It might be her last time with Case, the only time they would be free of the conflicts that kept them apart. They left all their power struggles, all the social differences, all the mistakes they'd made on shore; or so she thought.

Catarina understood how the ancient Mayans could believe in time travel. That's exactly what this felt like. The bay and the wind took her to an enchanting world separate from the world of clocks. A private universe where she and Case could create any reality they desired.

Desire! It poured into her from a place so deep and locked up, she let out a sob. The sound of it was lost; but, the feeling of it caught on the wind and blew into Case's heart.

"What's wrong?"

"Es hermoso, so beautiful I can't breathe." Catarina's shoulders shook a little. She shed her troubles in the tears that she wiped away. She suspected Case saw them and appreciated that he let her cry out whatever needed to be out.

An hour later, the sleek craft slithered into still waters. The little lagoon was silent. All life was sleeping.

"Look at the Mayan moon." Catarina's disembodied voice carried clearly on the night air.

"What makes it a Mayan moon?"

"Look." She pointed. "See the rabbit on the surface? He is Ix Chel's companion." She did not mention the rabbit's symbolic connection to fertility.

"Who is Ix Chel?" Case tied the sails.

"You remember, Mayan goddess of the moon." Catarina listened to Case tie the sails and toss out the anchor. She turned her head towards the splash it made. "Is the water deep here?"

"I might could touch bottom, but you couldn't."

Catarina gathered the courage to look up at Case. His silhouette towered over her. Raw sexual energy surged in the air. *Should I reach for him?*

Case broke the spell; he spoke softly. "Come over here by me. I'll tell you star stories." Case arranged the deck pillows on the floor of the boat so they could lay face up to the sky.

The unobstructed beauty of sparkling heavens brought new tears to Catarina's eyes. "I hate it when I am such a girl."

"I love it when you are a girl!" Case lifted her head from the pillows with one hand and slid his arm under her shoulders. He pulled her into his chest, kissed her hair and moved his other arm to enclose her.

Catarina relaxed under the magic of his salty smell. She allowed herself to run her hands over his tight forearms and wondered what he did to make them so hard with muscle under his warm skin.

"Tell me about this Ix Chel, protector of women. Do I need to be worried about her?"

Catarina giggled, "No. She liked men and all the man gods wanted her, all but one. Every time she chased after him, the tides would rise, creating floods that ruined the crops and caused much death. Her father disapproved and struck Ix Chel with lightning, killing her.

The ledgend says that for the next one hundred and eighty-three days, hundreds of dragonflies surrounded her body. They fanned her and sang to her until she came back to life. She eventually married her love; but later, her husband accused her of having an affair with his brother and threw her out of the sky."

"I can tell you admire her. Why is that?"

"She was very brave and continued her life on her own. Abuelita says that when you reach out to touch the moon, Ix Chel will make your wishes come true." Catarina did not want to discuss her secret wishes with Case, so she changed the subject. "You were going to tell me about the stars."

He pointed out the Big Dipper and Little Dipper, showed her how to locate the North Star and helped her distinguish between a star and a planet. When she had trouble sorting out the snaking shape of Scorpio, she raised herself on her elbow, pointed her finger and allowed Case to trace the shape of the dragon with their two hands.

"I see it!" Catarina continued to point while Case let his hand slide down her arm. He paused for a lingering kiss to the inside of her elbow. His fingers grazed her neck, her bare shoulder and came to rest on the side of her breast. She arched into his hand and turned her gaze from Scorpio to his poet's lips. In that instant, her choice was made. There was no fight left in her. She surrendered her body and her heart.

He kissed her as though he understood the decision her body had made. His hand moved to cup her breast. All of the energy swelling between them since the day they met collided. The impact forced Case to move over her, crushing her with his weight. They grasped each other in the depth of the kiss. Their legs entwined and they instinctively began to move in the rhythm of man and woman. It was as though all lovers ever drawn together by the power of the universe were inside them. They were mixed, melded and lost.

The only force strong enough to break Catarina away was the urgent need to feel her bare skin touching his. She pushed his shoulders away and he knew to slide the straps of her sundress down so he could move it to her waist. He sat astride her and let her raise his shirt as far as she could before he took over and stripped it from his body. He let her hands explore his chest, then his belly. Her fingers traced the line of hair that disappeared into his shorts below his navel. He watched the movement of her torso as she caressed him. He groaned and dropped his mouth to her breasts, giving each its turn. Catarina grabbed his head and pressed it tighter, encouraging the nips and tugs.

She felt the absence of his mouth as air touched the dampness on her nipples. He stood to step out of his shorts and she watched him linger above her, devouring her body with his eyes. When his eyes moved to hers, their gazes locked in agreement. This was to be an intentional act. It wasn't something happening in a moment of lost confusion. It was a declaration for both of them. Case dropped to his knees beside her in reverence.

"Case." His name was Catarina's prayer. She could feel his mouth next to her ear. She could feel his breath on her neck as words murmured from his lips.

"I want you to love me. Love me. Love me." He repeated the request over and over, chanting to the rocking of his body. The remainder of the cotton sundress was an insignificant barrier to the hard demand that assaulted her most sensitive place without entering her. Case ground into her until his rhythm became the rhythm of her blood. He covered her moans with his kisses. He scraped her nipples with his teeth. When he felt her temperature spike, his hands moved inside her to extend his own pleasure and to torture her.

Torture her he did. The delay of penetration twisted her anticipation to a level of tension she had never dreamed of. She slipped back and forth on the brink of orgasm multiple times. Any one of these would have been the best she ever had.

When Catarina began to loose control, Case eased her to her side to face him. He moved his leg over her hips and pulled himself into her. This time he groaned with her. He kept the pace slow, the penetration shallow, then deep. He denied himself. He repeated the agonizing, alternating pattern until the satisfying, final chain reaction ignited. Their sounds became more audible, then more and more ragged until primal cries erupted into the dark.

* * * * *

Awareness came to Catarina when she felt Case harden and move inside her again. Their desperate hunger had only paused, not abated. Her face was cradled in the hollow of his chest. His breath spread through her tousled hair. Her body had not lost its prime and it was easy for Case to arouse her instantly. No words. No thinking. No talking. No kissing. She began to move against him, helping him. Her hands moved to his buttocks and she clutched him closer. Case followed her lead and slid his hands down her back to her buttocks, gathering her with the most tender strength she could imagine.

He was hard all over. His thighs were rocks; his abdomen was a mass of rippling bulges; the sinews along his sides into his back were strung like tight cords. She touched them all. She reveled in the feel of them. Hardness surrounded her, inside and out. The sensation began to overwhelm her; and imperceptibly, she let Case take over. Now, she was helpless in his arms, another stroke, another stroke, and another. She began to convulse with pleasure.

Case managed to maintain a few more plunging strokes before joining her rapture. His skin was covered with the sheen of sexual exertion; a growl replaced his heavy breathing; he gripped her in the position of male possession and poured himself into her.   Even after the peak passed, he remained hard inside, rocking her through her aftershocks that subsided into peace.

At first the cooling night felt good to her hot damp body.   When she eventually shivered, Case reached for the stack of beach towels and covered her. He kissed her silent, swollen lips and pressed her body into his skin while they slept.

Chapter 22

Fun in Heaven

A seagull squawked, calling his friends for a predawn fishing trip. The deck of the fiberglass boat that felt just fine to Catarina last night was unyielding to her aching muscles this morning. She gave a tiny smile, for some of the aching places were very pleasurable.

Case was sprawled across the deck like a dead man. The beach towel covered his groin and one thigh, leaving the rest of him for Catarina to enjoy. She studied the lines of him, his brow, his jaw, his lips. His shoulders were square. His biceps had sharp definition even in relaxation. She watched the small rise and fall of his sleeping belly and marveled at how alive he was, how vital he was and how glad she was she let herself have this night.

No matter what came of it, in this moment, she was joyful. The smile got bigger and bigger until it seeped out in a giggle. Now, she was hungry! She got up, wrapped herself in her towel and carefully descended the steps to the cabin below deck.

There was a bathroom on the boat with a toilette and she freshened herself as best she could. She washed her diaphragm and replaced it. Catarina and Case were far from through with each other. She could still smell sex on herself and she liked it. Something new happened last night. Catarina fully enjoyed being female for the first time. She didn't resent her passions or the man that satisfied them.

"Catarina!" Case's groggy voice sounded above the gulls.

"Down here." She could hear him growl through a stretch to work out the kinks of sleeping on the deck. She knew he was still naked and her imagination fired.

"What's for breakfast? I'm starved! My steak from last night is long gone."

As Catarina appeared from below with a plate of fruit, bread and cheese, Case was stepping into his shorts. He pointed to the new turquoise swimsuit and sarong she wore smiling with approval. They devoured the food as if it would be their last meal. Even the instant coffee tasted wonderful and they watched their first sunrise together.

Catarina noticed when Case cocked his head to watch the breeze play with the sarong. He seemed to be waiting for the beautiful cloth to give in and expose her leg. When it did, he caressed her thigh.

"We are different now," he said.

"Are we?" Catarina felt a tug of war, hope and resistance. Case was an impulsive, mercurial man. She knew the feelings he had at this moment would not last. She scolded herself. *Let it go. Take this only for what it is; it's good.*

"I've wanted you from that first morning I met you in the field shack. Now I'm falling in love with you." When Catarina looked away from his face into sky, he asked gently, "What do you think of that?"

She dropped her head. He was close enough to take her face in his hands and raise it, forcing her to look at him. Her eyes were glassy.

"I'm sad," she whispered.

"No!"

"If you let these feelings between us just be a.....just what they are, that will be best. If you try to make me think it is more, I'm not sure I can survive when you leave me."

"I won't leave you." He brushed a wild curl from her face. "I've decided not to take the cruise on *The Merry Maker.* There is too much I want here."

"I'm scared."

"You can be scared; you can't be sad. Because I'm the happiest I have ever been in my life!" He jumped to his feet and with his arms outstretched, he boomed the words to the bay, "I'm in love!" He frightened a flock of gulls and Catarina as well.

"You're ahead of me. You are going too fast. Can you wait for me?"

"Yes." His confidence did not console her. "Now, I need a swim. Come with me."

He took her hand and helped her up from the deck. He made a ceremony of removing the sarong, kissing her hips around in a circle as the unwinding fabric exposed her flesh. His arms surrounded her for a kiss while he leaned, leaned, leaned starboard. He teetered on one foot and dropped them both over the edge and into the water.

"Ahhgah!" Catarina's shriek gurgled as she went under. The water was almost as warm as the air, so it wasn't unpleasant, just a surprise. Her first word when she came up was "Asno!"

"What do you mean?"

"You're a jackass, Gringo." She clung to the swimmer's ladder attached to the side of the boat.

"You can't call me Gringo any more, Catarina. I'm not just any man, now."

"I'll call you whatever you deserve to be called!" She pushed her hair out of her face.

Catarina saw the familiar devil that appeared in Case's blue eyes. She saw a glint of danger and recognized what she was stirring up. She shrieked again and desperately scrambled to get back into the boat. He was too fast, too strong and too determined to make her laugh.

When he pulled her away from the safety of the ladder and she needed his help to stay afloat, he started playfully touching her intimately. He was easily strong enough to tread water for the both of them. He slipped his fingers into the elastic of her bikini, gently pinched her bottom, successfully untied the halter top and whisked it away in a tug of war. When she started to sink, he rescued her. When he kissed her mouth, laughter replaced tension and sadness was the last thing on her mind.

Sounds of an Evinrude motor interrupted their caresses. "Fishermen," Case said.

"Where's my top?" There was panic in Catarina's voice. She tread water while Case dived for it, twice.

"Can't find it in time. Get behind me. Stay

Susan LeMiles

close." Case recognized Bob and his fishing buddies.

"What's with this guy? How does he manage to show up at exactly the wrong moments?" Catarina put her hands on Case's hips and stayed very close. Her breasts brushed back and forth against his back with every swish of his arms.

"Hello, there!" Case's tone was barely cordial.

Bob's rolls and his Speedo were covered with a denim shirt today. He had white Nosekote splotched across his face to protect him from the sun. "Are you catching any fish?"

"Not fishing today. Just swimming," Case said. Catarina smiled painfully over his shoulder and hoped no one would ever guess what he was hiding.

Bob's flat-bottomed Skooter glided in a slow circle around Case and Catarina. Case kept pace with the turns making sure he was always between Catarina and the men.

"I'll bet a guy like you knows some sweet fishing spots around here. Got any suggestions as to where to go?"

"Just follow the birds."

"Follow the birds?"

"Yeah. The birds know where the bait fish are. The big fish know where the bait fish are."

"Oh. That makes sense." The three men nodded in agreement.

"You guys better get going before all the pelicans are done with breakfast." Case's suggestion clearly sounded like a dismissal.

"Yeah, thanks for the tip." The motor on the Scooter revved and the fishermen waved goodbye. As they sped away, Catarina heard one of the men laugh and say, "Honeymooners."

Catarina peeked around Case's shoulder. "Oh my God, where's my top?"

"I'll get it. I think I saw it; I just didn't have time to grab it. Let me boost you up on deck."

"No! I'm not getting out of the water without my top. You find it!" She clung to the ladder and assured him she was fine.

He swam back to the spot of his playful crime and came up with the top after the first dive. He shook his head to get the hair out of his eyes, hooted and triumphantly swung his trophy in a circle above his head.

It took longer than necessary to get the top back on. Catarina needed help staying afloat and his hands kept slipping in between the drifting fabric and her firm round flesh. Her nipples were erect from the danger of discovery and the water. It seemed Case would never give up the view.

He finally climbed into the boat and pulled her in too. The towels that were their covers last night, served to dry them before they went below to search for more food. Good sex and salt water play made them hungry. They opened sodas and found cans of tuna in a cabinet.

Case was too tall to stand erect in the cabin. He folded himself into the booth that served as a dining table while Catarina fixed sandwiches and opened chips. They sat on the same side of the table, enjoying the closeness; and while they ate, they both kept glancing through the open door to the sleeping quarters in the aft cabin. The queen-sized bed looked restful and inviting.

"I think I would be more comfortable stretched out in there." Case pointed to the bed.

"Oh, you would?"

Case's intent was to have her in that big soft bed, but gentle waters moved the boat like a cradle. His body finally needed something more than it needed Catarina.....sleep. He watched her through his heavy lids. She purred in early slumber. His last thought was one of wonder that his life was starting to make sense.

* * * * *

Whonk.....whonk.....whonk. The boat rocked and the thudding sound alarmed Case. He was instantly awake. Someone was trying to board the boat! His awkward tumble to the place he knew Skipper kept a flare gun woke Catarina. He clamored half way up the steps and periscoped his head three hundred sixty degrees. Nothing.

Carefully, Case stepped out of the hold and walked the perimeter starting at the bow. He held the gun close to his chest, controlled and alert. His shoulders relaxed when he spotted the intruder. A molded plastic lawn chair bobbed and bumped hard against the boat with each swell.

"Case? What's the matter?"

"Nothing, it's fine. We're being attacked by furniture." He reached overboard and hoisted the villain chair to the deck. "Someone probably lost this in the last storm."

Catarina popped out of the cabin and gasped, "You carry a gun?"

"It's just a flare gun. All boats should have flares."

"Do you shoot fish?"

"No, it's in case you get lost or stalled, so the Coast Guard can find you." Case was puzzled at how little Catarina knew about the water. "I'll show you how to fish. Want to catch our own dinner?"

She nodded, intrigued. "I never caught a fish."

"Let's go; I know a better place than this for trout." Case hoisted the anchor and started cranking the mainsail. He felt strong, rested, proud. He was a man capable of providing dinner for his woman. This was his world and he was sharing it with Catarina. His whole persona swelled; after all, he had just protected her from a lawn chair.

By dusk there were six trout fillets, salted, peppered and waiting on a plate. Case set up a grill rigged to hang over the side of the boat. Another plate piled with sliced mangos, papayas and limes glistened in the sunset. *What more could a guy need? A lawn chair.*

Case positioned his new chair close to the grill so he could cook his fish and watch Catarina open one of the bottles of wine. She poured some for each of them.

"Hey, stemware."

"Señor Skipper is a very romantic man; I can tell. Perhaps he has a lady friend, someone he would bring out on a cruise like this?"

"Skipper? No. These glasses are for the tourists, people who rent the boat."

211

"I think he is a romantic; look at everything he did for us. I should introduce him to Abuelita. She believes in love."

"Do you believe in love, Catarina?" He watched the smile fall from her face. It wasn't the sign he wanted to see. "Sixto says you don't."

"I don't know any more."

"If you don't believe in love, do you think you could believe in me?"

"I never thought of it that way. No lo creo."

Since she still didn't know, Case decided not to pursue the matter. Dinner sizzled and popped on the grill. He let the wine trickle down the back of his throat seeking the pleasurable sensations of a moment ago. He didn't remember the sunset having this many colors or food tasting this good. Even the music coming from the radio was brighter. It was because of Catarina; he knew.

"Today is Sunday," Case said.

"Yes, it is easy to lose track of time out here alone." Catarina smiled and sipped her wine.

"I have to have the boat back in time to restock it and get it cleaned up for the customer on Tuesday."

She sighed and went to sit on his lap. She ran her fingers through his hair and he leaned into her hand enjoying her touch. While his eyes were closed, she initiated a kiss which he took over. He pressured her mouth, played with her tongue. She whispered into his mouth. "We have tonight then."

"It's not going to be just tonight, Catarina, you'll see." Case wanted to ask her to marry him right then and there. Right this minute! But he was afraid she would say no. He could not let that happen.

Catarina loved him. He just had to let her figure it out for herself.

Their relationship had raced from infatuation through desperation to passion to playfulness. The desperation phase was hard on him, wanting her without knowing if she wanted him. Now with their passion acknowledged, they could play. This was where he could convince her that he was the man who could make her happy.

The fish was delectable, the mangos sweet as candy. Catarina liked the papaya better than Case did. He gallantly gave her the last piece of fish. She poured him the last bit of wine.

When Case doused water on the fire, the charcoal exploded with pops and smoke. Catarina took the plates below while Case propped the deck pillows up for another evening with the stars. They settled into each other's arms, a step closer to being a couple than yesterday.

"Abuelita taught me about the Mayans. Who taught you about the stars?"

"Skipper. He was in the Marine Corps and then the Merchant Marines. He claims to have flown to the farthest star out there himself."

"See, he is a romantic. Is there a love story in the stars?"

"Yes." Case thought this question was encouraging. "And it is better than that sad one you told me last night."

"I want to hear it."

"Andromeda." He pointed to her in the sky, "was an earthly princess that was so beautiful, the queen of the gods got jealous. This queen, Juno, was so angry about Andromeda's beauty that she got her husband, the king of the gods, to send a sea monster to ravage the coast of Andromeda's country. The devastation was so bad that Andromeda's father consulted a sorceress to see what could be done."

"What's a sorceress?"

"I guess, sort of a magician. Listen to the story; you'll like it. The magician tells Andromeda's father that he must sacrifice his daughter to make the queen happy."

"Sacrifice his daughter? These people were like the Mayans."

"So Andromeda is chained to a rock in the middle of the ocean where the sea monster can get her."

"Like Ix Chel's father."

"Luckily, a prince, named Perseus, was flying back from killing a different monster and saw Andromeda struggling for her life. Without realizing it, he fell in love. Even her tears were sexy."

Catarina started to ask a question. Case put his finger to her lips to shush her.

"Don't ask how he could fly. That's another story." Case changed his voice and started a dramatic presentation of dialogue. "Perseus called down to her and said, 'You should not be wearing such chains as these. You should be wearing the chains of love. Tell me your name, where you are from and why you are tied up here.' Andromeda resisted telling him anything."

"Maybe she thought it wasn't any of his business."

"I don't know if she was shy or afraid of the monster or just terminally stubborn." Case shot a

214

meaningful look at Catarina. "But, Perseus almost crashed and burned hovering around her trying to get her phone number. Do you want to hear this story?"

"Sí." Catarina fell silent.

"Just about this time, the waters around Andromeda's rock started churning; the waves started crashing over her getting her all wet and Perseus said, 'Man! You would look good in an orange string bikini! Soon, the sea monster appeared."

Case paused the story when Catarina slapped his chest, then he continued. "To save his love, Perseus knew he must attack the monster. After a long bloody battle, he managed to kill the monster, rescue Andromeda and marry her. They lived happily ever after."

"How did he kill the monster?"

"I think he shot him with a nine-millimeter.....a gun."

"And they were happy?"

"Well, there they are, together in the sky, forever. Look, to the north. There she is lying on her rock, and right next to her is Perseus. See his sword and the monster's head he is holding?"

"Did they kiss?"

"I'm sure they did." Case rolled over on top of Catarina and kissed her breathless. He didn't even try to keep his hands from roaming for it had been almost twenty-four hours since they made love. He was already in a panic to have her again. He wanted this night to be spent in the bed, like it should be. He planned to stay awake all night and love her until morning.

He propped his weight on his elbows and settled himself in between her legs. He used her bosom as a pillow for his chin and stared into her eyes. He picked up a curl and tickled the side of her face with it. He kissed her breasts through her sarong. His fingers played with her mouth until she parted her lips to take a taste. It drove him wild and he held her face in his hands to possess her with the kiss he wanted.

Case rolled to a sitting position taking Catarina with him. He wanted to symbolically carry her over the threshold and into the bedroom, but the opening to the cabin was too small. He held out his hand for her to accept and they climbed down into the cabin together. The overhead light burned in the galley. They left their clothing next to the table and entered the darker bedroom. They slithered between the soft sheets and their whispers overlaid the exploration of each other's bodies. Case propped himself up on one elbow to watch her while she touched him.

"I've never tasted you," Catarina murmured.

Case was amazed when she pulled back her hair and slid down his body. She teased him mercilessly. The feathery kisses and rhythmic motion she inflicted caused him to lose control immediately and his semen spilled over onto the sheet.

"Catarina!" He convulsed and pulled her into his groin. "That's not the way I wanted it."

She laid gentle kisses along his stomach and up his chest. "I can wait."

"No, you will have to suffer my hands until I recover. It's your punishment." He placed her on her side like he did the night before and played with her until his miraculous recovery was complete.

When they finally lay in the quiet of each other's arms, Case understood the phrase "and the two shall become one." He could not tell where her skin ended and his began. He was sure she was asleep when he heard a scared little voice.

"I don't want to; but what if I fall in love with you tonight?"

"Well then, you will wear that orange string bikini for me tomorrow."

She pinched him and they fell asleep laughing, tangled in each other, peaceful.

* * * * *

Catarina felt her lover stir in the night. He was her love now, whether she stated it or not. She didn't understand why the words choked in her throat like they did. They just wouldn't come out. If she was going to be happy, she was going to have to be a lot braver than this.

Chapter 23

While We Were Sleeping

Catarina woke alone in the big bed. She slid her arms across the sheets to where Case had been sleeping. They were cool so he must have been up a while. Being with him wasn't like she thought it would be. True, she was physically satisfied, but there was an emotional peace that was new.

Since Logan, Catarina felt damaged inside, broken and permanently rearranged. She resented her body's stirrings and the phantom aches she could not control. Physical attraction to a man made her feel alone. That was the reverse of the way desire worked for most women.

Last night, knowing what a man wanted and giving it to him on her terms made her feel wonderful. Ironically, expressing her physical passion with Case made her feel connected to him in a way she did not know existed. When she lost control with him, she discovered that she was completely at peace with the truth of loving him. *Is this where trust comes from? Is this what love feels like? It must be.*

She toyed with the idea of letting him know that she loved him.....or not. Maybe actions would speak louder than words. She looked at the orange string bikini tossed on the dresser. She pictured Case's potential reaction to seeing her in it and could feel his hands on her bare, bare body. She reached for it and put it on.

Catarina took one last glance in the mirror. She was practically as naked as any of the wildlife on the beach. Well, Case would like it and it would definitely send the message of how she wanted to spend the day with him. Would he see it and remember what he'd said last night, that if she fell in love with him, she would wear it?

A muffled voice that was not Case's drifted down into the cabin. Catarina reached for the sarong and wrapped it tightly around herself. No one but Case was going to see her dressed in this bikini. When she reached the top of the galley stairs, she heard Case's wary question.

"Logan, what can I do for you?"

"Need to come aboard, Becker. Got something to talk to you about." Logan stood on the bow of a Coast Guard patrol cruiser. Besides Logan and two Coast Guard officers, there were three armed men representing the Sheriff's Department.

Case tried to keep things light. "I promise those fish I ate last night were the legal size." Catarina could tell Case's easy manner covered his readiness for trouble. When she stepped into Logan's view, his thin lips curled a smile.

"Well, Miss de la Alvarado, I can't say I am surprised to see you. Did you two have a nice weekend?" Syrup dripped from his voice.

"Logan, I think your jurisdiction ends over there." Case pointed toward the Texas shore. Facing down six armed law officers didn't look like good odds to Case. He stepped back and allowed Logan and another officer to board the *Everlovin'*.

Catarina felt a crawl run up her spine. She never felt safe when Logan was around; but she always knew what he wanted. The fact that he was being so aggressive with a man like Case produced sickening dread. She'd seen Logan execute personal vendettas before, usually against the penniless and powerless. He must have something terrible on Case to ambush him like this.

Case said, "Get it done, Logan. I've got to get this boat back to Skipper this morning."

Logan held out a photo for Case to see. "You know this man?"

Case's stomach lurched. It was a crime photo. Blood trickled from a hole in the middle of a man's forehead. His jaw was slack with death. Even in the black and white picture, Case could tell the man had been dead for a while. It was not pretty.

"Know him?" Logan prodded again.

"I met him once, don't know him. What's his name?"

"This is Jonathan Pender."

"What happened?" Case handed the photo back to Logan.

Logan ignored the question. "How did you meet him?"

"Picked him up off the corner where braceros wait for work. He did some odd jobs for me."

"Perfect. Case Becker, you are under arrest for the murder of Jonathan Pender, money laundering and drug trafficking." Case was already in handcuffs when Logan approached Catarina.

"You, Catarina de la Alvarado, are under arrest for conspiracy to commit murder, money laundering and drug trafficking."

Logan instigated a small struggle with the malicious intent of dislodging the sarong. By the time he put the handcuffs on Catarina, the sarong had slithered to the deck and her almost naked body was on display for all the men to see. Logan stood behind her, ran his hands over her shoulders and slipped his arms around her waist. He hugged her to him, continuing the mock struggle.

"Settle down, now. I wouldn't want you to lose that top." Logan looked at the other officers and raised his eyebrows in pretend horror just before he gave them a quick wink.

"Logan!" Case's voice was steel and ice. A vein protruded at his temple and his jaw line visibly ticked. "You have no idea what you are doing."

"Yes I do. I'm apprehending a criminal whose fingerprints connect him to the scene of a murder and to money used to purchase transportation for illegal drugs. As soon as I have Catarina's fingerprints, I can confirm an eye-witness report that she purchased a truck with money you gave her." Logan reached down to pick up the sarong; he draped it around Case's neck. "Get in the cruiser."

"What about Skipper's boat?" Case asked.

"It's impounded, suspicion of being used in drug trafficking." He looked at the Coast Guard officers and said, "Seize it. We haven't figured out how Skipper's involved; but we will. Let's go."

Catarina was numb to the leering stares of the officers. Her skin was locked in recoil at Logan's touch. Everything was happening so fast, unbelievable, surreal.

The only words that echoed clearly, were Logan's....."the money you gave her." The money hiding behind the wall in her closet at home was Case's money! The money that freed her to love him was so dirty it led to murder. Catarina could feel herself slipping into shock. When Logan pointed to a bench seat in the Coast Guard cruiser, she sat. He shoved Case down beside her. She looked through Case as though he didn't exist.

The cruiser sped across rough waters. The wind picked up and Case and Catarina were seated in the front of the boat where the pounding against the surface was merciless. Her spine felt as if it would break every time the bow lifted and slammed the water. Catarina's head began to hurt. The lurching was so violent she had trouble keeping her seat on the bench. Case threw his leg over her lap to steady her. Logan sneered at the protective gesture, but let it go.

The sarong around Case's neck blew to the bottom of the boat and was soon soiled with saltwater and footprints. Catarina closed her eyes to protect herself. It was the only safety she could find. Her eyes were still closed an hour later when she felt the engine slow to approach the dock. Now, she was aware again, of her nakedness, her aching bones and Case's betrayal. Logan loved humiliation. He should really enjoy parading her around like this. Holding her tears took all the strength she had.

The cruiser bumped against its slip at the Coast Guard Station. Her eyes fluttered open to see a gathering of law enforcement officers, reporters and curious observers.

Case leaned and spoke in her ear. "Catarina, don't worry about this. I can fix everything. I just want to make sure I do it in front of an attorney. Catarina? Do you hear me?"

Logan lifted her by her arm. "Don't count on it, superhero. Catarina knows who can take care of her in a tight spot, don't you, baby?"

* * * * *

The ride to the Brownsville court house was wretched for Case. He and Catarina were forced into separate cars. He knew Logan was filling Catarina's head with poison, twisting the story into lies that might never be undone.

The driver of Catarina's vehicle made an unnecessary turn taking her on an alternate route. The last thing Case saw happening through the back window of her vehicle was Logan placing his arm around Catarina in the back seat. Case boiled with helplessness. He kicked the seat so violently that the policeman in the passenger seat drew his gun and stuck it through the grate between them.

* * * * *

The Cameron County Jail holding cell was full of last night's drunks and tomorrow's repeat offenders. It was impossible to keep a place like this clean. Nasty. The cell door clanged and an echo filled the concrete halls.

"I want a phone call!" Case demanded to the back of the guard's head.

"You ain't gettin' no phone call." A rough, muscle-bound man paced the length of the cell. The sleeves were missing from his shirt as were a few teeth from his mouth. Twenty-odd prisoners gave the man a wide berth. He was not as tall as Case; but his beefy, slick muscles bulged out of the torn sleeve holes and scars on his face pronounced him volatile and dangerous. He placed his face close to Case's and hissed. "I ain't got no phone call, so you ain't gettin' no phone call!"

"Case Becker, your attorney is here, come on." A guard opened the cell door. Lucky break, Case thought. He had a lot more important things to do rather than fight this crazy guy. But, how could anyone have found out about his predicament so soon? Maybe the Becker Rescue Services dispatcher heard something on the police scanner. He followed the guard down the hall to a private interview room.

What the hell? Nothing could have surprised Case more than to see the Speedo-modeling, tourist fisherman waiting for him in the interview room. In honor of the seriousness of a murder arrest, Bob had donned some rumpled khaki pants. He did still have on his fishing shirt and flip flops. His hairy arms cradled a worn brief case.

"I saw you honeymooners get picked up this morning. Figured you could use some help from an ambulance chasin' lawyer. Bob Barker, criminal defense attorney from Austin." He smiled big and extended his meaty hand.

Chase took it. "My family has an attorney."

"I don't think you need that kind of attorney. I've read the charges." He waved a folder in the air.

Case explained. "It's all a mistake; I can explain. I just did something stupid."

"Which is the mistake? The little murder thing or the drug trafficking thing?"

Bob's smartass response didn't sit well with Case. "I didn't murder Jonathan Pender! I'm not involved in drug trafficking. But I have screwed up my life." Everything he had built with Catarina in the last forty eight hours was vaporizing. When she found out the whole truth, she would never forgive him for betraying her. Of all the impulsive, destructive lies he could have come up with. He just never thought he would get caught; and Bob was right, the Becker family attorney never handled anything like this.

"Want to tell me about it?"

"It's pretty dumb."

"I'm listening." The attorney settled in the straight-backed chair, looked over the top of his reading glasses and waited while Case searched his mind for a place to begin the story.

"I guess I believed I'd fall in love, someday; but I didn't believe in love at first sight." He snickered at himself. "I fell in love with Catarina de la Alvarado the moment I saw her. We're not exactly from the same social world. My family is in business; her family members are undocumented fruit pickers." Case shook his head. "She's proud. She would never take anything from me, not money to help her go to school, not a kiss, not a flower."

"You weren't lovers?" Bob gave Case a lawyer's skeptical look.

"We were together one time before this weekend. She threw that back at me too! It was a disaster. She didn't want anything to do with me. The relationship wasn't going to go anywhere, so I decided to bail out, quit trying. I still wanted to help her go to school, get an education. That's what she really wanted. She deserved it. I've never seen anyone work so hard for something, want it so much." Case paused. "I had the money; I didn't need it."

"So, what did you do?"

"I took a hundred thousand dollars out of my account and paid Jonathan Pender to accidentally lose it where she would find it. I knew Catarina wouldn't turn it in to the police because of her immigration status. I planned to leave town and forget her. I've signed up to crew for a couple sailing the Caribbean for a few months."

"You had one hundred G's to spare? Good God! Didn't your banker have questions?"

"They know me. I told them I was buying a boat."

Bob noted the amount of money in a file. "What happened next?"

Case's words stuck; he cleared his throat. "She came to me. She changed her mind and came to me. I don't know why and I don't care!"

"And you took her out on the boat."

"Yes." Case shuddered recalling Catarina's smile, her willingness, the intimacy and happiness they shared.

"Where did you get the money?"

"Inheritance. My grandmother Becker left everything to me, all the money, all the real estate, the business too. My dad, my step dad, runs the business, but his last name is not Becker even though everyone thinks it is."

"I'll need a copy of that probated will." Bob started designing the case in his head.

"I'm not worried about this legal mess. But, I've lost Catarina, haven't I?"

"I couldn't say. She's proud and you're right; you're dumb. Doesn't sound good to me."

Case's spirits sunk lower. "Can you handle things for her? See she doesn't get deported? I'll pay you. She can't stop me from helping her with that, can she?"

"Let me get you out of here first. That Border Patrol guy, Logan Dell? I feel something strange coming off of him. He could be a problem."

"Yeah, he's got a reputation for jumping outside his jurisdiction, railroading cases; and....."

"And, what?"

Case leaned forward, put his arms on the table and looked under his eyebrows at Bob. ".....and he and Catarina have a history."

"Uh, oh." Bob made a face at that news. He wrote down the name of Case's banker, information on the dates of the cash withdrawal and contact numbers for his office. "By the way, do you have an alibi for Saturday night between six p.m. and eleven p.m.?"

"Yeah, I do. We both do.....a good one. Catarina was on stage singing at the pavilion on the island and I was with her."

Chapter 24

Getting Out of Jail

"Son of a bitch!" Logan hurled the stapler. It made a deep dent in the metal file cabinet right next to the dent it made the last time he lost his temper.

"Cool it, Logan!" Captain Kennedy picked up the stapler from the floor. "I'm not cleaning up another one of your messes. If you go off into the twilight zone again, you're on your own."

"Case Becker is involved in this murder. I know it, and his little band of Alvarado groupies too." Logan could feel his mind hurtling towards uncontrollable rage. He liked it when he got to this point. It made him feel so alive, to lose control of himself and gain control of those around him. Sweet.

"You need to stay out of the police's way. It's their territory. Besides that, all Becker's bases are covered. With the bank records and alibis, it's over."

Logan's jaw clenched and the muscles in his face moved in response to the pressure on his teeth. "I'll figure it out. In the mean time, the de la Alvarado family is going to get a personal guided tour of hell."

He slammed his trooper's hat low on his brow and stormed out the station door to make his prophecy come true.

* * * * *

"Get in the car, Case. Now." Bob's command was military. Intense.

The pale green colors of a Border Patrol sedan swooshed into Case's vision just before its screeching stop blocked their exit from the County Jail parking lot. It didn't seem as though Logan was coming to apologize.

"Case, let me handle this. Get in the car."

"Don't try to manage me, Bob." Case stood waiting for Logan. He wanted to see just what he was going to have to contend with and he didn't want Bob filtering the information.

"Don't get used to the fresh air, Becker. I'll get you for the drugs if not the murder." Logan's face was puffed, sweating with mania. The green sedan rocked when he slammed the door.

"The case is closed," Case said.

"My cases aren't closed until I close 'em. You may be out for now, but the Alvarado's problems have just started."

Case's stomach flipped. "If you hurt Catarina....."

"Shut up, Case!" Bob was loud enough to interrupt the words before they were spoken. "Logan wants a threat. It's exactly what he wants."

".....or you'll what?" Logan's shoulders relaxed.

He sneered. "I won't have to hurt Catarina. I'll find a way to get the state to kill them all."

The attorney must have been more nimble than he looked, for he appeared between Case's fist and Logan's face just in time to receive the impact of Case's punch. Bob reeled backward and grabbed his nose. "Shit! Case, get in the car!" Blood spurted onto Bob's shirt. "I'll hit you back, I swear I can!" He pushed Case into the car and scrambled around to the driver's side. He gunned the motor, threw it into reverse and backed out of the parking lot, over the curb and into the street.

Case watched Logan march into the jail where Catarina still waited for help. He felt his eyes sting. Never in his wildest imagination could he have foreseen consequences to his actions like this. What made him do it? Give Catarina the money. Was he just intent on winning, exerting his power over her? He certainly managed to fool himself into thinking he was helping her. When he examined his motives, they did seem more like some kind of revenge for her rejection rather than benevolent giving. He was sick, inside and outside; and he had no plan to save her.

* * * * *

Catarina stared at the faces of the three men sitting at the table with her. The interview room at the jail was stuffy; or was it just that she couldn't breathe after seeing Sixto ushered into the room wearing an orange jumpsuit that matched hers? She started crying the moment she saw he was a prisoner too. She hadn't stopped.

The presence of Bob the fisherman was also a shock. She wondered if Bob remembered watching her hovering behind Case in the bay without the top of her swimsuit. Had he seen anything? Everything? Now, he was her attorney? She would have to bear it for she and Sixto both needed him.

Her attention turned to the third man, a stranger, Case Becker. Catarina discovered the truth about something Abuelita had always told her, that there is a thin line between love and hate; and hate him she did. With all the power her strength could give her, she hated him. She watched him, all fresh, showered and smelling of good intentions.

Bob spoke without eloquence. "I've got some good news and some bad news."

"I don't want him here." Catarina's voice shook.

"You are all in this together. Your defenses are connected. You need to talk to each other." Bob knew he was going to have to be gentle.

Sixto slid his chair close to Catarina's and put his arm around her. "No llora, es bueno. Estoy aquí." As he murmured assurances and comfort, his eyes told Bob to continue.

"The murder charges against Case and Catarina have been dropped. The bank evidence is solid as to where the money came from and your alibis are unshakable. The police have nowhere to go with that."

"Sixto, do you know what he did?" Catarina's voice accused, judged and sentenced Case in one question.

"Yes, he told me.....it was wrong." Sixto looked at Case without anger.

Bob ignored her outburst and continued. "Catarina, you are being deported immediately."

"No! I start school in less than a month!" She threw off Sixto's comforting arm.

"That's not going to happen." Bob explained. "There will be no visa. The worst news is that they have a lead indicating that there's evidence in Sixto's truck that will connect him to the drug trafficking charges. They have impounded it and have a search warrant."

"What?" All three of them reacted in unison.

"Whatever is there was probably planted. But, Sixto doesn't have an alibi for the night Jonathan Pender was killed, at least not one that is currently on this side of the river. Seems one of those drug sniffing dogs has a serious interest in something inside your truck, Sixto. They are searching it now. If they find anything, police are going to pursue the murder and drug charges against you."

Catarina exploded in a rage of Spanish language invectives. Her words echoed back and forth against the concrete walls - mentiroso, asno, embustero, bastardo. She quickly realized Case couldn't understand what she was saying and slowed her rant to include English. "You are a liar! You betrayed me; you let me trust you and you betrayed me! I will never forgive you for making me what I hate the most.....a liar to myself and my family! Look at me, you liar!" She slapped the table and wished it was his face. "I thought that money would help my family."

Case raised his eyes to hers and mumbled, "I thought so too."

"Most of all, I thought it would free me from being dependant on any man so that I could love someone! You ruined it all! Look what you have done to Sixto. You have stolen every dream I ever had and hurt every one I love! And I helped you because I lied too, to them and to myself!" The truth lay in silence on the table in front of them.

The three men waited for her to calm down. Finally, Catarina whispered, "Does Abuelita know?"

Bob's voice was steady, purposefully soothing. "Yes, Case and I visited her. We told her. She asked if you need anything."

"I need him out of this room." She stared through Case as though he were already gone.

"It's more important to start taking care of these charges against Sixto."

"I can't help do that if I'm not even in the country."

"I'm working on getting a stay against your being deported. I want you to be close by," Bob explained. "There is not much we can do today, but I'll be back tomorrow to get you released."

"I want to write Abuelita a note. Can she bring me some things?"

"Maybe, depends on what they are."

Catarina wrote a note in Spanish and passed it to Bob. She folded it so no one else could see. "This is private, right?"

"Yes, attorney-client confidentiality."

"From him too?" Catarina thrust her chin towards Case.

"Yes, from him too." Bob looked at each of his clients and decided, "We're done for now."

Catarina and Sixto were taken back to their cells. Bob packed his briefcase and Case stared at the wall.

Case asked, "What about Skipper's boat, is he going to get it back?"

"The Coast Guard conducted that search; it was legit. *Everlovin'* is already safely home. You asked me another question yesterday. Want an answer?"

"What?"

"You asked me if you had lost Catarina." Bob snapped the latches to his brief case closed. "I think you had better make other plans for your life. She's not going to be in it."

Chapter 25

A Mystery Solved

The dog reacted just the way Logan knew he would. He hovered around Sixto Terrazo's impounded truck, racing from one wheel well to the other. He danced and barked, alerting his handler that what he found was something important.

Mack was an expensive German shepherd with years of training. He was the premier drug enforcement officer in Texas. More arrests were made as a result of his work than any other ten law officers combined. He was disciplined, wore a badge on his harness and six stars of commendation studded into his collar.

Logan loved to watch Mack work. Mack could run down a suspect with a quarter mile head start. He was a magnificent animal. Trouble was, Mack was more intelligent than most damned humans. *It would be a shame if I ever had to kill that dog.*

Logan sidled up to Mack's handler. "He does love his work, doesn't he?"

"Yeah, this must be a big haul; I've never seen him so excited. Mack. Come." The handler clipped the leash on the dog and rewarded him with affection. "Mack. Sit. Mack. Stay."

Logan walked over to speak to the officer searching the interior of the vehicle. "Come on, quit wasting your time in the back seat. Check those wheels first. Mack really liked them."

Logan knew what they were going to find. It would be exactly 40 ounces of fine grade, uncut cocaine. *All I have to do now is let the dominoes fall. Sixto's alibi will never hold up. Those wetbacks he claims he helped move furniture are never going to show their faces. I'll have him for the drugs. I'll have him for the murder. Careful, don't smile too big.*

The hubcaps popped off easily. "Shit! What the hell is this?" The officer conducting the search wretched. Mack jerked his leash from the handler's grasp and ran to examine the decayed remains of four frogs, their juices puddeling on the garage floor. The stench was heavenly to Mack. He was the only one of the search crew that didn't cover his nose and curse. The other hubcaps each held their share of sixteen frog bodies, the heads, the brains, the guts, the bones, the blood and the squinty eyeballs.....no legs.

* * * * *

Bob's laughter echoed off the walls of the jailhouse interview room. Red-faced and happy, he slapped Case on the back and leaned over to Sixto. "I don't know what kind of god you pray to, but I want to meet him!"

Sixto didn't get the joke. "I pray to God.....the regular God. What do you mean?"

Case could not think of anything that would be this funny in this situation. "Shut up, Bob. Tell us what's going on."

Bob squelched his laughter, but it squeezed from the edges of his pretend sober mouth and serious eyes. "I have the results of the search conducted on your truck, Sixto."

"Yes? Yes? I am innocent?"

"They found sixteen murder victims." Bob was laughing so hard he could barely speak.

Sixto's face contorted in disbelief. "Murder victims! They were looking for drugs!"

"Frogs!" Bob spat the word out with lungs deprived of air from laughing. "They found sixteen dead frogs in your hubcaps. No drugs, just frogs." Bob put his hands on his stomach to still the shaking fat.

"What's the matter with you? They are trying to kill me. It's not funny! I need a different lawyer!"

"No, no you don't. I'm just an old man in need of a good laugh." Bob wiped his eyes and took a deep breath. "I talked to the officer who did the search on your truck. It was pretty funny. Logan Dell was there, just so certain they were going to find drugs. 'Mack The famous drug sniffing dog' was dancing around making noises, telling everybody he struck gold. When they took the hubcaps off your truck, they were full of stinking, squishy, dead f....." Bob choked on the word again. "Mack raced over for a gourmet lunch, and Logan was so mad he kicked the dog like it was his fault. The handler said Dell was really loosing it. Mack was the only one that wasn't afraid of him. Bit Logan good." Bob let the news sink in before he asked the two men. "Why do you think Logan lost it like that?"

Case logically filled in the story. "Because he planted drugs in the truck himself."

Bob continued. "Right. Not only has his evidence in the drug charge collapsed; but your alibi for the night Jonathan Pender was killed showed up. Sixto, the only thing they have on you is illegal entry into the U.S. and you know the penalty for that."

"They send me back to Mexico." Sixto relaxed in his chair; but it was going to take more time for him to recover from the scare of a murder charge.

"Will he get his truck back?" Case asked.

"Probably not. It'll disappear in paperwork when he leaves the country."

"I'll keep an eye on it for you, Sixto. Maybe I can claim it for you," Case offered.

"It's your truck; you bought it."

"This isn't over." Case was dead serious. "Somebody's got those drugs."

Bob shook his head. "I don't care who's got the drugs."

"Sixto and I care. I know who went frogging Saturday night."

* * * * *

Case knew Logan Dell was heartless enough to hurt anyone, even a ten-year-old boy. The man was unraveling a little more each day. It wouldn't take much of a detective to find out who played a practical joke on Sixto Terrazos. Alberto would have bragged to half the neighborhood by Sunday morning. *He better be home. I need to talk to him before Logan figures it out.*

Case pulled up to the house where María and Alberto Sanchez lived. Relief came when he spotted Alberto sitting on the wooden steps drawing pictures in the dirt with a stick. "Hey, amigo. Que pasa?"

"Nada." Alberto hunched his shoulders and dug his bare toes into the dust. His usual smile was absent and he didn't look up from his drawing.

Case sat down on the steps. "You don't look so good. Something the matter?" He gave Alberto a minute to think.

"Sixto is in jail. I think it's my fault."

"Well, Sixto is getting out of jail. Things are going to turn out OK. He does have to go back to Mexico, though; Catarina does too."

"Sixto is not in trouble any more?" There was a little hope in his voice.

"Well, not as much as he was. You and I still need to talk about something. Want to go get a raspa?" Alberto managed a nod. "Tell your mother."

"Mama! El Gringo is taking me para una raspa." The two friends walked down the street together. The snow cone hut was more like a hot box containing one person, one ice shaving machine, and 25 bottles of syrup guaranteed to make your lips whatever color you chose. Case chose strawberry. Alberto chose grape. They continued their walk down to Resaca Park where they sat at the table where Case and Catarina used to meet to study.

"Catarina and I ate a snow cone here one time."

"What color did she get?"

"Strawberry."

Alberto noisily sucked the juice from his paper cone. "Did you have your date?"

"Yes, we did."

"Did you get married?"

"Ah.....no." The knife resting in Case's heart twisted slightly. "Catarina doesn't want to get married to me."

"Why not? We like you - Mama, Abuelita, Sixto and me."

There was no way Case was having this conversation with a child.

"Alberto, I know you put frogs in Sixto's hubcaps. Why did you do that?"

"It was just a joke; you know I like jokes. I thought it would be funny. I didn't know he would get put in jail for it. We didn't kill the frogs to be bad; we ate the legs. Their purpose in life was to be our dinner. Are we in trouble with the police?"

"No, Alberto, you are not in trouble. In fact, those frogs saved Sixto from being in worse trouble." Alberto finally looked at Case. "Alberto, was there something in the hubcaps when you opened them to put the frogs in?"

"Maybe."

"No maybe. Was there something? You're not in trouble; but, we still need to help Sixto."

"I think Sixto would be in trouble if I told you. It was something bad."

Case marveled that a ten-year-old would recognize cocaine. "Did Carlos and Javier know what it was?" Alberto's answer was a shrug. "What did it look like?"

"Powder, like what goes on a baby's butt."

"Do you know who put it there?"

"I don't know. I thought maybe it was there when Sixto got the truck or maybe Sixto put it there. That's why I threw it away."

"Did you see anyone around that might have put the powder there?"

Alberto hesitated. "That man, Logan Dell was there. I think he put the powder in the wheels. We had to wait 'til he left to put the frogs in."

"How do you know it was Logan? Do you know him?"

"He drives by our house all the time to look at my mother. I don't like him. He looks at her funny. He looks at Catarina funny too."

Pictures of Logan's hands on Catarina's bare body exploded in front of Case's eyes. He would never forget that morning of the arrest. He had no answer for what to do with this rage; maybe it would pass with time, in about twenty years. For now, Case just knew rage wouldn't protect Alberto.

Case prodded further. "Did you see Logan touch the truck?"

Round eyed and innocent, Alberto nodded, yes.

"Alberto, I don't think Logan Dell is a good man. I believe he put that powder in Sixto's truck to get him in trouble on purpose. And, I think he will try to get his powder back from you." Case did not want to scare the boy, but he wanted Alberto to take him seriously.

"I can take care of myself!" Alberto puffed up his skinny chest. "I can take care of my mother too."

"Yes, you probably can. And Carlos, maybe he can take care of himself too, but, Javier. Can Javier take care of himself?"

"Not so good," Alberto admitted.

"If you show me where you threw the drugs away, we can take them to the police. They are going to ask you where you got them. You have to tell the truth. And you have to tell them you saw Logan do it. Are you brave enough?"

Alberto's solemn raspa-stained lips quivered as he said, "I am."

Chapter 26

Goodbye

The contents of Catarina's bag supplied meager comfort against the uncertainty she faced. Abuelita included the items Catarina requested in the note she sent from jail. She was grateful for the coins that she knew came from the cow cookie jar. But, who would pay Abuelita's phone bill without that money?

A bus scheduled for Vera Cruz idled at the curb. Its visible heat and fumes enveloped the deportees with a blanket of black exhaust that would kill them in an enclosed area. Catarina covered her nose and mouth. She stood in her assigned place behind a sawhorse barricade in a loose semblance of a waiting line. She knew she looked as bad as everyone around her, unkempt and haggard. Time in jail didn't make you pretty or provide uninterrupted sleep.

Catarina looked at the people around her. Many didn't seem the least bit concerned about their situation. Deportation was just part of the survival game they played. They came to the U.S., worked while they could, got caught in a round up, went home to Mexico, came back, worked and started the cycle all over again. It was routine.

Feelings of isolation assailed her. Her pride in her independence and willfulness disintegrated as she faced the fact that even if she had not shared her troubles with her family, she'd always had all of them close to her, loving her. She was adrift without them.

The momentary hope of love and happiness with Case was gone too. It was as though those starry nights happened to someone else, and she'd just heard about them. Today, the only experiences that were real were the horrors of the last two days; and the fact that at some point during the torment, her logical mind separated and took control of her errant heart. It told her not to lament the loss of a man who didn't exist. Case Becker was not who he seemed to be. Catarina shivered in the heat.

Leaving the country with no news of Sixto was the worst punishment of all. With less than twenty-four hours between the time her criminal charges were dropped and the availability of scheduled transportation to Mexico, her attorney had no time to get her deportation delayed. It was happening, now!

There would be no one to meet her in Vera Cruz and it was seven hundred miles from the tiny mountain village where relatives she had never met lived. It would take days, maybe weeks for Abuelita to get a letter to her at the house of her uncle. *I will have to find someone to let me use their phone and call Abuelita when I get there.*

She wished Bob, or even Case would miraculously appear to let her know what was happening to Sixto. As much as she despised Case Becker, her instincts told her that he would not abandon her brother. She was grateful for that.

That's when Catarina spotted Logan Dell advancing toward her on the sidewalk.

"Well, Miss de la Alvarado. This is just too bad. I'm going to miss you, darlin'." He sported a deep, fresh scratch across one eye and a bandaged hand.

Catarina's skin crawled. Once again, she found herself in a situation where she felt she had no choice but to go to him. She swallowed her pride and walked to where Logan stood on the other side of the barricade.

"Tell me about Sixto." She hated that she sounded panicked and helpless.

"Oh, information like that is going to cost you. I need a goodbye kiss." Logan looked to the guard as though he sought support in his negotiation.

Catarina could taste him before he touched her; but the bitterness of Logan's mouth would be better than leaving with no news of Sixto. Logan couldn't hurt her here in the daylight with all these witnesses. She set her teeth and took a step towards him.

"Umhum!" Logan smirked. "Would you mind holding this?" He handed his trooper's hat to the guard standing beside him. He grabbed Catarina's wrist, roughly pulled her to his chest and moved his hands to her behind.

Catarina let him thrust his tongue into her mouth and take what he wanted until she felt his hand start pulling up the back of her skirt. Enraged she bit his lip and shoved herself free. Logan kicked away one of the barricades and started after Catarina. The guard grabbed Logan's arm long enough to prevent Logan from striking her but was shaken off.

Logan waved his finger in front of her face. "No biting....."

"But you like biting, Logan." Catarina knew she was taking a chance baiting him like that. She couldn't help herself.

Logan put the back of his hand to his lip and saw there was no blood. "Well, maybe just a little." He winked.

Catarina looked over her shoulder at the other passengers. A few were watching; most were more embarrassed than she was and turned their heads away. She looked back at Logan.

"Tell me." Catarina demanded.

"Tell me." Logan mimicked her voice, then changed his tone. "You know, Catarina, things don't have to be like this. I can take care of your brother's problems and yours too." He took his hat back from the guard and rotated it in his hands. "I've got this little rent house. Could set you up. Get your visa straightened out. You could go to school, like you want to. We could be together....." His voice trailed off like he really wished for the picture he painted. He leaned into her ear to whisper, "Maybe I could talk to Jan about a divorce?"

Catarina leaned away from him; she did not believe any of it. What was that look in his eye? She remembered Jan's bruises, the sadness in her eyes and Case's concern for her. Catarina knew her instincts were right about this man. She had to get away from him for good.

"No, gracias. Nunca mas." She knew she wasn't going to get news of Sixto now. Catarina trembled as she stepped backward and attempted to join the line of people slowly boarding the bus; but she wasn't fast enough.

Logan grabbed the handle of her bag and jerked her back. "Guess I'll have to search your stuff then." He peered into the bag before he stuck his hand inside. "Let's see what we have here. Food. I guess you need that. Lady things." He gave her a nasty leer. "What's this book?"

"It's for teaching English with pictures." Catarina reached for the battered, warped notebook. Logan swung it out of her reach. The pages crackled when he opened it to the middle; and Catarina feared it would come apart in his hands.

"Oh, isn't this sweet, a dried flower. Not supposed to take plants across the border with you, ma'am." Logan rolled the fragile petals of the gardenia between his thumb and forefinger and watched the fragments float to the ground. He sniffed the perfume left on his fingertips and smiled. He popped the notebook closed, examined the faded Mayan etchings on the front and back covers and considered his options.

Catarina waited, willing herself not to think of the loose pictures of love and hope lying inside the front cover. Discovery of those would make the dictionary seem personal and important. She would loose it.

Logan decided the notebook was worthless and handed it to her. Catarina snatched the book and the bag to her breast and ran to the bus. As rude as it was, she pushed her way into the door in front of a man with two small children.

Logan finally paid her for the kiss with news of Sixto. "I'll miss you, Catarina! You keep in touch. You might want to come back for Sixto's execution. Start saving up to have his body shipped home!" Logan placed his hat on his head. He spoke to the guard still standing next to him. "Yeah, she is a hard one to let go, beauty to stir my cock, brains to challenge my mind and pride to squash. Yes siree, the perfect woman."

* * * * *

When Logan pulled into the parking lot of the Border Patrol Station, he saw Captain Kennedy, Case Becker and María Sanchez's boy, Alberto, coming out the door. Case had his hand resting on Alberto's shoulders; the captain was shaking Alberto's hand. *That's worrisome.* Logan figured the lost drugs were already sniffed up some junkie's nose. *Surely the little bastard didn't find them and turn them in.*

Logan saw Captain Kennedy spot him and point. The Captain's voice carried over the distance between them. "Logan, come to my office. Need to talk to you."

Logan watched Case and Alberto descend the steps and eye him cautiously. *Well shit! Time to dance.*

Chapter 27

Hermina

It was hard for Catarina to remain quiet when she wanted to scream. A scream would feel so good, let out all the dead hopes, dissipate some of the rage. If she could just expel the air that was rank with the anger she bottled up inside her lungs, if she could make room for oxygen, then she could think about what she was going to do when she was dumped in Vera Cruz.

The motor of the bus droned on. An old man in the seat behind Catarina snored like someone was strangling him with a wire. Each crescendo was followed by a pause of silence just long enough to ignite a spark of hope that the snore would be his last. The next wave of snoring always came. *How can anyone sleep with that going on?*

Yet, Catarina seemed to be the only one awake. Even the old man's wife slumbered comfortably beside him. She wore a skirt sewn of the same calico cotton that his shirt was made of; and she held his rough, work-scarred hand in hers.

Catarina tried to relax, but her racing mind would not slow down. Her feelings whirled in alternating circles of anger, fear and blame.

The sleeping girl next to Catarina sighed, twisted in her seat and nestled her head on Catarina's shoulder. Catarina didn't want to be touched and she started to wake the girl when she looked at her face for the first time. She felt a tug in her heart, for it was as though Catarina was looking at a snapshot of herself from happier days.

The sweetest smile curved the girl's full lips. How old could she be, sixteen? For Catarina, that age was a long time ago, before she lost her belief in love, before Case, before Logan. The girl snuggled and smiled broader in her sleep. Catarina observed the long lashes and unlined skin. *What is she smiling about?*

The snoring man changed positions in his seat. Quiet descended. She rested her head on the head of the girl beside her; a flow of peace from the young girl seeped into Catarina, and finally, she slept.

* * * * *

An urgent moan woke Catarina. The sound had come from her own throat. She felt flush, warm, a little disoriented. Her fingers touched her lips and the tingle that shot through her told her she was having an erotic dream. She was thankful she couldn't remember it. It was dark outside and the motion of the bus had changed to twisting and turning, as though they were traveling through mountains. Catarina wondered how long she slept.

The young girl beside her was also awake. "Buenas noches. Como está?" she asked.

"I don't know yet." Catarina pushed her hair out of her eyes.

"I didn't wake you at the last rest stop. You were sleeping like the dead. How long has it been since you slept?"

"I don't know, a long time. I feel awful, like a hangover, but without the tequila." Catarina tried to stretch. "Oh! I have a cramp!" She massaged her calf.

"The driver said we would stop every four hours, so it shouldn't be long before you can get out."

"What time is it?" Catarina massaged her leg and the pain began to ease.

"I guess about ten o'clock. My name is Hermina. What's yours?"

"I'm Catarina, Catarina de la Alvarado."

"You cried a little in your sleep. That man, the one who kissed you on the sidewalk, did he make you cry?"

Catarina snapped her head up. The squeeze in her stomach replicated her body's reaction to the original repulsion to Logan's mouth.

"I cried?" She touched her cheek to check for evidence.

"Sí."

"You are very bold to remind me of that. Muchas gracias." Her sarcasm was clear. Maybe she wasn't going to like this girl after all. That serene smile was still there resting peacefully on her face! It was pretty before; now it was irritating. Hermina expected an answer. Her eyes did not waver until Catarina relented.

"No, it wasn't him. I stopped crying for that man long ago. He still tries to hurt me, but now, he is hurting my brother.....and another." Catarina's voice dropped.

"Ah, your brother. And this other, is he your true love?" Hermina had the expectant look of a hopeless romantic.

Catarina hesitated as doubts flashed through her head. How would she answer this question? In this moment, with this stranger, what would she say? How many miles away from him did she need to be before it was safe to look at her feelings? She swallowed the lump in her throat. Her words were halting. "El Gri.....his name is Case Becker." The sound of his name made Catarina's eyes sting.

"You love him." Hermina pronounced, wise and all knowing.

"I don't want to.....and I'm not going to." Catarina looked sideways and noticed the girl did not seem convinced. "Can we change the subject and why do you smile like that? Are you happy to be going back to Mexico? Is that home?"

"I smile because of what I am taking with me." Hermina gazed down and caressed a small bulge in her belly. "Un bambino."

"You're pregnant!"

Hermina giggled. "Sí! It's wonderful!"

It took one second for irritation with Hermina's meddling to change into concern for the little mother to be. Catarina was wary. "Does the father know?"

"Oh, sí, I left him a message."

A message? Catarina's fears were confirmed. The baby's father wouldn't even talk to Hermina.

"He was hiding when I got taken for being illegal."

"Does he know where you are going?"

"I don't think so; but, Enrique, he will find me. We are in love."

Hermina's words, "We are in love," rang hollow in Catarina's ears. What a sad awakening was in store for her new friend. Maybe this was why they ended up on this bus together. Catarina could be there for Hermina when heartbreak came and Enrique did not. They could comfort each other and damn the basic nature of men. God knows, Catarina had no one else to turn to. She looked out the darkened window. All she could see in the glass was her own reflection. She looked awful.

The trip through the night was boring, but being with Hermina made it tolerable for she was a delightful companion. Catarina shared her food. They played hearts with Hermina's deck of cards. Hermina had a little picture of Enrique inside a locket that hung around her neck. Catarina saw the soft, dark eyes of a man who looked gentle and quiet. Hermina explained that the other side of the locket was for a picture of their baby who she already loved more than life itself.

Hermina told stories of slipping back and forth across the Rio Grande with her parents since she was five, old enough to pick cotton. She never went to school. She could read a little Spanish, no English. Her family never tried to integrate themselves into America, and life revolved around family, simple joys, and surviving poverty.

The young girl was so open with her feelings, so joyful in spite of her uncertain future that Catarina found herself sharing too. Their stories were very different. Catarina didn't remember how she came to the states. Abuelita told her that after her father died, her mother took her and Sixto back to Mexico until a friend of the family left the house on Camino Ratama to Abuelita.

The three of them came to live with Abuelita. Catarina existed happily and invisibly throughout childhood until Logan Dell noticed her, seduced her and made her life hell simply because she was beautiful and she wanted to get away from him.

"Can you tell me about Case Becker now?" Hermina's voice was gentle, testing.

The air went out of Catarina's body, leaving her deflated. Case's face appeared in her mind, and she shrugged her shoulders. "It makes me a little sad that I don't have a picture of him to show you. I thought I wanted to forget him completely. After talking to you, maybe it would be nice to remember some things."

"Tell me the moment you first knew you wanted him." Hermina was eager to hear the story. "You know what I mean, that instant when your soul connected." Hermina nodded her head in encouragement.

"I don't know for sure. I guess the moment I got scared was when he first kissed me. It was in a storm. There was thunder and lightening and wind....."

Hermina sighed. "Kissing in the rain." She closed her eyes in ecstasy. "When else did you know?"

Catarina realized that this was high entertainment for Hermina. She dropped her voice to an intimate whisper. "I knew I couldn't resist him one night when we went to the beach to watch the stars. A

255

Susan LeMiles

drunk man threw up on him; that's another story. But
he had to take off his clothes and clean them in the
ocean. The waves washed over him in the moonlight.
Every time a wave receded, I could see his knees and
everything above. He was.....he had.....majesty."

"Stop, stop! I can't stand it!" Hermina hugged
herself, clutching at the sleeves of her blouse.

The woman behind Catarina popped up to hang
her head over the seat and breathlessly and said, "I can
stand it! What happened next? Was he, you know,
ready for you?" Catarina felt a hot flush rise. She
arched her neck backwards to discover the woman's
face dangling upside down, much too close to her head.
She looked back at Hermina and said, "I'm afraid that
between the kiss on the sidewalk and this, I'm going to
arrive in Vera Cruz with a disgraceful reputation."

"So you were together that night, under the
stars; and what happened?" The woman was begging
for more.

Catarina arched to look at her again. "I'm done,
end of story. And that's what it was, just a story."

"Please." The woman reached for Catarina's
hand.

"I'm going to the bathroom." Avoiding the
woman's grasp, Catarina climbed over Hermina from
the window seat and headed for the bathroom. She hid
there until another passenger banged on the bathroom
door in desperation.

During the wee hours of the night, the bus
wound its way through the Sierra Madres. Each twist
in the mountain road took Catarina further and further
from Case. Closer and closer to nothing.

Catarina was reluctant to go to sleep again. Every time she closed her eyes, visions of Case and their starry nights invaded her subconscious. The neat wall of separation between her head and her heart broke down. This sweet agony was Hermina's fault. That brat of a romantic forced her to think about all the sensations, aches and tastes of being with Case. She lured Catarina into stirring up memories of moments when he was generous. He was generous with his laughter, his knowledge, his body and, yes, his money.

A thunderous idea exploded in Catarina's mind. Case gave all those things away and never expected anything in return. He never once asked or even implied a debt of any kind. What made him do such a foolish thing, carrying that generosity into such a destructive act?

She thought of the initial sparks on the morning they met. When did they both become fools? When did that attraction grow into the desire that neither of them could abandon even though nothing could come of it? There must have been a point of no return. Catarina closed her eyes and drifted into a dreamy semi consciousness that floated her until morning.

Catarina woke when her body fell forward as the bus came to a full stop. The interlude between her old life and her new one was over. Catarina renewed the vow to forget Case Becker; for whatever life held for her next would not be served well by obsessive thoughts of El Gringo.

The shwish sound of the bus door opening prompted everyone to stand. Stiff with inactivity, they collected their belongings and shuffled down the aisle and out the door into the unknown that waited just outside in the Mexican sunshine.

Catarina complained as she followed Hermina down the bus steps. "Why do they bring us all the way down here?"

"Because it takes us a lot longer to get back to the U.S. They know most of us will go back. It's too easy if they just send us across the border to Matamoros."

Catarina blinked against the light. Her eyes adjusted to the scene of milling strangers in a strange place. She knew she was going to be alone; she just underestimated how empty she would feel. Hermina searched the passing faces with an air of expectation. The bond between the two women forged the night before by sharing secrets led Catarina to make a decision. "Do you have a place to stay?"

"No, do you?" They walked a few steps to get out of the way of other passengers exiting the bus.

"No, but I do have a little money, maybe enough for one room. We would have one night to figure out what to do next."

Hermina threw her arms around Catarina. "Gracias, mi angel!"

"Hermina! Hermina. Hermina!" The girls turned from each other to the direction of an urgent voice. Catarina watched as Enrique swooped Hermina into his arms. He kissed her hair. He kissed her cheeks. He kissed her lips. Words of love, apology and commitment tumbled in Spanish for all to hear. The little gathering of remaining passengers clapped in approval. Hermina danced a little circle and stuck out her tummy, proudly displaying her bump.

Enrique held up his hand signaling the people to quiet. He fell to his knee in front of Hermina and simply said, "Marry me."

"See, Catarina, I told you he would find me! Enrique, how did you get here before me?"

"You were on a slow bus. I was in a fast car!" Enrique beamed up at her. "Marry me, Hermina, right now."

"Yes!" Hermina dropped to her knees giving Enrique an embrace that knocked him over. The people, all in need of an uplifting moment, cheered and congratulated them.

Catarina had a catch in her throat. She scanned the crowd for Case, knowing he would not be there. Hermina had her Enrique and he was everything she believed him to be. Catarina was glad to be wrong. There before her was evidence of love. Could it be that love was real, just impossible for her? Whatever the truth, tonight Catarina would be alone. She heard a gentle question.

"Señorita de la Alvarado?"

"Sí?" She turned her head to see a man dressed in a Mexican business shirt, un guayabera. He bowed slightly at the waist.

"Allow me to present myself. I am Jaime Reyna.

"Señor Reyna?"

"I am here on a mission from Señor Alfonso Carreras, a favor at the request of your grandmother."

Was this hope? Were there strings attached? Catarina telegraphed her anxiety.

"Here I have a letter, a record of a phone conversation, and some money." The man offered an

259

envelope. "Read it and you will see." He bowed again as she took the letter.

> Catarina,
> I am sure you remember meeting Señor Carreras at our home in May. I have told him of our bad luck and he has agreed to help. He owns a resort on the island of Zacape, close to Tulum. Your English is good. You know history. There is work for you with the tourists there. You will have a place to stay and a job as long as you want. His manager, Señor Reyna will take you there. Please let me know that you arrived safely. I found the bag in the wall of the closet. I returned the money as you requested in your note. Case asked for my forgiveness and I gave it to him. Remember, no good man will wait forever. Do what you must. I miss you every day.
> > Love,
> > Tu Abuelita

Catarina crushed the letter to her chest and looked at Señor Reyna. She expected tears to come; but there were none. "Thank you," she said.

Hermina called. "Catarina! Enrique has a priest; we're getting married right now, just like he said. Please, come. I need someone to be my maid of honor." Hermina wrapped her arms around Catarina as though they had known each other for years.

Catarina glanced at Señor Reyna. "Do we have time?"

"Of course."

"Señor Reyna, where I am going, will I need any of this money?"

"Not really, just for whatever personal items you want."

"Good. I need to buy a wedding dress for a girl who believes in love."

* * * * *

The wedding was held in a little chapel on the grounds of the Our Lady of Assumption Cathedral. The guests included twelve recent deportees from the U.S. The bride had a wedding gown befitting the romantic that she was; and Señor Reyna made arrangements for a wedding supper at the inn of a friend.

"A toast!" Señor Reyna stood and raised his glass. "To true love; may we all find the person who will make us believe." He reached into his pocket and brought out a hotel room key. There were aaahs around the table. He hoisted his glass and drained it before he dangled the key in front of Enrique. "You begin your new life tonight, compliments of our host, the gracious provider of this wedding supper, mi amigo, Manuel Gomez." Manuel stuck his head around the corner from the kitchen and waved to the group while the wedding party applauded.

"And for us, Señorita de la Alvarado, it is time to leave. I must be back at the resort tomorrow to greet a large tour group. Lo siento, it's business."

"Forgive me; I didn't know," Catarina said.

"I didn't tell you. Call me Jaime, por favor."

"Thank you, Jaime, for letting me stay and for giving Hermina and Enrique such a gift. They deserved a wedding night they will never forget." Catarina quickly said her goodbyes and followed Señor Reyna. When she reached the door, she turned for a last look at love.

Hermina and Enrique had everything she and Case did not - mutual respect, a common purpose and above all, trust. Even if Catarina wanted to, there was no way to repair all the damage done to her relationship with Case. It was over.

As her eyes met the bride's for the last time, Hermina touched her fingertips to those sweet smiling lips and blew Catarina a kiss.

Chapter 28

Life Without Catarina

Case slapped his alarm clock; but the damned thing kept ringing. The phone. It was the phone. He fumbled for the receiver, knocked it off the bedside table and recovered it from the floor.

"Hello."

"Becker! You good for nothing bum! Sleeping in the middle of the day."

"I love you too, Skipper. What do you want?"

"Where've you been? I've been counting my boats every night; I haven't lost one since the last time I saw you."

Case stretched inside the sheets of his bed. "I've been trying to engineer a little twist in a business deal. It's not going so good; so I'm looking for a backup plan."

"Have you heard from that little girl you like?"

Why couldn't people drop this? No one would leave him alone! Abuelita, María, even Jan asked him about Catarina regularly. Case's mother even surprised him. When she found a melted piñata, a bull with one

263

leg missing, lying in the corner of his living room, she asked him, "Have you heard from that lovely girl that got deported to Mexico?" How did she know about a relationship he'd never mentioned?

Alberto was the worst nag of all. "When is Catarina coming back? Why aren't you getting married? Will you take me to see her?" Case's patience was wearing thin.

"No. I haven't heard from her. What do you want, Skipper?"

"Remember the Higgs? The couple wanting muscle to sail with them for a year?"

"I thought they left six weeks ago."

"They did. The guy I set 'em up with bailed out in Antigua."

"Why is that?"

"A girl. Higgs said he thinks that was the guy's intent all along. He was just looking for a ride to Antigua. They don't want to just pick up someone they don't know down there. They asked about you. Want the job?"

Case sat up in bed. This was exactly what he needed, escape. If he couldn't solve his problems or let them go, he could leave them behind. He could replace the fog in his head with salt spray and fresh air from another continent.

"Yeah, I'll go."

"Good. They want to fly you down as soon as possible. When can you leave?"

"I never got a passport."

"Dammit, Becker!"

"I didn't think I'd need it." Case threw off his covers and put his feet on the floor. "Don't worry; I'll

264

drive to Houston tonight. If I walk the application through, I can have it in a couple of days. Skipper, you know how charming I can be. Can they wait?"

"Yeah, yeah, charming. They'll wait."

"Hang up, Skipper. I'll call you as soon as I get back. And Skip, thanks."

Case threw a change of underwear and shirts into a plastic garbage sack. He started to make a mental list of things he needed to do before he left for Antigua. *I'll buy a real suitcase. I'll take my scuba gear. I'll call my mother when I get back from Houston.*

First, Case stopped at the Becker Rescue Services fleet yard to pick up the latest package of documents on the sale of the business and trade the wrecker for a smaller vehicle. Parking was difficult enough in Houston without trying to maneuver through traffic in the giant he drove every day. He moved his stuff into the back seat of a company sedan and tried the air conditioner. *Good, one that works.* He checked the gas gauge, full.

As he adjusted the rear view mirror, he thought of one other thing he would like to do. He hadn't been to the migrant school in weeks. He wanted to say goodbye to Delores García and the kids.

* * * * *

The field shack was gone, burned to the ground. Mrs. García leaned against her Chevy, staring at the black spot on the earth while children dug through the ashes with sticks. When Case walked over to join her, she shook her head.

"When did this happen?" Case asked.

"Must have been last night. It was fine when I closed up yesterday."

Case kicked a large hinge that used to be mounted on the door. "We know it wasn't bad wiring since it had no electricity."

"Mrs. García turned to Case. "Who would do something like this on purpose?"

"Oh, I guess someone could have been careless with a cigarette; but more than likely, it was someone with a grudge against me, or Catarina. Probably no way to prove it."

Lola spied El Gringo; she ran to him with arms spread open for Case to pick her up. "My pencil is gone."

"I know, sweetie. I'll get you another pencil; don't worry." Case hugged her tight.

"I miss you."

"I miss you too."

Lola kissed his cheek. "Have you been practicing you're A's?"

Case chuckled. "Yes, I have; and I'm getting better every day."

"Me too!" Lola seemed delighted that the two of them had not lost their connection. Case put her down and she scampered off to play with the other children.

Mrs. García opened her car door to leave. "I can't keep this up by myself, you know."

"I'll resupply the school. Can you find another location?"

"It's not that, Case. I can't keep up the pace. I'm neglecting my family. I can't be here any more. What made you come by today anyway?"

"I wanted to say goodbye. I'm leaving on a long trip, maybe a year."

"Really? Why so long? It won't take that long to go get Catarina."

The necessity to explain more than he wanted to explain irritated him and reinforced his need to get away. He looked at the blackened tree that he and Catarina used to water. He couldn't think of anything that would make him stay in The Valley.

"Delores, don't start on me. I'm going to crew on a private yacht for a year."

"You're going to leave Catarina in Mexico? Shame on you."

"She's fine. Her family says she's fine. I am moving on to the next adventure. I need things to be the way they used to be; women are too complicated."

"You may be moving on; but you're still a changed man, Case Becker. With or without her, a changed man."

"What do you mean?"

"Being loved changes people; it makes them notice things. You think you would have ever noticed someone like Lola before you knew Catarina? You think you would have ever found out why you couldn't read without Catarina?"

"Delores, Catarina may have changed me; but it wasn't because she loved me."

"What makes you think that?"

"She told me, more than once." Case touched the scorched tree and a shower of blistered leaves fell to the ground. "There are things I need to be forgiven for and she won't do it."

"You're wrong. Believe what you will." Mrs. García argued. "Who am I? Humph. I'm just the little old lady who saw you both get struck by lightening the day you met."

Chapter 29

The Passport Office

Case checked into the Holiday Inn in downtown Houston just after midnight. He tossed his garbage sack luggage on the floor of the bathroom and bounced on the edge of the bed to test the mattress. He flipped through the television channels, watched the end of a movie he had already seen and stared at the packet of documents lying on the dresser. *What the hell.*

The envelope was sealed with tape and required the use of Case's pocket knife. The cover letter confirmed this was the final offer; and since the package had been sitting on his desk for two weeks, the offer was only good for three more days. The price wasn't too bad. All the signature lines were marked with little X's.

He shuffled through the pristine pages of the contracts, scanning for general content, like Catarina taught him to do. He found nothing about his new ideas or the possibility of his remaining at the company after the sale. They had turned him down without even

269

talking about it. He tossed the papers on a chair.

That's just fine with me. Case wasn't disappointed. By the end of the day tomorrow, he would have the travel documents he needed to crew on *The Merry Maker*. Cappie and Lila Higgs were newly retired, newly rich and they wanted a seafaring adventure with no itinerary. Island hopping through the Caribbean, discovering new places, meeting new women sounded like an excellent antidote to love sickness.

Men with loose ends were perfect for this kind of job. Case could go back to his meandering ways. There would be no pressure to take over the family business, no need to persuade Catarina to forgive him, no dress up dinners to attend with Sharon. *Screw it. All I have to do is show up at the dock in time to swim out to The Merry Maker before it gets too far from shore.*

The Higgs seemed pretty loose. They indicated he would have his own small stateroom and could entertain an occasional guest if he wanted to. *This is everything a man could want. Isn't it?*

What he really wanted was Catarina's forgiveness. Hell, he didn't blame her for not wanting to ever be with him; but it hurt to know that the one person on earth who made him feel whole, hated him.

He wondered what she was doing tonight. Was she already sleeping? He searched his mind and found the image of Catarina the way she was when he first loved her, an angel carrying a birthday cake surrounded by a halo of sparking light.

She wanted one simple thing, to be a teacher. His rash act took the opportunity away from her and he could never give it back.....or could he?

* * * * *

How many miles must a man walk from building to building, floor to floor and back again to get an emergency passport processed? The final stop was supposed to be this barren room with fluorescent lights where Case waited for two hours.

"Here it is!" The clerk's fluttery lashes indicated she might like to flirt. "One passport in the name of Case Hudson Becker. I wish I was going with you, wherever it is."

Case looked at her name tag and produced a dazzling smile. "Thank you Eileen." He opened the document to check for accuracy. Yes, the picture and address were his. "Eileen, would you mind helping me with something else?"

"I'd love to." Now she was definitely flirting.

Case leaned on the counter between them and assumed a secretive attitude. "Where can I check for a birth certificate for someone born in Harris County?"

Eileen whispered back, "It's on the third floor; want some company?"

"I thought you'd never ask." Case gave her a grin he was sure would seduce the devil herself.

Without taking her eyes off Case, Eileen screeched her announcement to her supervisor in the next room. "Mona! I'm taking my break now!"

Case and Eileen got on the elevator together and when the door closed, they were alone. Case noticed his new companion eyeing the stop car button and supposed she was wondering if he was going to push it and make a pass at her. *Stick with the grin and the eye contact. Got to take this long shot. What if.....*

Eileen leaned seductively against the wall of the elevator. "You know you can't get a copy of someone else's birth certificate, don't you?"

"But you can, can't you?" Case hoped. "It's probably not even there, but if it is, it sure would make some people very happy."

The elevator door opened and they stepped into the hall. Eileen looked at Case thoughtfully before she took his arm and led him to the church pew styled benches lined up against the walls. "You wait here. What's the name?"

All pretense of flirtation fell away with Case's answer. He practically said the name with reverence. "Catarina de la Alvarado, about twenty to twenty-four years old."

"Well, hell, I should have known it was something like that." Eileen's disappointment was still good natured. She shrugged and turned to go into the records room.

"Eileen," Case called her back. "There's another name too. Her brother, Sixto Terrazos, maybe three or four years older than her."

"What do you think I am?" Eileen cocked her head and placed her fist on her hip.

"I hope you are a miracle worker; because, I need a miracle in the worst way." He overheard Eileen loudly justify her presence in the records office.

"Hey! Guys. I need to do a little research. Mind if I help myself?"

The anonymous reply was, "No problem."

Case sat down to wait. People came and went. These benches must be purposefully uncomfortable to make sure no one wanted to linger. Case changed positions several times. He watched the second hand on the wall clock swoop round and round.

He finally made watching the clock a game, closing his eyes, trying to open them at the very instant the needle swooped past the twelve and the minute hand popped to the next marker. He was impatient the first twenty four times. He concentrated on relaxing. Three more times; that was better. He had his timing down pretty good now and the next time he opened his eyes, he expected to win the game. The second hand would be resting on twelve. Instead, Eileen's pink sweater blocked his view.

"Come on," she said quietly. She held a plain manila folder.

"You got it?" Case wasn't yelling, but his big voice echoed loud in the hall.

"Hush," she hissed at him.

And, Case did as he was told. He studied the floor while they waited for the elevator to come. It felt like an eternity before the doors slid lazily open. The car was packed. Eileen greeted someone she knew who forced enough space for the two of them to squeeze in.

Eileen remained calm as she marched out of the building and down the street towards the parking garage. She must have found something or else why the secret service act? Case's heart was pounding; he actually felt like he was in some kind of danger.

"My car is in this lot. Do you want to go somewhere?" Case needed to see what was in that folder soon.

"I just don't want anyone to see me give this to you. I could lose my job." She looked around carefully; and when she was satisfied there was no one to witness her crime of uncertain consequences, she shoved the folder at him.

Case looked at the ceiling; a prayer flitted through his mind. His hand shook as he opened the folder. There were two certified copies of birth certificates. One was for Sixto Terrazos born November 8, 1939. One was for Catarina de la Alvarado, born September 20, 1942. Of every hunch he ever had, of every long shot he ever played, this was the best, the very best payoff he would ever get! A reason for Catarina to forgive him.

"God, Eileen, thank you!" Case couldn't believe what he was seeing. It was too easy. "Are they real?"

"Yep, good as gold. Feel the little raised seal in the paper? Why didn't they come get these themselves?"

"They don't know they exist. They think they are Mexican nationals."

"Come on; that can't be."

"After Catarina was born, her father was killed in a farming accident. Their mother took them back to Mexico. Then, when she married again, she left them with relatives on the border. I guess they just took up the migrant worker life. I don't know for sure." Case ran his finger over Catarina's name like it was her skin he was touching.

"Why did you do it, Eileen, take the risk?"

"Well, first there was that look you gave me

when you asked. Then there was the look you gave me when you said her name. All women are suckers for love, even if it is not their own. I've seen love eyes before. Do you know you are in love with this girl?" Eileen's flirty behavior morphed into sympathetic understanding.

"Yeah, now I do. Unfortunately, I don't think even this birth certificate is going to win me her heart. But, it is going to get a very smart lady into college so she can become a teacher." He threw his arms around the startled clerk and kissed her on the mouth.

Eileen turned as pink as her sweater. "Get out of here before I push you into the stairwell and take your clothes off." She pushed him away laughing as she fanned herself with her hands.

Case took two skips and ran to his car. He wound his way down the ramps of the multilevel parking garage to the street. When he turned into the traffic, he spotted Eileen walking back to her office. He gave a quick toot on the horn and when she looked toward him, he blew her a dramatic kiss goodbye. She caught it in mid air, held it to her heart and rolled her eyes.

Case's mind was racing. This discovery could change everything between him and Catarina.....or nothing. He had to be prepared for that too. How would he get the documents to her? Could he see her face to face? Should he mail it to her? Would she come home and get an American passport? Would she stay in Mexico? Would she forgive him? Would he ever see her again, hold her again, taste her again?

That thought did it! His body broke through the carefully erected emotional walls he built to protect himself from feeling anything about Catarina. He wanted her. He looked down at his lap. It showed. Just how many speeding tickets was he willing to get between Houston and home? The answer was several. *Calm down, Case!*

Chapter 30

Logan Cracks

The largest ranch in the United States lay between Houston and The Valley, ten million acres owned by one family, the Kings. The long road through it stretched before Case, making a hypnotic drive straight to the tip of Texas. There was no traffic and no gas for one hundred miles of deserted wilderness. There were no turns; the road was flat and built for speed. Case intended to take advantage of it.

He looked down at his speedometer as soon as he saw the revolving red lights behind him. A hundred and three miles per hour in a seventy mile per hour zone? He would never be able to talk his way out of this one.

Case slowed to pull over and stopped on the shoulder of the highway. He killed the motor and got out his wallet. He watched in the rear view mirror while the State Trooper readied himself to ticket his catch.

The trooper walked the slow walk of the law when they had you and they knew it. His boots crunched the gravel when he stopped at Case's window.

"Good afternoon, officer. Was I speeding?"

Case had this routine down pat. It was always best to play innocent and cooperative when you were caught without a good excuse.

"Could I see your license and registration, please." It was a statement, not a question. Case handed the man what he wanted and waitied for him to examine it. "You are Case Becker?"

"Yes sir, I am."

"There is an all points bulletin out on you. I've got instructions to detain you."

"For what? Speeding is not a felony!"

"No, not the speeding. It's for your protection. There has been an incident concerning a man named Logan Dell. He's made some specific threats against you."

"What threats? Don't I look like I can take care of myself?" Case might be afraid of being unforgiven by Catarina, but he was not afraid of Logan Dell. "What's happened?"

The trooper leaned on Case's car and looked down into the window. "Well, Internal Affairs got enough evidence on him to charge him with some shenanigans involving drugs. When they tried to arrest him at Cantina Los Indios, he went psycho."

A hand of fear grabbed Case's throat; he didn't really know where Catarina was. "Has he hurt anybody yet?"

"Just the three officers that tried to arrest him. Pistol-whipped 'em good. One's got a broken leg, too. He's the one that told us who Logan was going after next."

"Who's that?"

"You."

Driving the speed limit behind a State Trooper's car was not Case's idea of appropriate action. He was edgy, antsy. His intuition told him that Logan's deranged craze wouldn't wait for Case Becker to show up to be the next victim. Someone was going to get hurt and the closest, most vulnerable people were Abuelita and María Sanchez. Case stuck his arm out the car window and made a winding motion telling the trooper to speed up. The man stubbornly shook his head no.

Case's fears gnawed on him for 20 more dull miles. He looked at the police scanner that all Becker Rescue Services vehicles had. He turned it on and searched for the frequency used by the local police. He wasn't close enough to pick up anything yet, but it wouldn't be too long. Meanwhile he listened to the scanner buzz and crackle and fidgeted to the rhythm of the irritating sounds.

When the scanner did pick up a transmission, Case heard an address he recognized. He listened briefly to the codes used by the dispatcher; he understood them all. The grip of fear in his throat was gone now. Case knew what to do with the adrenaline that electrified his body.

His vehicle's instantaneous acceleration caught his State Trooper escort by surprise. Case did not even acknowledge the man as he swerved around the vehicle and swooped by. He read the trooper's lips, "Damnit Becker!"

The revolving red lights following him were irrelevant. Case knew he needed to get to the pink house on Camino Ratama before Logan did.

* * * * *

Case heard the women's screams before he came to a complete stop. He bolted through Abuelita's decimated garden. There wasn't a flower or a bush that wasn't uprooted or beat into the ground. The front door was bashed and broken; but it still held. Case could hear Logan beating on the back door. Abuelita and María frantically begged Logan to stop and implored God to help.

Case banged on the front door. There was blood on the handle and the frame. "Abuelita, María, it's me, Case, let me in!"

"Dios! Dios!" A tear streaked Abuelita opened the broken front door. "Mis flores. Mira mis flores hermosas!"

Crack. Sounds of splintering wood announced an imminent breach of the kitchen door. Case pushed the women out the front door. Pancho Villa, snarling and vicious, snapped as Case picked him up and dropped the little varmint into a brown paper grocery bag sitting on the counter. Case exited the front door just as Logan crashed through the back.

Case collided with his State Trooper escort coming up the walk. "You've got a gun; take care of that." Case nodded his head and pointed with his chin to the rabid man lunging through the front door.

Logan spotted the trooper and abandoned his mad mission. He turned back into the house, smashing everything in his path. By the time he made it to his car parked behind María's house, the State Trooper had called for backup and was in fast pursuit.

Case held the two shaken women. He kissed the top of Abuelita's head and listened to María tell him how scared she was. Abuelita, forlorn and frightened, walked over to her chain-link fence and wove her fingers into the rough wire. "It takes a bad man to murder flowers."

"Abuelita, Logan Dell murdered his wife this morning." Case shot his eyes to María.

"We were next!"

"Yes, and if they don't catch him, Catarina is in danger too. Where is she?" Case didn't want two hysterical women on his hands, but he wanted them to be frightened enough to leave town.

María answered, "She is with our friend, Alfonso Carreras. She works at his resort in Quintana Roo, El Palacio de las Antiguas" in México.

Case laid out his plan. "We are going to go see Captain Kennedy; he'll be the first to know if they catch Logan. If they don't catch him, I am putting you two on an airplane to San Diego. You can catch up with Sixto and Alberto there."

"Abuelita wiped her tired eyes and said, "We have no money to go to San Diego."

"We'll get it from a victim's assistance program I know about. It will be fine." That wasn't exactly a lie. In that flash, the Becker Foundation for Victims of Crime was born. "Come on, get your purses and identification."

"Where's Pancho?" Abuelita looked for her little dog.

"Right here." Case raised the sack. The paper crackled as Pancho heard his name and raised his head over the edge of the paper bag. With blinky, bulgy eyes, he looked up at Case and clearly expressed his gratitude. Then he showed his teeth.

* * * * *

Captain Kennedy laid the phone back in its cradle. He looked at Case first, then the police detective in the room. "He slipped across the border. They lost him."

The word "Shit!" was only the first curse from Case's mouth.

"I'll get in touch with the Mexican authorities," said Detective Benson. "This will take forever. He can disappear down there fast." Benson was a neat freak, glossy shoes, perfect Windsor knot in his tie, probably got a new haircut every two weeks. This was the kind of man who never broke a rule in his life. International protocol was going to be safe with him.

Captain Kennedy looked like he was going to be sick. "I just wish I had reined him in a long time ago. God knows how many times I covered for him. I should have seen it coming. I just thought he was a capable officer with some quirks, some personal problems."

He took a moment to swallow his remorse. "We arrived first at the murder scene. When Internal Affairs botched the arrest, we sent a unit to Dell's house and to the florist shop to see if he would show up either place. I just don't know how he got to her so fast. It was fresh. I've never seen anything this brutal. He beat her to death, then stabbed her twenty-seven times. It didn't even look like she defended herself." He rubbed his mouth to cover his emotion. He rubbed his eyes and wiped the sweat from his brow.

"We found this at his house. Looks like some kind of list of people who have 'done him wrong.' He's been keeping it for weeks; see the dates?" He extended the paper to Case. "Couple of the names you won't recognize, but most you will. See, there's your's, right there, and there.

There were entries in a notebook for every day since Case and Alberto turned in the packages of cocaine. The names were scattered in a random and meaningless pattern through the dates: Alberto Sanchez, Case Becker, Sixto Terrazos, Catarina de la Alvarado, María Sanchez, Rita Terrazos, Jan Dell. In the last two weeks, Jan's and Catarina's names appeared with increasing frequency. Jan was dead and the last three entries read "Catarina de la Alvarado."

A wildfire of burning fear and rage swept through Case. His mental picture of Jan, dead and mutilated, morphed into Catarina lying in a pool of blood. Case's throat constricted; and he punched the wall.

Usually, in a crisis, he was in total control. He could act on his own, do what was necessary to save a life. Case knew exactly how fragile life was; and he always dealt with death when he had to. But Catarina's death would be the same as dying himself; and there were no do-overs.

"I want this guy bad," Captain Kennedy sighed.

Case laid the notebook down on the desk. "Then go get him." Case heard his own voice, but really could not feel himself speak. The captain's helpless answer inflamed Case even more.

"We have to go through channels. I can't break a dozen international treaties and agreements by charging into Mexico chasing him."

".....I can," said Case.

The two law officers stared at Case, then checked each other's eyes. In silent agreement each turned to attend to his own duties. Maybe Kennedy and Benson wouldn't break the rules themselves; but this time, they would let someone else do it.

Case walked to the hallway where María, Abuelita and Pancho waited for him. He picked up Pancho and asked, "Pancho, have you ever been on an airplane ride?"

"Oh, mi Dios, they didn't get him!" María held Abuelita tight.

"No. He got away, slipped across the border. I need you to go to San Diego like we planned. I can't be worried about you. Logan has escaped to Mexico, and I think he will go after Catarina. I've got to stop him."

Abuelita reached to touch his cheek. "We'll go to San Diego. You take care of Catarina."

"Hey, Becker!" Kennedy stuck his head out his office door. "Remember, we can't help you.....and we don't know you."

Chapter 31

Resort Life

Catarina learned to count her blessings from her Abuelita. Whenever there was not quite enough money or a sadness invaded their lives, they would turn to this ritual and share, noting the good things in life until they felt better; and they always did.

This morning, Catarina needed help. She was flirting with Montezuma's Revenge for the fifth day. She wasn't recovering from the emotional and physical stresses of the last few weeks. She loved her new job taking tour groups through the ruins at Tulum. The stories stored in her mind poured out of her heart with increasing embellishments that enchanted listeners, hungry for history to come alive. If it were not for the routine of that daily obligation, she would spend all her time in bed.

Blessing number one, the practice of siesta was sacred in Mexico. Time did not flow the same here. Sitting by the pool watching iguanas lunching on hibiscus flowers and sunbathing next to the tourists was a perfectly acceptable activity, even during business hours. Time was no longer her enemy.

Blessing number two, she didn't have to worry about money. Her two room suite on the resort grounds of El Palacio de la Antiguas was the nicest place she had ever lived. This was the only resort on the small island nestled next to the Yucatan Peninsula, and Alfonso Carreras owned it all - the island, the resort, the town, the bank, the golf course and the docks where cruise ships off-loaded tourists to shop and scuba dive several times a week. For Catarina, the resort was a protected world of uncommon safety and seclusion. She was not required to be so strong here.

Blessing number three? The attention from her host interrupted her obsession with Case Becker. Case's intimate presence in her mind was made sharper by his absence from her life. Her thoughts were an endless, whirling confusion of physical desire and emotional pain. Case had not called or written, but neither had she. It seemed they both would manage to go on with separate lives.

Alfonso was busy during the day, doing whatever upper-class Mexican business men do. He disappeared regularly to Mexico City, held secretive meetings with seemingly important men. Most were Mexican, but many were from other countries and brought their families and entourages with them. Catarina entertained the wives and children. Everyone was required to enjoy their stay at El Palacio de las Antiguas.

Many nights, late, when the heat of the day subsided, Alfonso invited Catarina to dine with him on a private patio next to his personal quarters within the resort.

From there they could hear the marimba band entertaining the guests, but they did not have to watch or suffer the company of the revelers. The resort's first class food and service were stepped up another notch for its owner.

Conversation with Alfonso was intriguing. He studied history, was involved in funding excavations of ancient Mayan sites and was expecting a government appointment to the country's Board of Tourism. Catarina's horizons were expanding.

Alfonso did not just talk about the past. His favorite topic was the future of Mexico; and he was making it more and more clear that he wanted Catarina in his personal future as well.

Catarina preferred talking about the future of the Mexican university system. Education was her dream, her purpose on this earth. Exploring that world with Alfonso was easy, fun. He had so much power and so many ideas.

When talk turned to a personal future, she felt herself shrinking in size, trying to make herself invisible. In these moments, Alfonso was always kind. She bade him good night whenever she chose and retired to her suite alone.

Letters from Abuelita were regular. She fed Catarina's need for family news with facts and details twice a week. From Abuelita, Catarina learned the part Alberto and Los Lobos played in Sixto's release. Every time she saw a frog hop across the resort gardens, she laughed and thanked God.

The news about Logan concerned her. He was suspended from his job pending the results of an investigation of missing evidence. In the last letter,

Abuelita sent a tiny newspaper clipping regarding a brawl at La Cantina Los Indios. Drugs were involved and Logan's name was prominently mentioned. Logan was asking the family where to find Catarina and he was seen going through the mail at both Abuelita's and María's houses, presumably looking for a letter from Catarina with a return address.

When Sixto was released and deported, he decided to re-enter the U.S. by way of California this time. He thought it best to be far away from Logan. María worried for Alberto's safety and sent him to live with Sixto in San Diego. Catarina knew that would please both Sixto and Alberto. She smiled and wondered whether or not the two would ever discover their true relationship.

Alberto's letter was the one she read over and over again. Through the eyes of a child, Catarina received news of Case.

Dear Catarina,

I will go to California to live with my friend Sixto. My friend El Gringo says I need to go away for a while. He got me a ticket to go there. He says he will miss me. He says he is going on a boat around the ocean. I think it is because he is not with you. He is not happy any more. How far is California from where you are. Mama says it is very far from her. I will not be with her on my birthday or Christmas.

Your friend,
Alberto

Loneliness has a weight like no other condition. Catarina felt heavy. Case was moving on; her close, loving family was scattering. She folded Alberto's piece of school notebook paper and pressed it into a wooden letter box.

The nausea assailed her again. She went to the bathroom to throw up. She didn't. This sickness was beginning to concern her. Montezuma's revenge didn't last this long. She mentally counted the days of her woman's calendar. The results made her gasp. María said the diaphragm wasn't one hundred percent effective. Case's appetites tested it to the limit and the device had failed.

Catarina stared at the suffering face she saw reflected in the mirror, then spoke to it aloud. "Perhaps you should start listening when Alfonso talks to you about the future."

* * * * *

That afternoon after work, Catarina stopped at the nicest dress shop on the island. There were two outfits she liked; she bought both of them. It felt odd to simply walk into a shop and choose anything she wanted, beautiful dresses never worn before by someone else.

Her favorite of the two was a coral color. It softened the new gray-green tint of early pregnancy in her complexion. The jersey fabric clung to every curve. Before dinner, she spent extra time wrestling her hair to sit on top of her head, allowing curls to fall in random places. Her arms were bare; she had no jewelry. This look was a distinct departure from the tour guide's attire she usually wore every night for supper with Alfonso. She wondered if Alfonso would get the message.

She passed the mirror as she left her suite. The glimpse she caught of herself confirmed that she planned well. The dress caressed her body with every step she took towards the patio where Alfonso waited.

The only thing she hadn't planned was for Alfonso's reaction to remind her of Case's reaction the day he saw her in María's black swimsuit. The difference for Catarina was the way she felt about it. The day of the swimming lesson, she felt humbled, embarrassed, scared. Tonight she felt powerful and sad.

"Buenas noches, Alfonso."

"Catarina, you delight me!" Alfonso rushed to pull her chair out for her. By the time he seated himself, he was slightly breathless.

Dinner was more lively than usual tonight. There was extra energy in the conversation, more laughter. Alfonso sent a request to the band; and when the strains of a waltz floated over the stucco wall, he asked Catarina to dance with him. It was the first time he ever held her. Catarina felt strange, but not bad.

"Could you get used to this.....my touch?" Alfonso bent low to be closer to her ear. Catarina could not speak, but found a way to answer by caressing the back of his neck as they slowly moved to the music. Alfonso closed his eyes and allowed himself a subtle smile.

They had an extra glass of wine; and when conversation trickled away, Alfonso covered her hand with his. "Would you mind going inside with me? It will be proper. Samuel will go with us." Alfonso indicated the silent waiter who served them every evening. "I want to show you some things that belong to my family."

"I would love to see them." Catarina let herself be led into Alfonso's home. Its simple elegance reflected the man himself. Catarina recognized authentic artifacts of Aztec and Mayan life. He paused in a hallway to name the people in six dark portraits that traced his lineage from the time of Maxmillian and Carlota.

Their destination was deep in the center of the residence. Alfonso unlocked a narrow door at the end of the hallway. Behind it were steps descending into darkness. Alfonso flipped a switch but no lights came on. "Forgive me, I have trouble with the electricity down here. The original wiring was not done well," Alfonso apologized. "Sometimes it connects and sometimes it doesn't. We're still working on this, aren't we Samuel?"

"Si, Señor." Samuel lit two oil lamps. He handed one to Alfonso who led the way. Samuel carried the second and walked behind Catarina as they followed the winding stairs that sank into cooler and cooler earth. Soon their steps started to echo. Was it the increasing chill that made goose bumps on Catarina's bare arms or was it the eerie feeling there might be other women chained down here?

She tapped Alfonso on the shoulder. "You're not engaged in white slavery, are you?" She was only half joking.

Alfonso didn't notice her concern. He laughed.

"Spooky, isn't it. Look, we're here." Before them was what looked like a walk-in vault, the kind you might see in a modern bank. Alfonso sheltered the view of the lock with his body as he dialed the combination. A click sounded, and Alfonso stepped back swinging the mammoth steel door with him.

"Samuel, wait here. Come, Catarina. Let me show you the family jewels." Alfonso flipped the switch inside the black void. This time the lights came on.

Catarina blinked at the brightness. Someone must have looted a Spanish galleon! She walked over to touch the gold ingots stacked on shelves. Mayan and Aztec artifacts, so perfect and valuable that they could not be displayed to the public, lived in glass cases lining the wall. There were crumbling parchment documents, original letters signed by Santa Anna and a set of jeweled dueling pistols labeled "Maxmillian."

"Alfonso, are you telling me you are descended from pirates?"

"It's dazzling, isn't it?" Alfonso carefully watched her take in the sight. "No, my ancestors were not pirates, although some of the jewelry does date back to the time of Queen Isabella. He walked to a counter height glass display case. "This necklace once belonged to Empress Carlotta. Sadly, she didn't get to take it back to Austria with her. It was, sort of a gift to my fifth great grandfather for his part in the revolution."

"I assume it was given to him by the winners, not Carlotta herself." Catarina wondered what miseries the peasants of Mexico would have been spared if the necklace had been dismembered and the diamonds, rubies and gold turned into schools and hospitals. The irony of such wealth residing beside such poverty as she personally experienced wouldn't leave her mind.

"Much of this is of historical significance only, not gold, but treasures all the same." Alfonso showed her Aztec armor, a carved calendar and a sacrifice stone. Catarina was drawn to the Mayan relics and found a codex that included the goddess Ix Chel.

"Catarina, it is important to me that you neither be too impressed by this or.....or repulsed by this."

Catarina flashed her eyes from the treasures to Alfonso. "You are proud of your heritage and your possessions. Why should you care what I think?" Her neck was stiff; her stomach felt funny; the lights were too bright and made her squint. She felt something building up in the room and wasn't sure she wanted to know what it was.

"I care because I have a very important question I want to ask you." Alfonso picked out a small chest of fine black leather. He opened it and gazed at the contents. He turned the interior of the chest towards Catarina revealing twelve diamond rings. Fractured rainbows jumped, jittered and blinked, scattering bits of light throughout the vault.

The center stone of the smallest was three carats. The largest was too big for Catarina to even guess. A marquis cut on a simple band rested next to a pear-shaped heirloom she recognized from one of the family portraits. Alfonso reached into the velvet lined box and plucked a ring with a rectangular center stone and two dozen other diamonds surrounding it.

"This is a rare radiant cut. To cut so many facets requires a flawless, deep stone." He held it up to the light to show her the depth of the cut. "My great grandmother wore this one from the day she married until the day she died." He extended it to show Catarina the inscription, "'José and Juana 3-14-1896.' My important question is.....which one of these rings would you like to wear?"

Chapter 32

One Hero Required

There was no sign marking the airstrip as the home of Charlie Rose Aviation. Case drove directly onto the tarmac and parked close to the newest of the three airplanes resting in the sun. He strolled up to the crop duster and did a pilot's check as if he performed it every day.

Truth was, his friend Charlie taught him to fly the little plane in secret just to help out when one of the regular pilots stood too close to a cotton field. The guy got sprayed with full strength pesticide and was in the hospital a week. Charlie had a contract with a deadline to fulfill and Case was always available for an adventure.

Case dusted and sprayed the fields that were far away from electrical wires and residential subdivisions. The risk of discovery was as big a thrill as the inherent danger in the job.

The dirt air strip was deserted. Charlie's motorcycle was parked behind the three sided corrugated tin hanger. Case could see Charlie asleep, draped over a camp cot in the back of the hanger. A greasy green "gimme cap" rested on his face. Charlie didn't exactly run a high-class operation; but, he made ends meet by dusting cotton, doing mechanical work on other people's planes and selling pesticide, defoliate and aviation gas.

Case tossed his oddball collection of weapons and supplies into the back compartment of the plane - flare gun, spear gun, deer rifle with scope, ammo, set of fisherman's fillet knives, rope, Rand McNally road map of Mexico, canteens of water, candy, chips, jerky. Most were things he did not know if he would need.

The two most precious items he laid in the empty copilot's seat, the file folder he picked up in Houston and what remained of the one hundred thousand dollars cash that Abuelita returned to him. There was no room in the plane for the ugly monster of guilt for what he'd done to Catarina's family. Case would leave that behind.

The engine roared, Case looked at the wind sock and drove the plane to the south end of the runway. He started his taxi; and when he saw Charlie dash out of the hanger to chase the plane down the runway, Case smiled and waved a friendly goodbye.

"Becker! You don't have a license! Come back here. This isn't funny!"

Case could only see a pantomime of punching fists and moving lips. He couldn't hear a word. It wouldn't have mattered anyway. He felt the lift under the wings and soared into the air. The Mexican border was only two miles away.

"Damn it, Becker, you stupid ass! You better be back in two hours. You don't know how to fly in the dark!"

Case checked his instruments, then questioned his sanity. He had gas, but didn't know exactly where his next tank would come from. If luck was with him, he would find the little air strips he had heard of close to the hunting and fishing areas he marked on his Rand McNally. If not, he would die in this episode of daring-do just as his mother always predicted he would. He unwrapped a candy bar.

From atop the levee, an observer watched the soaring plane. The man's sweaty hands clutched the sticky steering wheel. There was still blood under his fingernails from the morning's kill. He knew exactly where that plane was going, or at least close enough. He reached inside his shirt pocket to retrieve a grubby, smudged envelope. The return address read, "El Palacio de las Antiguas, Zacape, Quintana Roo, Mexico."

* * * * *

The inside of the safety deposit box vault at El Banco Nacional de México was cool and clean compared to the smelly streets of Zacape. Case tossed most of his cash into the rented box. On second thought, he considered the elegant sapphire ring worn by the bank's clerk. He reopened the box and took out another five thousand dollars. He closed the box again

297

and shoved it into the wall to resume its anonymity among the rows of other boxes. He called the clerk to lock it.

She was proper and deferential to Case despite his worn and disheveled appearance. His beard was scruffy, his hair was askew from sleeping in the cockpit of a crop duster and the ever present cut off shorts shouted "I don't give a shit what you think!" She handed him his key.

"Where did you buy your ring?" Case asked. She held her hand out for him to inspect it.

"It was a gift, of course. I think it came from La Casa de Luces Hermosas." Her pride in the treasure was obvious and the dreamy look in her eyes told Case she had a lover. "It is on this street, four doors down. You have someone you want to surprise?"

"Oh, I will be the surprise. I need a gift to make it easier to accept."

She purred, "I love a little mystery. Who is she?"

"That is a secret." He smiled that devastating smile. "But, you can tell me how to get to El Palacio de las Antiguas."

"Ah, Señor Carreras, un hombre muy importante. It is east, on the island."

"Muchas gracias, Señorita, Adios."

Case blinked at the harsh light outside the bank and turned toward the jewelry store. He found it and peered in the window. It was a classy place with several well dressed customers shopping inside, some local, some tourists; the salesman had on an expensive tailored suit.

Case reached into his pocket and pulled out cash to carry openly in his hand. He knew how to be taken seriously. When the salesman looked up, Case shook the money like a bullfighter's cape. The salesman excused himself politely and sprinted to open the door for his new customer. He treated Case with an attitude usually reserved for royalty. "Bienvenidos, Señor. How may I help you?"

"I want to buy a sapphire ring."

"Something for yourself, Señor?"

"No, a lady's ring, with maybe some diamonds."

"Certainly, this way." The man led Case to a glass counter of sparkling choices. "Sapphires come in different shades, you know."

Case needed no sales pitch, no haggling over price. "Let me see that one." He pointed to a fat circlet of yellow gold with a large, medium blue, pear-shaped stone. It was unusually set with the sapphire placed off center. The sapphire rested to one side with a scattering of twenty diamonds - tiny, small and medium ones, trailing throughout precious, intricately spun metal. To Case, the design looked like a shooting star in the night sky. The ring lay on the velvet display cloth and called his name. He answered, "How much?"

Case climbed into his rented four-wheel drive Jeep. His next tasks were to buy some clothes, obtain a room at El Palacio de las Antiguas and find Catarina. He dreamed of the hot shower he planned for himself.

Alfonso Carreras was so important to El Banco Nacional de México that the clerk must have called him the moment Case left the vault. A stranger needing a large safe deposit box and hunting for El Palacio de las Antiguas was an event of note.

By the time Case arrived at the resort, both a suite and a dinner invitation awaited him. Case had to sleep; there was no option. Satisfying his curiosity about Carerras and finding Catarina would have to wait until dinner.

Chapter 33

Dinner for Three

The coral dress Catarina wore to dinner last night got quicker results than she bargained for. The second dress, tonight's dress, was even more provocative and was perfect for her determined mood.

It was a clear turquoise, strapless delight that revealed all of her shoulders and a little of the inner curve of her swelling breasts. She stood in front of the mirror. She let her tousled hair down to caress her bare skin. The effect was purely devastating. Alfonso didn't have a chance.

She needed to decide whether or not she would seduce him tonight and secure the future or whether it would be more proper to wait.

She contemplated life with Alfonso. She would never want for anything. He would be expected to have mistresses at his level of Mexican society, though she could have no lovers. She would have a long leash in many other ways, freedom to raise her children as she saw fit, freedom to work in the world of education. Still, it would be a leash all the same.

She had to decide soon. It would be hard enough to explain a scandalous early birth of their first child. She wondered how a clear blue-eyed baby would be accepted. Would Alfonso pass it off as a freak of his European ancestry or be suspicious enough to delve into family history looking for some forgotten blue-eyed forefather? "Well, I can't think about that tonight." She was talking aloud to herself a lot these days.

Alfonso was handsome, intriguing, a prize. Sexy? Yes. In time, maybe she could love him. But he could never own her soul. He could never live in her blood, for there was someone already living there, someone she didn't want.

* * * * *

Samuel led Case to the private patio where his host, Alfonso Carreras, waited. Seeing a familiar man in white linen clashed harshly with Case's expectations. A family friend of Abuelita's should surely be older, decrepit, married! Instead, Catarina's benefactor was the vital, mysterious man Case had seen at the Cinco de Mayo party, the same man he saw talking intimately with Catarina at Cantina Los Indios. The same man that aroused strange, possessive urges he was unaccustomed to. This did not feel good.

"Señor Becker. Welcome. Una margarita?" Alfonso extended his hand; Case accepted it. The handshake was perfect, strong, not challenging. "I am Alfonso Carreras. You look surprised."

"I am. I never expected you to be someone I met before. Well, not met, but seen." They sat down at the table. "You will not remember me; we were not introduced."

"Of course, I remember you, Señor Becker. You are the man who left the Cinco de Mayo party early to take Catarina and María to see fireworks. Did your evening turn out well?"

Where is this going? Case decided he better find out quickly. "Yes, the fireworks were spectacular." Samuel placed a margarita on the table. Case's nerves were on alert; adrenaline made every sense acute. He heard a marimba band warming up; a frog chirped in the banana trees along the stucco wall and smells of fajitas sizzling wafted through the air.

Case picked up the glass, looked Alfonso directly in the eye and toasted, "Salud." The two men assessed each other as newly discovered animal rivals in the wild.

Case wasted no time getting to the point. "So, how do you know the de la Alvarados? It seems odd for a man like you to visit such a humble home in a border town in Texas."

"The connection between our families is very old," Alfonso began. "Do you know her name is Rita? Catarina's Abuelita? She was my grandfather's mistress."

Alfonso was so matter of fact that Case was shocked. He took another sip of his margarita and waited for more explanation.

"I think they loved each other from childhood. Her parents worked on one of our ranchos, a laundress and a stable hand. The arrangement as a mistress was the best they could do to be together. When my grandfather's marriage began to fail, the family blamed Rita. They got rid of her."

"Why did you go to the trouble to find her?"

"My grandfather never lost touch with her. He always tried to send her money, take care of her. She would accept nothing. He knew when she married, when her daughter was born, when she was widowed, when Sixto and Catarina came to live with her." Alfonso sighed over the old memories.

"Rita was very kind to me when I was a messy little boy that no one had time for. She taught me what love looked like. I've always checked on her. When her husband died and she had two grandchildren to take care of, she finally let my grandfather give her that little house on Camino Ratama." Alfonso leaned back in his chair. "I made the arrangements myself."

Case sipped his margarita and asked, "Does Catarina know this story?"

"I think so. She is as stubborn as her Abuelita, no?" Alfonso grinned. "I wonder how many generations back that streak of pride goes."

"That explains why I saw you talking to Catarina one night at Cantina Los Indios."

"Yes. That night, I asked her to be my mistress.....she declined." Alfonso sipped his drink. "Last night, I asked her to be my wife. Can I expect your congratulations when she accepts?"

Case remembered how it felt the time he was hit directly in the chest by a ball off the bat of a kid that went on to break Babe Ruth's home run record. He thought he would never breathe without pain again. He struggled the same way now. After another swallow of

304

his drink he managed to calmly say, "Catarina always knows what she wants."

"Ah!" Alfonso brightened. "Here is the lovely Miss de la Alvarado now. Darling, we have a surprise guest."

Case was barely prepared. The collision with her eyes brought him staggering to his feet. The way she was dressed couldn't possibly be for him. That turquoise dress was for Alfonso. The fresh, unpretentious beauty Case remembered had been replaced with a stunning, understated sophisticate. She was a siren, sent to steal his brains away and leave him speechless. Of all the dangerous things he'd done, all the risks taken, all the narrow escapes, now, Case knew what it felt like to die.

For Catarina, the earth tilted sideways before the floor fell away. She felt herself falling; but oddly, did not reach the ground. She watched the scene before her shift to gray, then fade to white. The touch of Alfonso's hand on her arm made her realize she was not breathing. Just a second ago, Alfonso had been across the room. Now he was guiding her to the table set for three. Her vision began to clear. She was about to sit down to dinner with both the man she was going to marry and the man her body desired more than oxygen itself.

Alfonso pulled out her chair and seated her. "Catarina, you know Señor Becker."

She concentrated on a deep breath. "Sí." Samuel appeared at her side to lay a napkin across her lap. "Señor Becker, you have business in México?" The floor was still moving under Catarina's feet.

Alfonso interjected, "No. No talk of business. First, we will dine and enjoy the company of our guest. Then, the business." It was a gracious command that anticipated no resistance. Catarina looked into the empty plate on the table in front of her. Case nodded to Alfonso in assent.

The business of settling down to dinner did not take long enough, and quiet overtook them quickly. Someone had to say something, anything. All three started to speak at the same time. Alfonso deferred to his guest. "Señor Becker, my apologies."

Case cleared his throat. "Catarina, how are you?"

"Muy bien, gracias." Catarina observed Case's new clothes. The resort look became him. She had never seen him in anything so elegant. The tan slacks hugged his legs and hips, smooth and tight. The blue silk shirt tapered against his body revealing enough to make her hand tremble when she reached for her glass of water.

"Tell me about your work here at the resort." Case purposefully moved his foot to touch her toes under the table.

Catarina prayed Alfonso did not notice her sharp intake of breath. She moved her foot, turning in her chair away from Case. "I am a tour guide. I take guests to Tulum to see the ruins."

Alfonso interjected, "Catarina is fantastic. She knows the intimate stories of the places and the people who lived in history. In just a month, she has become our most requested guide." He touched her beautifully manicured hand while Case's knee found her thigh.

They sat at a round table, just the perfect size to accommodate a triangle of conversation. Inane details of their lives unfolded, driven by harmless questions and vague answers. It was as though Catarina was participating in two separate but simultaneous events. One, a casual dinner with friends. One a visceral upheaval of confrontation and danger, each event unacknowledged by the other. Disconnected. She marveled at the phenomenon without comment. Case lost his napkin from his lap, retrieved it and trailed it across her ankles. *Damn you, Case!*

While Catarina silently argued out her blistering displeasure and anguish at Case's sudden appearance, the men talked about the hurricane developing in the Gulf, sailboat racing tactics and the virtues of reef preservation.

By the time a dessert of flan and mixed berries arrived, the scenario of "dinner with friends" had won the contest and Catarina was more relaxed. She attributed it to Alfonso's expert manipulation of the art of conversation.

"And, now, what is your business in Mexico, Señor Becker?" Alfonso was ready to let the scene play out and Catarina's apprehension returned.

Case addressed Alfonso. "You know the circumstances that brought Catarina back to Mexico?"

"Sí." Alfonso settled himself in his chair.

"The Border Patrol officer involved in deporting Catarina has been caught dealing in drugs, blackmail, and now murder." Case looked at Catarina. She gave him her full attention. "This man killed his wife yesterday and the local police have good reason to believe that Catarina is next. We believe he is already in Mexico."

Tears sprung to Catarina's widened eyes. She thought of pretty, sweet Jan, the waif who somehow remained innocent and hopeful in the face of her husband's sins. She was gone? "What happened?"

"They don't know exactly. Trouble has been brewing since you left. They tried to arrest him on charges regarding missing evidence and drug trafficking. He flipped out, beat up three officers and escaped. He got to Jan and murdered her. Before they caught up with him, he was at Abuelita's house.

Catarina grabbed the edge of the table. She had a new reason to hate Logan Dell! "Mi Abuelita!"

"She's fine. I got there just as Logan broke into the house. María was with her; they were both scared, but fine. I put both of them on a plane to San Diego to meet your brother. It's you the authorities believe is in the most danger."

Of all the things Catarina dreamed could bring Case to México, this wasn't it. She stopped to speculate on his tendency to need to rescue the women in his life. "You're blowing this out of proportion. Logan wouldn't murder Jan; surely it was an accident. He wouldn't come all the way down here for me. I'm not that important; and he has no reason to hurt me if he did."

"You don't understand, Catarina. Logan Dell is not just the bully you think you know. He's cracked. Every dark thing you ever saw or suspicioned about him is spilling out. Everyone has watched him fester for years. I feel guilty for not stopping him myself; I knew he was hurting Jan. Did you know he beat Jan so badly she had to be hospitalized five times in the last three years? The last time, she lost their baby."

Catarina shook her head no. She wouldn't accept it. "He won't bother me here. I'm safe."

"Jan's dead and there was no accident. It was brutal; she didn't even defend herself." Case paused to give Catarina time to believe him. "Catarina, he is on his way down here. He left a list with your name on it."

Alfonso came to attention. Case was glad one of them took him seriously. "What do you mean, a list?"

"I mean the police found a list of people Logan Dell intends to kill. Catarina's name is on it five times."

Alfonso calmly moved into action. As always, he was the man in charge. "Samuel! Get Rodolfo, pronto." He looked at Case and explained, "My chief of security. Señor Becker, why are you here on this matter instead of the authorities?"

"American police notified the Mexican authorities the moment Dell crossed the border and I'm sure you will be hearing from them, in a couple of days. I could get here faster with less red tape. I believe Dell is so dangerous that it couldn't wait."

Alfonso tapped the edge of his wine glass and said, "I agree. Señor Becker, if this happened yesterday, how did you get here so quickly?"

"I flew; I have a passport."

"Do you have a stamp on that passport recording your entry into México?" Alfonso's question was answered with silence. "I appreciate your sense of urgency in delivering this warning to us. You must have deep feelings for Catarina to take such measures when a phone call would have sufficed."

Catarina watched the sparks snap between the two men. "Oh, it is nothing, Alfonso. Señor Becker's family has a business, Becker Rescue Services. He thinks he should rescue people whether they want to be saved or not. He can't help himself."

Catarina and Alfonso confronted Case as a unified couple. Case looked from Alfonso to Catarina and back again. "I see you both don't think I should be here. You're wrong. Catarina is in danger."

Alfonso stood up. "Nonetheless, you have accomplished your mission, Señor Becker. My business office has informed me that the resort is fully booked for the rest of the week. You will have to check out in the morning. I know you won't want to be here when the police arrive. How will you get back into the U.S. without being noticed?"

"I really think Catarina is better off away from El Palacio de las Antiguas. We have reason to believe Logan knows she is here," Case insisted.

"Actually, she couldn't be safer anywhere in México. I have extensive personal security forces. My contacts with the police will be invaluable. Even the military will be at my disposal should that be necessary. Portions of this resort have withstood every hurricane and revolution in the history of México. Trust me; one gringo criminal will not be a problem."

Catarina agreed. "I feel very safe here. I'll be fine." What she really meant was that she didn't feel safe with Case Becker. Even if she hated him, she knew she would be in his arms as soon as they were off the resort property.

Samuel came to whisper in Alfonso's ear, then left as discreetly as he had arrived.

"I have a man," Alfonso began. "Pablo Pusas, very efficient. He will be here by morning. He will keep you safe, Catarina." He took her hand and covered it possessively with both of his. "Until he arrives, you will stay in your suite."

Catarina withdrew her hand. "I don't need a babysitter!"

"You do need a bodyguard, an experienced one. Por favor, do as I ask."

Although there was no condescension in Alfonso's voice or face, Catarina knew this was no request. She saw everyone around Alfonso grant his every wish, obey every spoken or unspoken command. Now it was her turn to fall into place. Would he be a kinder master than Case Becker?

Catarina looked from one man to the other, first Case, then Alfonso. Both were trying to protect her the best way they knew how. She felt each held a pillow ready to cover her face, control her, smother her.

Her need to escape both of them made her mentally run through her options. No good choices. She was fed up with both of them, bickering over her like they had some claim! She was about to explode. She was about to cry. She could afford to do neither. In keeping with the former civil tone of the evening, Catarina excused herself.

"Gentlemen, I'll leave you to work out my supervision on your own. I'm tired and you are more interested in impressing each other than protecting me." She was up from the table and on her way to her room before Alfonso could stop her or Case could curse.

Catarina didn't care what those two said or did to each other. She was tired, confused and angry. Her soul rocked between joy and horror in seeing Case again. Somehow she knew he would not leave her alone tonight. He would be knocking on her door or rapping on her window. She needed to start planning now how she was going to get rid of him.

Then, an impulse struck her. Why wait until he showed up at her room? Why not get rid of him this very minute? She spun and walked back to the table.

"Alfonso, my answer is yes. I would be proud to wear your great grandmother's ring."

Chapter 34

Temptation

The phone in Catarina's room stopped ringing at midnight. She lost count of the number of unanswered calls. Each time she checked with the operator, she learned the call was from Case. Now, the phone's silence screamed in her ears.

There were not enough chores, magazines or Spanish novellas in Mexico to blot out the memory of the look on Case Becker's face when Catarina accepted Alfonso's marriage proposal. It was funny that she didn't remember the look on Alfonso's face at all. She did remember Alfonso kissing her to seal his possession.

She threw the paperback novella she was reading at the silent phone. Its bell pinged in protest. The exertion helped a little and proved what she already knew, that the only relief from her fidgets and insomnia would be physical activity. She got out of bed and exchanged her pajamas for one of the designer swimsuits in her closet, grabbed a towel and quietly left her room.

313

Alfonso wouldn't like her leaving her suite. He was taking the threat on Catarina's life seriously. *Too bad; I don't belong to him yet. I need a walk and a swim. And, I'll do my tour tomorrow, whether he likes it or not!* She decided to avoid the pool and club areas; there were too many people to tattle on her to Alfonso. She stayed away from the lighted paths and sneaked through the lush landscaping and groves of palm trees.

If she did not believe Logan Dell was after her, why was she so jumpy? Case Becker, that's why. He was somewhere on this property, lying naked on a bed wanting to be with her. She knew the room number; he'd left it in several messages. All she had to do was knock on his door.

He was close; she could feel him in everything she encountered. The band in the cantina played a number she and Case had danced to at the pavilion on South Padre Island. She could imagine his body moving rhythmically to the beat. The night air held the smell of his breath; every brush of a leaf felt like the trail of his fingers down her arm.

Catarina's heart skipped a beat; she thought she saw him in the shadows leaning against a palm tree. When she got closer, she discovered that the unknown man was with a woman. He embraced the woman and gave her a deep, passionate kiss that sent a jolt directly through Catarina's core to the place where her wicked swimsuit made a high legged v. She hurried her steps to give the couple their privacy.

She was almost to the soft sand that led to the beach when she heard a rustle behind the oleander hedge. Suddenly she was aware of how vulnerable she was, leaving her room alone at this time of night. She heard the click of a gun. She froze. Logan couldn't be here! Her skin crawled and she literally felt her hair rise on her scalp. Muted steps and low murmurs came in her direction.

She darted behind a stack of beach umbrellas and chairs that sunbathers rented during the day. She dared not breathe until two of Alfonso's security guards strolled by. One was smoking a long brown cigarillo and he passed his lighter to the other. The second man used the butane flame to light his smoke. After he took his first long drag, he closed the stainless steel lighter. Click. The acrid smell of newly lit tobacco relaxed Catarina.

She felt silly and scolded herself for letting her imagination run wild. From her observation post at the umbrella stand, she watched a group of night divers returning from their adventure. Flashlights bounced crazily around the dock as they struggled with tanks and weight belts. They'd had a good time and practiced the stories they would tell their friends when they got home.

Catarina was jumpier than ever and thought about returning to her room; but the moon was bright, the guards were close by. There was someone swimming about one hundred yards off shore. The kissing couple was strolling arm in arm towards the far end of the beach. All the activity convinced Catarina that she was safe enough. Any of them could hear her if there was trouble.

Warm, crystal waters of the Caribbean bathed her feet, her ankles, then her thighs. She swished her hands through liquid that was as warm as a bath. Then she lowered herself under. She broke the surface with her face to the stars, letting her heavy hair pull back from her face and drip down her bare back.

She watched the man swimming horizontally to the beach beyond the third sand bar. Back and forth he swam, from the edge of the resort on the north to a point about a quarter of a mile to the south. He took long, strong, powerful strokes that Catarina would recognize anywhere. Case propelled himself from one point to the other, his endurance seemingly inexhaustible.

Catarina was mesmerized; she could not leave. On some level, she knew that before she could marry Alfonso Carreras, she had to prove to herself that she could resist the magnetic sexual vortex of Case Becker.

The dark figure swam towards the shore; and when he stood up in the water, his muscular silhouette looming in front of the moon, Catarina walked toward him.

It took a couple of minutes for Case to notice her, but only a second for him to recognize her. He gradually slowed his advance until he came to a stop in front of her. His hair was slicked back like hers, as if they had been swimming together. He stood so close that anyone observing would have assumed they were at the resort together, on a lover's trip. So far from the truth. It had been six weeks since they had been together, and they had never talked of the events that destroyed them. Catarina steeled herself for the test that began with staring into those blue, blue eyes. She knew how impossible he could make this.

Case reached for her hand and Catarina avoided him by turning to walk out of the water. When she reached the place where she left her towel, she picked it up and dried her face. When she handed it to Case, he ran it over his hair, then rubbed the towel down both his arms while he inspected her from head to toe.

"No bikini?"

"I told you; I don't like bikinis."

He spread the towel on the sand. "I thought maybe you'd changed your mind; you've changed in so many other ways."

Catarina snapped back, "I don't owe you any explanations."

"Are we going to talk?"

"Yes." Catarina sat down beside him. It was a dangerous place to be, on a beach towel, under the Mayan moon, beside the surf, looking up at the same stars that covered them on the night they had the most erotic sex of their lives on the deck of the sailboat *Everlovin'*.

"How did you know I was out here?" Case asked.

"I didn't; I just needed to get out of my room. The phone kept ringing." She paused for effect. "I was restless."

"Me too." Case looked at her; and although his meaning was completely clear, she ignored it.

Catarina fought for how to initiate the closure she wanted in their relationship. It was too difficult a task so she took a sideways approach. "I need to thank you for everything you did for Sixto, getting the lawyer, watching out for him."

"I didn't do it for you. Sixto and I were friends before I knew who you were." Case sounded irritable and itching for a fight.

"I know. All the same, I am grateful." That line

of conversation was dead; she would have to find another. It was suddenly quieter and Catarina realized that the band at the cantina was taking a break. "Shall we discuss your behavior at dinner tonight?"

Case exploded with the real question. "Catarina, I want to know if you are really going to marry Alfonso Carreras!"

"And I want to know why you lied to me!" Alarmed at their outbursts, Catarina looked around to see if anyone heard their raised voices.

"Are you?"

"I'm committed to him."

"Catarina, you haven't done anything yet that can't be undone."

"He is a good man."

Case turned his body to face Catarina and forced her to hold his hands. "I'm sure he is a good man, not to mention a very rich one.....have you slept with him?"

Catarina snatched one of her hands away and tried to slap Case. He was too fast and caught her wrists midair. She struggled and his grip tightened slightly. She glared at him and wanted to spit a lie in his face. She wanted to tell him yes. She settled for, "It's none of your business!"

"It wouldn't matter to me.....I still want you." Case slowly moved his arms around her forcing her hands behind her back. He placed his mouth close to hers, but would not steal a kiss that was not his. He whispered into her lips, testing her. "If you'd slept with him, if you loved him, you'd be back in that museum he calls a home and in his bed right now. But you're not. You're out wandering around on the beach hoping to run into me." Case's hold on her gentled.

"You arrogant, gringo asno." This time, Catarina was able to wrench her wrists away. This was going to be an emotionally bloody fight. "I'm not in his bed because he respects me."

"You know being with him wouldn't be anything like what we had."

"Everything will be different than what we had; I can trust him!"

"Trust him? To do what? Trust him to not love you? Not make demands on you?"

"He won't lie to me!"

Case sat with his arms propped on his knees. He dug his toes in the sand. "So there it is. You won't forgive me for being stupid. You'll throw everything away. You must have no idea what love is. You think being with Carreras will put you in charge of your life? You think you're going to control him?" Case gave a sarcastic half laugh.

"I don't want to control him; I just want to control what happens to me!" Catarina's upper lip remained stiff and unyielding. The band started playing again and a singing voice doing a fair imitation of a Cuban artist floated from the club to the beach.

Case leaned back on his elbows and studied the sky. "I think I've figured it out. If you forgive me, there is nothing to keep us apart."

"I want you to leave in the morning, like Alfonso asked you to." Catarina was unmovable.

"Catarina, giving you that money turned bad because of Logan Dell. I gave it as an anonymous gift, the only way I could get you to take it. Is being anonymous the same as lying? It didn't feel like it at the time." He waited for a crack, a tic in her face, a

319

Susan LeMiles

change of heartbeat, anything. "Catarina, I was drowning before I met you; you changed everything for me.....I've never actually told you I love you....."

"And don't. I really want you to go." Case didn't know that hearing the words "I love you" actually made it easier for Catarina to leave him, because that's exactly what Logan Dell told her years ago. Thank God Alfonso wasn't foolish enough to have tried that line.

Still, the word "love" living in the air between them made her light headed. Case had presented an entirely different view of his actions and considering it was like letting acid eat at her carefully constructed shell. It made a ragged hole in her soul where the raw energy of the man sitting next to her could seep in and assault her again. Her heart flipped in her chest; she calmed it with a deep breath and a toss of her half dried hair.

"I'm right, aren't I? If you forgive me, you'll want to be with me."

Catarina stood up. She'd resisted him, but she'd had all the temptation she could stand. "I'm serious, Case." She pulled on the edge of the towel; but he wouldn't move.

Case looked up; she was standing over him as icy as the last time she told him she didn't want him. "Still all locked up. Tied in knots over hurts that happened so long ago you don't even know what they are. You know, Catarina, one of these days, you are going to tell me to leave you alone; and I'm going to believe you mean it."

Catarina left Case sitting on the towel, the incoming tide starting to wet his feet. What was her

320

definition of closure? Did she think she could brush a man like Case off with a quick "So long; I have other plans? Oh, by the way, I'm having your baby." She stomped up the beach toward her room.

"Señorita?" Jaime Reyna stood up from one of the umbrella chair rentals. "Por favor, allow me to escort you back to your suite."

"Oh! Thank you, Jaime." Catarina flushed violently, embarrassed that her night's escapade was exposed. They fell into step, making their way around the edge of the cantina and pool toward Catarina's room. They walked in silence until they reached her door; he opened it for her and she turned to confront him.

"You were watching me."

"We have all been told to watch you." He gestured to indicate the entire resort. "I'm glad it was me who saw you. No need for Señor Carreras to know."

"Nothing happened."

"I know; just unfinished business." Jaime understood.

"Sí, it's finished now."

Jaime arched an eyebrow and gave that slight bow at the waist he gave her every time he saw her. "Buenas noches. Sleep well."

Catarina softly closed the door to her suite and leaned against it. The problem was, not all the business was finished. She'd railed against Case for lying to her and hated Logan for lying to her. Now, she was thinking of the lies she was telling, the lie that was growing in her own womb, the lie she was about to inflict on Alfonso Carreras. No matter what the consequences, she knew she couldn't live her whole life deceiving him like that.

If telling him the truth changed his feelings for her, she and her baby would be on their own. No embarrassing announcements had been made. If she was careful and humble, perhaps he would at least provide her a reference with another resort in Mexico. Maybe Alfonso's loyalty to Abuelita would save her once again.

Chapter 35

Touring Tulum

Case was enveloped in the aura of the ancient Mayan city of Tulum. Quiet swallowed the outside modern world, casting life into a historical perspective that clarified the fleetness of time.

Temple ruins hung over the Caribbean, perched on rocks held together by the roots of palms, vines and Spanish daggers. Azure waters were gentle here and lapped across white sands at the base of the great cliff. No visitor could stand close to these walls without hearing the whispers of the people who lived, fought, worshipped and loved within these stones.

The morning was heating and the tropical sun already beat on Case's uncovered head. The brochure he carried said Catarina's tour would go from Tulum to Dos Ojos, sink holes that led to vast unexplored underwater caves. They would end the trip shopping in Cancun. It was going to be a long, hot day.

Case stepped into the park's gift shop and bought a hat, a straw Panama style that added three inches to his height. He stooped to look in the mirror.

323

Can't hide from anyone in this. Case knew he wasn't the kind of guy who could slip around in a crowd unnoticed anyway. If he was going to be Catarina's protector until Carreras' man showed up, he didn't need to call unnecessary attention to himself. Case pushed the gruesome thoughts of Jan's crime scene photographs away and prayed Pablo Pusas was one bad ass soldier.

A stray boy stood by Case at the mirror. Clearly in awe of Case's size, his jaw was dropped and his head hung backwards on his shoulders. Case looked up at the brim of the hat from under his eyebrows. "Too much, huh." He put the hat on the boy's head. "Yeah, looks better on you."

The boy scampered outside to where his family was gathering to listen to Catarina's tour introduction. "Mom! Look what that man gave me!"

The easiest place for Case to remain out of sight was inside the shop. He watched Catarina through a curtain of wooden puppets dressed in peasant clothing and sombreros, dangling from their strings in the window.

She didn't seem right. There was no energy behind her pasted smile. Her enthusiasm was missing; not even the antics of a boy in a Panama hat made her smile. She kept taking deep breaths between sentences and looked obviously ill. Catarina dismissed the group to explore on their own, with instructions to meet in fifteen minutes back in front of the gift shop.

Case thought she was going to faint, but she stumbled into the public restroom before he could reach her. He was relieved when a grey haired woman in a red hat followed her inside. He would just have to wait.

Finally, the woman came out, smiling, but alone. Case approached her. "Is Miss de la Alvarado not feeling well?"

"Oh, it's nothing another seven months or so won't cure. She's pregnant." The woman gave a wise chuckle. "She just needs to keep a little something in her stomach. I gave her some snack crackers; she'll be fine." The woman checked Case's left hand for a wedding band. "I didn't see you on the bus. Are you part of our tour?"

"No, I'm not." His reply was barely audible for his mind was racing through the last few weeks. *Unless Alfonso Carreras had sex with Catarina on the bus that brought her to Mexico, that baby is mine!* This changed everything.

"Why don't you join us. She is a wonderful guide, such fascinating stories. I'm sure she wouldn't mind."

"She'll mind; but I'll join you anyway." *A baby! My baby!* What were these feelings gouging around in his heart? Loving Catarina made him feel strange enough. This.....this carried a primal, possessive intensity Case didn't know could exist for a man.

He couldn't make sense of the emotional twisting and turning in his guts; and his instincts turned to something he did understand, action. Logan Dell was no longer going to be a threat. From this moment forward, he was prey.

Case briefly contemplated a lifetime in a Mexican jail for murder. If he had to leave Catarina, he was going to leave her safe. Case would turn the tables. He would not wait for danger to find Catarina.

He would hunt.

Catarina stepped out of the ladies' room looking shaken and unsteady. She closed her eyes and smoothed her hair before she called her tour together.

Case joined the back of the group, standing directly in Catarina's line of sight. There was no way she could miss him, towering over the heads of the other people. There.....she saw him. One look at her face and Case could see she knew she was busted. He knew she was pregnant, and he knew the baby was his. Her face drained from pale to white and she stammered in the middle of her sentence about the ancient sacrifice of virgins.

"Does anyone have any questions? No? I'll meet you at the top of El Castille, that pyramid over there. See?" Catarina pointed to the tallest of the ruins; and like a gaggle of chatting geese, the tour group waddled toward the structure.

Case walked directly to Catarina. He did not reach out for her. She opened her mouth; but Case interrupted.

"You weren't going to tell me!"

"I was thinking about....."

"Doesn't this qualify as a lie, Catarina?" His deep voice ricocheted around the quiet of the park grounds.

"Case, por favor, my tour....."

"I was going to stay with you today; but I've changed my mind."

"You have no right to follow me around!"

"That may be true, since you don't belong to me; but you've got something that does belong to me and I'm not taking any chances with it." Case loomed over Catarina like the shadow of a storm. She was struggling for excuses he had no interest in hearing.

"Case, we'll talk tonight."

"You're damn right we will!" he thundered. "What are you doing working today anyway? You were supposed to stay on the resort."

"Case, I'm fine!"

"You're not! And, Carreras agrees with me. Do you see that man over there?" Case pointed to a man purchasing pistachios at the counter of the gift shop. "I'll bet that's Pablo Pusas, your new protector."

"He's just one of my group; how would you know?"

"Bulging armpits." Case tested his assumption. "Hey, Pablo!"

The man seemed to expect Case and pleasantly acknowledged his greeting with a nod.

"Catarina, I'm not waiting for Logan. I'm going after him."

"No, Case! You don't need to do that. If Logan shows up, let Alfonso take care of it, please."

"The only way Alfonso Carreras is going to take care of you and my baby is if I'm dead! If I don't come back, marry him. If you see me again, you are marrying me."

He turned to leave; but when he saw her dark eyes get glassy, he softened. "Your birthday is September 20, 1942." He reached into his pants pocket, then grabbed her left hand. He shoved the gold and sapphire ring on her fourth finger where a wedding band should go. "Your birthstone is sapphire, so I bought you one."

He watched Catarina twist the ring round her

finger. He held his breath, praying she would not take it off. He knew the ring was a risky purchase from the beginning. It was odd, unexpected, beautiful by anyone's standards; but it was a also a concrete symbol that the intangible living force between the two of them really existed, whether they spent their lives together or not.

"Abuelita told you."

"No, she didn't." He reached into his bag and produced the manila folder. "Here's something I want you to have. I followed a wild hair; you know me." Case forced the folder into her bag.

In spite of the fact he was so violently angry with her he could choke her, he thought about a kiss, just in case. There was a moment.....a long moment when that kiss was inevitable.

"Miss de la Alvarado, are you coming?" The opportunity was gone. Disconnected.

Case pointed to the folder. "Read it; you'll like it." He gave a quick nod to Pablo and never looked back.

Pablo followed Catarina discretely throughout the day. He had a cloak of invisibility he used at will. Whenever he saw Catarina looking for him, he stepped out of a doorway or moved within some shadow, letting her know he was close.

There was nothing about Pablo that attracted attention. He wore his nondescript clothing larger than what was stylish; but when Catarina looked closely, his square shape was packed with muscles and power. Once, he took off his sunglasses to wipe his brow and she saw eyes that had the look of someone who was used to killing. Catarina wondered how many times Pablo Pusas had killed and if Alfonso commanded it. She shuddered, for Pablo's presence made the threat she so lightly dismissed last night seem very real today.

The remainder of the trip passed quietly. The tourists were awed by the caverns of the cenotes. During their visit to Dos Ojos, an underwater exploration team was preparing to enter the labyrinth of caves and waterways underneath the Yucatan Peninsula. From one of the divers, Catarina's group learned of the beauty, danger and death that swirled underneath the land on which they stood.

When the Cancun merchants emptied the shoppers' wallets and the children were cranky, the guests of El Palacio de las Antiguas squashed their packages into the overhead bins and under the seats for the trip back to the resort. Last on the bus, Pablo took the seat across the aisle from Catarina while she counted heads. Satisfied that all bodies were on board the stuffy bus, she plopped in her seat and fanned herself with the manila folder. Any movement of air felt good.

Her exhaustion was as much from emotional turmoil as it was the day's trip and her guests' demands. Between every stop, every question, every translation with shop keepers, Catarina endured a war in her soul over her judgment of Case Becker. Her wrist flicked back and forth, the folder moving the air.

What is this stuff? Something to do with the school at Ito's farm? She remembered what Case said when he shoved the folder into her bag. "I followed a wild hair; you know me."

The folder popped when she opened it. There were two pieces of paper. The first looked like some kind of official document. She ran her thumb across a raised seal and saw the scrawling signature of a County Clerk.

She read through details that made her straighten and lean forward in her seat. Her lips moved and she mumbled the words aloud. "Birth Certificate: Father, Juan Ignacio de la Alvarado. Mother, Elena Giselle de la Alvarado. Baby girl, Catarina de la Alvarado, six pounds, ten ounces. Harris County Hospital. September 20, 1942."

A United States birth certificate! Catarina scrambled to the second page, an identical document in the name of Sixto Terrazos.

"Mi Dios." She looked at the birthstone ring on her right hand. Its presence vexed her all day. She'd taken it off a hundred times and finally settled for wearing it on her right hand until she returned it to Case.

If these documents were real, her old life was over. Surely Case wouldn't purchase birth certificates on the black market and pass them on to her as authentic, not after the disasters that followed his last deception. The fact that she considered the possibility that the documents weren't real warned her that she and Case weren't right with each other yet.

Catarina had been willing to spend seven years earning what she now held in her hand. In an instant, everything was different. The birth certificate represented freedom to work, study, teach, raise her baby, take care of Abuelita. The question now was should she do all of these things amidst a lifetime of power struggles with the unpredictable gringo who just handed her everything she always wanted?

Catarina took Case's ring off again, staring into the sapphire like it was a crystal ball with answers to her future. The bus hit a pothole big enough to bounce passengers off their seats and send the ring rolling down the aisle toward the back of the bus.

"I've got it!" The lady with the red hat swooped up the ring as it rolled by her seat. She steadied herself by holding on to the backs of seats as she made her way forward to Catarina.

"Gracias! I can't lose that; I need to return it."

"My name is Rosie." The woman placed the ring in Catarina's open palm.

"I owe you thanks again, Rosie, for the crackers this morning."

"How are you feeling?"

"Tired." Catarina tilted her head.

"Didn't I see a handsome man give that ring to you this morning? Here." Rosie extended a Polaroid picture of Catarina and Case standing next to each other. "You look good together."

Catarina looked around Rosie at Pablo Pusas. He was listening to nothing, looking at nothing.....hearing and seeing everything.

The photo caught the essence of a moment between Case and Catarina, tension and conflict. The picture was nothing like the soulful portrait of Enrique that Hermina wore in her locket; but it was a picture of Case, and Catarina was grateful to have it.

"May I join you?" Rosie asked. "It's a rocky walk back to my seat; this road is terrible."

Catarina moved her bag to the floor.

"That's a very unusual ring, a custom design. It looks like the sky on a starry night."

A dreamy smile twitched at the corner of Catarina's lips. "It was a starry night." She swayed in her seat to the bumps and jostles as the bus negotiated the battered asphalt.

"What are you going to do?"

"I don't know." Catarina flashed another glance at Pablo and adopted an undertone as she leaned closer to Rosie. "We have.....difficulties.....and, I'm engaged to someone else."

Rosie's round eyebrows raised and her wrinkled lips formed a perfect O. She shifted her eyes to Pablo and back.

"My protector." Catarina put her finger to her lips for secrecy.

Rosie whispered, "Old women know certain things. I don't care who the other guy is.....this one is the right one." Rosie punctuated her claim by tapping the picture Catarina held in her hand.

Catarina dropped the photo to her lap. "I meet the most opinionated women on buses. The last one, Hermina, said I should give him a chance. She was very young. What would she know?"

"I'm not young," Rosie argued.

Catarina shifted in her seat; she lifted her hair off her sticky neck and twisted it atop her head, holding it there. "My cousin María said I should grab him; my grandmother reminds me that he won't wait forever.....but, I just can't see us together."

"Look closer, Catarina."

Catarina raised the photo in her lap and examined the subjects. That couple did look right together. Her touch lingered on the figures caught in a moment of truth. Through the tension and conflict, she could see their hands reaching out to each other without touching; their bodies leaning forward; yearning etched their faces and proof of love leaped from the shiny paper.

"Do you see what I see, sweetheart?"

"You are a good photographer."

"Eh, so so.....This is the one." Rosie said it again.

Catarina felt, for the first time, that she understood how Case felt that day on *Everlovin'* when he bellowed to the sun, "I'm in love!"

Catarina's look of tenderness morphed into a grin; then came her musical laugh.

"What?" Rosie asked.

Catarina placed the ring of starry nights on the fourth finger of her left hand and held it up for Rosie to see.

* * * * *

Catarina passed a note to Rosie who felt for reading glasses that hung on a chain around her neck.

I want to see my fiancé before Protector does.
Can you help?

Darkness arrived before the bus pulled under the portico at Palacio de las Antiguas. Clever Rosie blocked the exit enabling Catarina to escape. Rosie

333

tripped, launching herself across the aisle; she sprawled on Pablo's lap, pinning him to his seat and covering his eyes with the red hat.

Catarina rushed through the lobby and down the stepping stones that curved around to her suite of rooms. In her haste, she collided with the front desk clerk. The contents of Catarina's bag and the clerk's daily paperwork spilled across the walkway.

"Anna! Lo siento!"

"Oh! Catarina! Here let me help you." Anna bent to retrieve sunglasses, lotion, and the folder.

"It was my fault; I wasn't watching where I was going." Catarina stacked Anna's papers as best she could. "I hope it won't be too much trouble to sort those out."

"No, it's fine.....I just left flowers in your room. Roses. They were delivered a few moments ago." Anna beamed.

Catarina let out a sigh and a wan smile. "Alfonso. He is going to charm me instead of scold me for going on the tour today."

"Alfonso es facinante; you are a lucky woman; he has chosen you." Anna spoke to Catarina with a new and subtle deference.

Anna returned to the lobby and Pablo appeared on the walk. He stepped in front of a contrite Catarina to take the lead, still on assignment. He had a way of constant motion that allowed him to survey all three hundred sixty degrees in three dimensions. Pablo saw everything, even in the night.

The outside light in front of Catarina's room was dark and Pablo's body went on alert. He held out his hand, snapping his fingers to indicate he wanted her key. She gave it to him without question. He turned the key in the lock; then cracked open the door. Pablo let out a soft groan, then a sigh of air that was much too long. It was the first and last sound Catarina ever heard him make.

He fell backward into Catarina knocking her to the ground; the back of her head bounced on the stone walk. Pain was instantaneous; and blinding fireworks ended in black. The last things she remembered were Pablo's heavy body on top of her, then something wet and warm seeping into her clothes.

Chapter 36

Approaching Storm

"Señor, we are closing.....the storm." A waiter pointed through an arch of the open air restaurant and Case watched a sheet of newspaper play chase with a plastic bag down the center of the street. Braids of garlic swayed in the quickening wind. Vendors folded up their sidewalk displays; street dogs trotted off to find shelter; and an old man covered a talking parrot who said "Buenas Noches" when the blanket slipped over the bars of his cage.

"One more coffee?" Case requested.

The town prepared for a gale. Hurricane Helen was headed for northern Mexico, but she would whip up plenty of rough water and high tides here off the Yucatan on her way to her final destination.

The waiter returned with a refill and the check.

It won't hurt to flash this news clipping one more time. "Have you seen this man?" Case extended the photo.

The waiter tilted his head to look at the man in the picture. "No, Señor."

The hunt for Logan Dell did not go well today. *Stop kidding yourself, Becker, this is going nowhere. You let your impulses run away with you again. You should be with Catarina, not out chasing the devil.* It was getting dark, and the pull to see that Catarina returned safely from Tulum was stronger than his vow to find Logan.

Case's heart swelled thinking of the girl holding a birthday cake surrounded by a halo of light. He willed her to keep the sapphire on her finger and to be waiting for him when he arrived at El Palacio de las Antiguas.

* * * * *

Case pulled his Jeep into the service entrance of the resort and walked around the bungalows until he came to Catarina's room. He would do his best to persuade her to leave with him in the morning.

The thought of being behind closed doors with her stirred the lust Catarina cast over him the night before. Weeks of abstinence flared in his groin and he had to adjust his pants. *Case, you dog; this is a life and death matter!*

The walkway in front of Catarina's room was dark. The wind curled around the corner of the bungalow whining on the tile roof. There were no lights on inside. Case didn't like that; he hurried towards her door. He tripped, then slipped on the wet stone walkway. He almost recovered his balance, but a vise like grip on his ankle pulled him down into a sticky pool of liquid.

When Case rolled over, he was face to face with Pablo Pusas. The invincible man that Alfonso Carreras trusted to protect his most precious possession used his last ounce of life to utter the name, "Dell."

Case entered a nightmare. A banana leaf slapped Pablo's face, covering and uncovering his open eyes while Case pried his ankle from the fingers of Pablo's death grip. Case was no stranger to corpses, but they were drowning victims and people who died in car wrecks. The fact that Pablo was murdered while protecting Catarina shook Case in his core.

He checked the shoulder holsters for Pablo's guns. Instead, he found gaping knife wounds in Pablo's chest. The guns were gone. Surely a man like this carried an extra. Case found nothing hidden in Pablo's custom-made boots.

"Catarina?" Case hissed. "Catarina?" He thrashed through the thickets of hibiscus and bird of paradise. Catarina's bag lay on the lawn beside the next bungalow. He reached for the manila folder, soaked in blood, while a scream shot through his head, *Catarina, don't be dead!*

Everyone underestimated Logan Dell from the beginning. To find Catarina, Case knew he needed all the help he could get, even if that help was from Alfonso Carreras.

* * * * *

"Carreras!" Case violently shook the gates to the private patio. "Carreras!!!" An edge of fear erupted as rage; it seemed to take forever for Samuel to appear.

"Señor Becker. You are not welcome here. My employer will not be pleased." Samuel turned on the patio lights revealing Case's bloody clothes. "Mi Dios!" he whispered.

"Where is Carreras?"

Samuel was fixed on the grisly sight, unable to respond.

"Donde está Carreras?" Case reached through the ornate bars and grabbed Samuel's shirt. "Pablo Pusas is dead; Catarina is missing.....Samuel?"

"La Ciudad de México, business." Samuel broke from his stupor and unlocked the gate.

"Have you seen anything strange, anyone who doesn't look like they belong?"

"There is a man, a man in the lobby, an angry man. He is looking for Catarina too."

"Americano?" Case struggled. What was the word for blonde? "Rubio! Un Americano rubio?"

"No, es de México; es moreno."

Case hadn't thought of the possibility Logan might have enlisted a local accomplice. Maybe ransom was the plan for Catarina. At least that would mean she was alive.

Case powered his way past Samuel and headed through Alfonso's quarters.

"This way," Samuel volunteered. "Un momento." He ran ahead of Case into a laundry room and reappeared holding one of Alfonso's white shirts. "Por favor.....the guests."

Case did not slow his stride but ripped off his
own bloody shirt, throwing it against the pristine stucco
wall. He shoved his arms into the long sleeves and
rolled them up without noticing the tight fit or the feel
of fine Egyptian cotton. He was still working the
buttons when he burst into the lobby.

Case peered through the wall of water falling
from the fountain, trying to identify the man slumped
into the couch. It would be good to know if the man
was armed, but time didn't allow for such luxuries.
Case would take his chances.

"Who the hell are you?"

The man stood to face Case.

"Sixto!"

"Gringo, your hands!"

Case looked at his forearms and fists covered
with Pablo's blood.

"Is that Catarina's blood?" Sixto's voice broke,
he felt for the couch.

"No. Carreras' man, her bodyguard. Sixto,
what are you doing here?"

"She's my sister; you think you are the only one
who loves her?"

"No." Case realized he was glad to see his
friend.

"María called to tell me about Jan Dell and that
Logan was coming here for Catarina. You said the
truck was mine. She sold it and wired me the money."

Case paced to the front desk and back. "Since
he didn't kill her on the spot, maybe he's got some sick
reason for keeping her alive. All I have is a trail of
blood that I hope is not hers. We've got to do
something now."

Samuel held out a map from the rack of travel brochures. "I know the island; there is no place to hide." He inserted himself between the two men. "Dell will have to get off of Zacape. Yesterday, we closed the ferry to anyone we don't know. If he came to the island in his own boat, he'll leave the same way."

"That's a start; he can't go anywhere tonight; the weather's too heavy," said Case. "They're still here."

Samuel spread the map on the couch. He pointed to the island of Zacape. "The Carreras family owns the whole island....."

Sixto and Case exchanged looks.

".....so, access is easier to control. If they make it to la isla de Cozumel, or worse, directly to the mainland, we'll lose them."

"Won't Alfonso's forces be able to help search by then?" Case smoothed the fold in the map.

"Sí, but Cozumel has many ways to get back to the mainland, a commercial airport, regular ferry transport and this time of year, cruise ships dock every day. If Señor Dell makes it to Yucatan, there are six thousand interconnecting, unmapped water caves to hide in, cenotes. The entire Mexican army couldn't find them. There are cenotes on Zacape too."

"Could they hide there?" Case asked.

"I don't think so; the entrances are under water; and the undertow there kills two or three scuba divers every year. Fools who don't know the waters go there because it is within sight of the land. It's easy to get in; dangerous to get out."

Case leaned over the map, turning it to orient himself to North. "Sounds like we better get lucky before the weather breaks.   How long do we have before the storm passes, Samuel?"

"Maybe an hour past dawn."

Case straightened his back and walked to the window, evaluating the wind's direction. A patio chair toppled and slid into the pool.

"We need to be a bird in the sky," said Sixto.

Case fixed his jaw and turned to Sixto and Samuel. "I can arrange that."

Chapter 37

Showdown on Zacape

Catarina awoke to the same sensations she last remembered, pain in her head and warm liquid flowing around her. The pounding was too excruciating for her to feel fear; there was no way she was going to open her eyes. One hand examined the back of her head. Yes, an astounding lump. The other hand searched the wetness and discovered a tide pool lapping at her face.

She forced one eye into a microscopic slit. Through the pink light inserting itself between her lashes, she watched a hermit crab make a real estate decision, abandoning his shell for a larger one resting next to Catarina's hand. The wind shoved ripples across the shallow pool; it whipped her hair into her eyes and stung her legs with sand. Was that moaning she heard her own? When she tried to raise herself, she cut her palm on black volcanic rock.

Jutting spikes surrounded her, creating a fantasy city of dark castles in white sand. An arching volcanic formation the size of a battleship loomed over the churning waters, its base hidden in hurling foam that

343

cascaded back into the sea. Waters raged rough here on a good day; with Hurricane Helen's help, the surf turned violent.

"Good, you're awake." Logan sounded eerily normal. "I didn't know how I was going to carry you to the launch over these rocks. They are practically made of glass." He bent to take off her shoes, throwing them far off into the black spires. "Sorry, can't have you going rabbit on me. I'd have to shoot a rabbit; not sure I want to do that."

Logan looked nothing like the crisp, clean shaven, uniformed man she knew. His hair hung lank on his collar; his cheeks bristled rough with stubble; and his eyes wandered, seeking an anchor for his drifting mind. Now, Catarina was afraid. Pablo was surely dead and Case would have no idea where to find her. She was on her own, her wits and Logan's insanity her only weapons.

She spoke with kindness. "I'm glad you don't want to shoot me. I have something to tell you."

Logan's mind strayed. "There's a hurricane in the Gulf. I wanted to leave last night but the wind..... dangerous.....dark."

"Yes, that was the right decision." She had to be careful. Every time she spoke, she risked setting off the inexplicable behavior that could end in her murder. Her morning nausea assailed her. Her empty stomach heaved with nothing but bile.

"What's the matter with you?" Logan asked. "I can't take care of a sick rabbit." He examined one of Pablo's guns, blowing sand from the barrel and testing aim on a honey bear at the edge of the salt jungle. The honey bear looked for breakfast while her hungry cubs trailed behind her. He spoke to the gentle varmint.

"Today is your lucky day, Little Lady. No noise. I don't want to be found." He pretended to shoot the honey bear and blew on the end of the gun barrel like a cowboy in a bad western movie.

Playing with Logan's fragile mind was a huge risk. Losing the game meant the end of two lives, hers and her baby's. Winning meant buying enough time for someone to find her. She closed her eyes and gave herself an imagined embrace from the man she loved. She felt his brazen spirit engulf her, giving her strength for a Case-like chance.

"Logan, did you ever want a son?"

Logan's head snapped towards Catarina. "How did you know that?"

"I wasn't sure. I was hoping you did." Catarina managed a careful, coy glance.

"Jan killed our baby!" His anguish was real; his face contorted with madness and regret.

Catarina swallowed another wave of sickness. "I just couldn't tell you before, because it would make trouble for you, being married."

"You're pregnant, from that last time we were together?" Logan's eyes widened and curiosity replaced the disconnected look on his face.

"Yes. I'm having your baby." Catarina's bottom lip quivered as she delivered her desperate lie and waited for Logan's reaction.

He squatted beside her, stroking her hair as he considered whether to believe her or not. "I'm not married any more. Things didn't work out for Jan and me." Logan looked through Catarina into some past event. "Maybe I'll keep you; I need someone." He pulled her close into a tender embrace.

Catarina's heart leaped; the deceit worked! She put her arms around his neck, and looking over his shoulder, she watched Logan's launch lift off the surface of the angry water and crash down between the rocks. Her mind raced forward to the next step. Leaving was still too dangerous; but now that it was light, Logan might ignore that. Catarina knew she could not get in that boat. If she left the island of Zacape, she was doomed.

Logan sat back on his heels. "We could disappear into Belize or maybe Costa Rica. I can raise a son right in a place like that, respectful."

"Family is very important." Catarina encouraged his fantasy.

"Did you know my granddaddy was a lawman, a Texas Ranger?" Logan caressed the old badge pinned to his denim shirt. His usual quick wink was a maddening twitch. His face slowly screwed up like he was crying, but there were no tears. He was in anquish and stretched his neck sideways with tortured emotion.

"He shot my daddy like a rabid dog. I was there; I can still see it like it is happening now." He whispered, "Crazy.....my daddy was. I'd love my son better than that." Logan's scattered focus finally landed on Catarina's face. "You have to do things exactly like I tell you."

Catarina looked down at her bloody clothes; she swallowed even though she thought it would be impossible, before she nodded and said, "Yes, I will."

* * * * *

Sixto followed the drone of the crop duster overhead. He leaned out the side of the jeep intermittently to check the plane's position.

"Gringo loco!" Sixto shuddered as Case fought the buffeting winds; the plane lurched and swayed overhead. No one in their right mind would attempt flying that tin can on a day like today. It was a good thing Case wasn't in his right mind, since they had no other choice, no other way to locate Catarina fast enough.

Sixto drove down the narrow road, dodging potholes as fast as he dared; in the distance the plane climbed high over the end of the island, flying a tight circle twice before soaring back towards Sixto and the Jeep.

Case aligned the plane with the narrow asphalt path and swooned low behind the tangled jungle in the center of the island; the wind tossed the wings to a breathtaking angle. Sixto was certain Case was going to crash. He heard the motor choke and sputter.

"Madre de Jesús!" Sixto sped up, racing to see. In an instant, the plane appeared directly in front of the Jeep. Its landing gear brushed the top of a tree as it swooshed close enough to vibrate Sixto's heart in his chest. He stomped the brakes, diving to the floor in preparation for the crash that didn't come. He popped his head up in time to see Case land the craft safely on the road behind him. Case taxied to a stop, turned the little plane and drove back to the Jeep. Sixto slammed his door and stomped to meet Case in the no man's land between them.

"Bastardo! You scare me to death!"

"I found them! Get back in the Jeep! You drive."

* * * * *

"They are looking for us." Logan pointed the gun towards the plane circling above then aimed at Catarina. "It's time to go."

Catarina rose and began the treacherous walk across the lava. She maneuvered around the rocks she could see and stepped on tiny glass knives she couldn't see waiting under thin layers of sand. She purposefully stumbled as many times as possible, cutting her feet and scraping her elbows. She stopped to wretch twice, blaming it on the baby.

The boat careened wildly; its bottom scraped the rocks hidden under the foam with every dip and swell. White waters swirled and eddied; rip tides sucked at Catarina's feet even in the shallows.

"Get in the boat!" Logan screamed.

Catarina considered her dilemma, getting shot for not getting in the boat or drowning when the boat sank. She checked for life jackets. None. Logan waved the pistol. Catarina reasoned that drowning provided a longer time line to death than a gunshot; she floundered into the boat with Logan. He bent to loose the line that tethered it.

A horn blasted from the road and the roar of a four-wheel drive sounded above the crashing waves.

Both Catarina and Logan looked to see a Jeep rocking across the stony outcrops, bouncing off anything in its path.

Pop.

One of the tires blew out.

Logan took a shot at the driver. A looming figure holding a spear gun folded out of the passenger side. Only one man would be strong enough to hold onto the frame of that lurching vehicle and lean out to take aim, Case Becker.

Catarina attempted to lower herself back into the water; but Logan grabbed her hair and pulled her back. Her cry drowned in the sound of fiberglass crunching on rocks. As soon as Logan managed to untie the line holding the craft, the massive current immediately twisted the boat in a circle, hitting every boulder on its way to the swirling waters at the base of the volcanic bridge.

Catarina sat low in the bottom of the boat, doing her best not to fall out. Logan emptied the bullets of Pablo's first gun toward the oncoming Jeep. Even his famous accuracy couldn't overcome the lurching of the boat. Every shot was wild. He threw the useless gun into the sea and retrieved the second one from its place behind his back.

The Jeep halted just short of joining the boat in El Mar de Caribe. The vehicle hovered over the water, one jutting stone preventing its fall. Both men jumped from the Jeep to the rocks. Sixto pointed Case's rifle at Logan. Case held the spear gun, relaxed at his side like a weapon he knew how to use.

"Logan, throw me the line. You know you can't beat this water." Deadly calm resided beneath the

349

surface of Case's command. Danger befitted him. He was always at his best in this place. "Even if you get to sea, the Mexican Navy is already looking for you."

Logan turned his head sideways like a curious animal and swung the gun towards Catarina's head. "We're going to be together.....Catarina, my son and me." The launch careened into the rocks. The bow rose, throwing Logan's aim away from Catarina.

Case took advantage of the split second opportunity, but the spear meant to pierce Logan's heart shattered the fiberglass bottom of the boat instead.

As the craft rolled into the rocks, the spear twisted with a screeching, wrenching sound, tearing a lethal hole in bottom of the boat.

Logan fell backwards overboard and began a losing fight with the current. Catarina barely noticed his head going under before her own battle began. Forces of nature sucking from down under pulled her deep beneath the surface, away from the noise of the crashing surf. Catarina remembered the swimming lesson.

Don't panic.
Go with the flow.

The force released her as magically as it had grabbed her.

She saw Case run toward the water. He was tying rope around his waist and shoulders as he screamed instructions to Sixto. Sixto responded, tying the other end of the rope to the front bumper of the Jeep. He got into the driver's seat and forced the gears into reverse.

Case ran up the beach before diving into the water. He swam with the current, allowing it to propel him towards Catarina.

Catarina was choking; she went under again. *Don't panic; he's close.* The boat bumped her shoulder, pushing her to a boulder. She grabbed the glassy lava just as the sucking on her body swirled her legs against Case.

"Here we go. Just like Persus and Andromeda, right? Happily ever after." Catarina nodded. Case removed the rope from his chest and looped it around her. His arms surrounded her, locked together with a twist of the rope around his wrists. The muscles in his forearms bulged, knotted and steady. Case motioned Sixto to pull them out. Saltwater stung her eyes, washed her cuts and filled her nauseous stomach. Catarina felt the tug on the rope and began to believe that they might live.

Suddenly she heard a sickening thud and felt Case's hands slide down her slick body. He shoved her into the momentum of the giant wave headed for shore and away from the descending hull and motor of the boat. Frantic, Catarina looked back in time to see the boat fall on top of Case. The motion of the water threw him against the rocks and the boat hit him again, crushing his chest.

Catarina watched in horror as the waters swept Case towards the rocks where she last saw Logan. Case was the strongest of swimmers; but injured, perhaps unconscious, he had no chance. It didn't seem that Catarina's invincible man fought the waters at all.

With less weight, the Jeep pulled Catarina onto shore and into Sixto's arms in seconds. She was exhausted, battered and weak; but she pulled the rope over her own head to free herself.

"Sixto, don't let him die!" She cried to her brother as though he were the god that answered such prayers.

Sixto didn't hesitate. He grabbed the rope, got back in the Jeep and drove closer to where the whirlpool sucked the waters into one of the underwater caves. He pulled the rope over his shoulder and ran towards his friend, for he would give his life to answer his sister's prayer. He thrashed through the surf, disappearing in the boiling water.

Catarina's head hung over the sand; she threw up the saltwater she'd swallowed and tried to catch her breath. *Not now! Not now! Please don't let me lose him now!*

She heard a pounding whoosh in the distance and squinted into the sky. Before the helicopter was close enough for her to see, three security cars from Palacio de las Antiguas pulled off the road. Men rushed toward Catarina. One man threw a blanket around her; three others ran to meet the helicopter. As it brushed the ground, Alfonso jumped from the passenger's side. He ran to Catarina, grabbed her and kissed the top of her head. He would not let her go when she tried to follow his men to the rope.

The line went slack. Free of its burden, the center of the rope curled upon itself and floated towards shore. Alfonso's men scrambled across the rocks and by the time they reached the rope, it was taut again. The three of them heaved in unison, pulling the body to shore.

"It's my brother!" Catarina broke loose from Alfonso's protective embrace. True, there was someone attached, but the head bore the blonde hair of Logan Dell!

"I don't think it's your brother," said Alfonso. "Stop," he commanded his men. "Don't bring him in yet."

One of the men lackadaisically observed, "But the rope, it's fraying on the rocks."

"So be it," said Alfonso.

It was fine with Catarina, too. She didn't care how Logan got the rope; she was losing both Sixto and Case.

This can't happen!

Her body seized with agony; she moaned as she dropped to her knees covering her head with the blanket.

"Señor Carerras! Aquí!" One of Alfonso's men appeared at the top of the highest point of the rocky extrusion. "Mira. Becker!"

Catarina threw off the blanket and ran toward the sound of Case's name. She was afraid to hope, afraid to cry out. She couldn't scale the battleship-sized rock without shoes; she had to pick her way around the base. When she reached the other side, she saw Sixto bending over Case giving him CPR.

Case was so still; Sixto was so methodical. It looked to Catarina like he was going through useless motions. She ran to Case's side and pushed Sixto away. She found her voice; she found her rage. She screamed and pounded Case's chest with two-fisted blows.

"You promised, happily ever after!" She hit him again, violently and again and again, until he coughed.

She sputtered his name, "Case!"

Case tried to rise and Sixto caught Catarina when she toppled from Case's body.

Case roared in pain. "That hurts! My ribs are broken!"

Alfonso eyed Case from atop the volcanic bridge. "Pain, that means you are not dead. That's good, I suppose."

"Señor Carerras. The rope, it broke. The man, he is gone." The messenger seemed only mildly apologetic.

Alfonso stood above the scene, gazing over the graduated shades of blue in the Caribbean waters. His silk slacks whipped in the wind and he adjusted his sunglasses. "There are many paths to justice, don't you agree, Señor Becker.....are you good with this one?" His eyes met Case's for the answer.

Alfonso dismissed his men. "No need to search for this man today. Look for him on Thursday down on La Playa de las Muertas. That should be enough time for him to join all the others on the Beach of the Dead.

Chapter 38

Alfonso

Alfonso observed Catarina, waiting for him to join her. She sat on the patio where the two of them spent many pleasant evenings getting to know each other. They'd laughed there, danced there and talked of the future. She smoothed her khaki chinos, crossed and uncrossed her legs. She adjusted the crisp white collar on her shirt and lifted her long hair off the back of her neck. Samuel offered to bring her refreshment; she declined.

Alfonso surprised himself; he thought losing Catarina would hurt more. He was truly enamored with this woman; but he was not going to fight for her. He opened the door to the patio; he'd made her wait long enough.

"Catarina? Here, let me look." Alfonso tilted her chin to check a bruise on her cheek. Now that she was cleaned up, her injuries proved much less serious than he'd feared. A slight swelling on her bottom lip added to its sensuality; the scratches would heal without scars.

355

Catarina adjusted her chair. "Thank you for moving me to the main hotel last night. The suite is lovely.....I owe you so much."

"You owe me nothing, Catarina. How is your brother?" Alfonso sat down with her at the table.

"Sixto is good."

".....and Señor Becker?"

"He's.....he's cranky, not a good patient." Catarina finally looked at Alfonso, a message written on her face.

Alfonso could read it clearly; but he saw no reason to make breaking the engagement easy for her. *I'm not that civilized.*

"I do need to talk to you.....about.....Señor Becker."

"Case," Alfonso offered.

Catarina let out the breath she'd been holding since Alfonso appeared on the patio. She reached for his hand, holding it in both of hers. "You know I can't marry you."

So simply stated, so painless for him, so agonizing for her. Alfonso covered her hands in his. "I know."

"I'm so sorry! In so many ways, I want to marry you; but I can't."

"Catarina, you know I've always loved your family, kept track of you. I knew there was something powerful between you and Case that night at Abuelita's Cinco de Mayo fiesta. What I saw happening between the two of you confused me, stirred my machismo. I had to try to win you. In truth, I thought I was the better man." He gathered Catarina into his arms. "We could have been good together.....except, that you are in love with someone else."

"Alfonso, I don't understand why you considered marrying me in the first place. A man in your position, your family?"

"Besides the fact that you are the most beautiful, intelligent, caring woman on earth?"

"Stop it, Alfonso. I come from nothing! Why?"

"You don't come from nothing. You come from your Abuelita."

Catarina tilted her head.

"My grandfather loved her with a passion that transcended every relationship I've seen in my whole life. I wanted that too. I want to feel that deeply, cry that hard, live that exhilaration. I thought maybe, I could find what they had with you." He shrugged his shoulders. "I was too late."

His sincerity melted her guilt; she touched his face when she said, "Alfonso, you honor me."

Chapter 39

Touch the Mayan Moon

Catarina tiptoed into the huge suite that she shared with Sixto and Case. Despite her efforts to silence the door, the latch popped. Sixto looked around from his place at the window; he held the birth certificates, one in each hand.

"Did you talk to Alfonso?"

"Sí." She whispered, so as not to wake Case.

".....and?"

"He said we could stay as long as we liked."

Sixto gestured at the luxury surrounding them. "Are you sure you don't want to marry him?"

"Sixto!" Catarina hissed at him.

"Kidding! Just kidding." He laid the birth certificates side by side on the coffee table.

"Are they real?"

"They're real. It would be too easy to prove if they weren't."

Catarina sat on the couch and traced the edge of the document with her name on it. "Why would our mother lie to us? Something so important."

"I've been thinking about that; I might know why." Sixto joined her on the couch. "She told me my father died before I was born; but I believe I remember a man. A vicious, violent man, muy malo." He unconsciously massaged his wrist. "Mostly, I remember how terrified of him she was. She told me to forget about him and that my name was Terrazos, like hers, before she married your father. De la Alvarado was a good man. It's too bad Abuelita never had a chance to meet him. When he died, we moved back and forth to Mexico. I barely remember those years."

"Then what happened?"

"I did like she said. I forgot about my father. I think she was protecting me, us."

"Do you think my father is dead?" Indignant, Catarina didn't know what to believe any more.

"I know he is; I saw the accident. Be glad you don't remember."

"Sixto, aren't you angry? This is the biggest lie a mother could tell her child! Life could have been so different for us."

"I'm going to trust that she did the right thing at the time. I'll probably never see her again to tell her this; but I've decided to forgive her." He put his hand on Catarina's shoulder.

"You think I should do the same, don't you? I'm much angrier about this than you are!" Catarina fussed with the birth certificate.

"I wish I had more of your fire, Catarina."

"What if you did have more fire, Sixto. What would you do with it?"

"I'd take this birth certificate and go marry María Sanchez."

"You would?" A slow smile spread across Catarina's mouth. "Why don't you?"

"She already said no."

"When?"

"Ten years ago, eight years ago and seven years ago."

"You should try again."

"I'm bored!" A bellow came from behind Case's bedroom door. He pounded the wall with his fist. "Come get me out of this bed!"

Sixto pointed towards the bedroom. "You have more than just our mother to forgive."

"El Gringo?"

"I thought you called him Case now."

"He barely tolerates me in the room. He doesn't touch me or make eye contact. It's like he's gone back home and left his body here."

"He's really banged up, Catarina. Give the man a chance. He's slept most of the last twenty-four hours."

Catarina rose to her feet and Sixto banged his shin on the coffee table hurrying to get up.

In Case's room, heavy curtains were drawn against the setting sun; the covers were thrown off the bed. Case was trying to sit up. Catarina took his ankles and gently swung his feet off the bed to the floor. Sixto slipped his arm behind Case's neck. Together they raised him to a sitting position on the side of the bed.

Case picked at the legs of his briefs. "It's hot." He threw off Sixto's hold on his arm. "I can stand up by myself." He expanded his painful lungs, slowly, preparing for the worst. By the obscenities he slung around the room, movement hurt as much as he'd feared. A chance look at his battered face in the mirror produced his favorite curse, "Shit."

He gimped his way into the living area on his own. Sixto followed, extending a pair of pants.

"Forget it. I'm not hurting myself to put those on." Case eased into a lounge chair.

"Here, I'll help you," Sixto insisted.

"Let me confirm your worst fears; your sister has seen me in less."

Sixto looked at the floor and slowly folded the pants. "You two need to talk. I'll just be out by the pool.....yes, the pool." The door shut itself behind him.

"If you're hot; do you want some ice water?" Catarina opened cabinets looking for a glass.

"I'm leaving tomorrow." His announcement sounded dry, final.

Catarina walked to the refrigerator for ice. "You can't travel yet."

"I have to get back to sign some papers. I turned the tables on those Houston big shots. My new attorney Bob and I figured out a way to convince their bankers that Becker Rescue Services was the stronger company. We are buying the Houston firm instead of letting them buy us. Becker Rescue Services is going to own them. We'll be bigger than ever. Wish I'd been there to see those lawyers' faces. I blew the job crewing on *The Merry Maker*; so it's a good thing I have work waiting for me back home."

Catarina listened to the string of announcements, but was preoccupied by her struggle with how she would tell Case that she was going to forgive him and that the engagement to Alfonso was off. Case might not care about either one now, but Catarina knew she needed to do it so she could forgive herself too. Then Case's comments turned personal.

"It takes a cold, determined woman to do what you have done." His words were judgmental, punishing.

"What do you mean?" She slammed the glass of water on the counter. He jerked at the noise and the corners of his mouth curved downward.

"Does your fiancé know you have Logan Dell's baby in your belly?"

Catarina took off the sapphire ring and threw it at Case so hard it left a new ding in his already nicked up forehead. She may have been willing to forgive him for everything else, but never this. She burst into tears and there was no hope of hiding them from Case.

Catarina ran to her bedroom and started throwing her belongings into a hotel laundry sack. She ransacked the drawers, and when she came to the swollen, wrinkled dictionary she and Case made together, she turned and threw it overhand through the door.

The book landed hard; its weakened binding gave way and pages exploded at Case's feet. He recognized the treasure that represented their entwined souls, and he moved as if he had no injuries. He was upon her in an instant, pinning her to the wall. She turned her head sideways so she wouldn't have to look into his eyes.

He whispered in her ear. "You did not call me; you did not write me; you did not send word to me that you were pregnant. Still, I assumed the baby was mine. You told Logan the baby was his. What am I supposed to think?" Case buried his face in her hair. "I want you more than anything in the world." He bent his knees, pressing his pelvis into hers. "You can feel it even now, how much I want you."

Catarina felt wild urges to melt into the rising hardness between Case's legs. Her responding body disturbed her. How could she rid herself of him if she couldn't be in the same room with him?

"Why, Catarina, why would you tell him that?" Case lifted his face from her curls and stroked her hair with desperate need to touch her anywhere since he could not touch her everywhere.

She trembled with rage, sadness or desire; she did not know which. "I was scared! I thought I was going to die! I lied to Logan to confuse him; I had to protect myself. I thought if I let Logan think the baby was his, I could buy one more minute, two minutes, three minutes more of living so you could find me. It worked. That lie saved my life and my baby's life. Case, Logan never touched me from the day I met you, no man has!"

He cupped her tear-streaked cheeks and kissed her with abandon. He crushed her chest with his broken body and released her arms to run his hands down her shoulders, over the sides of her breasts and to her hips. Catarina reveled in his taste, his smell and the sensations she would put behind her when she walked out of this room. Even though Case's kiss told Catarina that he believed her, she could not believe in him.

He winced and sucked in air as she pushed him away. She escaped the suite while he pleaded, calling her name.

"Catarina. Catarina!"

The door slammed.

Case followed her into the hallway, much to the delight of red-hatted Rosie. "Well, Mr. Becker, we meet again. How nice you look!" She scanned his bare legs and torso. She pursed her lips at his tight buttocks rippling in his briefs as would an artist appraising a statue. Then she noticed the tape on his chest and the cuts on his face.

"Oooh! What happened to you?"

"The story is long and I don't have time. I'll tell you about it later if you help me put on my pants."

Rosie raised her eyebrows and followed him into his room. When she bent to help Case slip into his pants, she declared, "This is the most exciting part of my trip! I can't wait to tell the girls in my bridge club! I bet they come with me next time."

Case exhaled air through his teeth when he had to stand on one leg. "Will you help me find Catarina?"

"If you promise to say the right things to her, I will."

"I wish I knew what the right things were. I can't open my mouth without screwing up."

"I told her you are 'The One.' She believed me. You tell her the same and she will believe you too. Trust me. I gave her a photograph I took of the two of you to prove it."

Rosie let Case steady himself on her shoulder while they walked slow baby steps down the hall, through the lobby and across the pool area. Night frogs were starting to croak and birds were rustling in the palms, settling to await the dusk. Rosie's eyes searched the beach while Case scanned the restaurant and bar.

"There she is, sitting in the sand. See? I think she is waiting for you, hoping you will come and make everything right." Rosie removed his arm from her shoulder and asked, "Can you make it the rest of the way?"

"Yeah." Case pointed to the hedge separating the pool from the tennis courts. "Rosie, could you get me one of those gardenias?"

When Case reached Catarina, he painfully bent over and placed the gardenia blossom behind her ear. She ignored him; when she did not offer to help him sit down, he straightened up. He stood letting the breeze and the sound of the waves do their work on his mind, calming him so he could be eloquent at his last chance with Catarina. He stared away from her into the rippling lights that rested on the water.

"Catarina, I believe we are meant to be together. We've been given this baby because we're both too stubborn to figure it out any other way." She sat frozen in the hot night, he wondered if she would shatter if he touched her.

"Catarina, I need to sit down, please."

She stood and allowed him to grab her shoulders while he eased himself to sit in the sand. They waited, not touching, not talking.

A full, pure white moon slipped between the thin line separating the ocean and the sky on the horizon. It rose into clouds of navy, royal and baby blue, colors left over from the sunset. Case lost himself studying the mysteries of the moon's surface.

"I see the rabbit," he finally said.

"What?"

"The moon goddess' rabbit, Ix Chel."

"The moon does seem closer here."

"I feel I can reach out and touch it." Case extended his arm, squinted his eye and aligned his hand to touch the Mayan moon. He addressed the goddess.

"Ix Chel? I heard you like men. If you do, I want you to grant me a wish. I want you to tell Catarina that I am 'The One' and that I want her to forgive me."

Catarina closed her eyes and her chin dropped almost imperceptibly towards her chest. She fingered the gardenia in her hair. "That's two wishes."

"I need you to forgive me," he said.

"There is a lot to forgive."

"I know. I'm hurting; can we talk about it lying down?" He pressed his hand into the most painful place on his ribs and they eased themselves back into the soft sand. They laid on their backs in separate poses, listened to the music of the waves and watched the moon ascend.

As they relaxed, the energy flowing between their bodies would not allow them to stay apart. The tips of Catarina's fingers involuntarily slipped toward Case's, one grain of sand at a time. When he felt her sweet presence with the hair on his arm, he seized her hand. His big body shuddered and he tenderly pulled her into his aching side. It had been a long time since they held each other like this on the sailboat, *Everlovin'*. They rested, testing the return to each other's embrace.

"I forgive you for seducing me on the beach."

"I seduced you?" He kissed her forehead and gave her a squeeze.

"Yes, you did. But the money? You are still going to have to explain how you thought that was a good idea."

"I told you; it was an anonymous gift to the school."

She raised herself to one elbow. "You did things that will be much more difficult to forgive than those two."

Case wondered what she could find to be angry with him now.

She leaned over his face and briefly kissed his poet's lips as she listed each item.

"I forgive you for making me vulnerable.....for cracking my shell.....for smelling wonderful.....for being beautiful.....for being kind to children.....and thirsty trees. I forgive you for not following me down here sooner, chasing me like you should have....."

"What? That's a two way street. And after the things you said to me?" Case's voice was husky.

"And that horrible comment just now, about Alfonso and Logan....."

"What about my list? I forgive you for not taking every gift I offered you. I forgive you for making me love you and then running away." He paused to lift his head and touch her lips with his. "I forgive you for not telling me about our baby. And I forgive you for telling the biggest lie of all.....that you don't love me." The challenge hung in the narrow space between them.

Catarina opened her mouth; no sound came out.

"If you lie to me again, it will be the last time."

Her eyes were glassy; she spoke slowly, uncertainly, forcing the words with her tongue like she was speaking a new language. "Yo.....te.....amo. I love you, Case Becker."

Case looked deep into her eyes and said, "I know you do, Catarina." He caressed her hair and pretended as if he were plucking something from the gardenia behind her ear. He placed the sapphire ring on the fourth finger of her left hand.

She smiled down at the glittering jewels. "Starry nights."

Case flattened her fingers against his and reached their joined hands toward the Mayan moon. He touched her palm against the surface and whispered into her hair, "It's your turn, Catarina."

Epilogue

The frayed rope trailed behind him like the tail of a kite. He flew on crystal waters taking an excursion through fantasy landscapes of underwater chambers and formations, eerie with intermittent beams of light and complete blackness. He was conscious even through an impact that temporarily paralyzed his diaphragm. Air pockets and the speed of the storm surge turned a certain fatal journey into a miracle for Logan Dell.

The last cave spit him out of its belly like the biblical whale. New currents caught him, carrying him out to sea. Fifty feet below, a school of barracuda eyed him through blue aquamarine. Logan ignored them and rolled to float on his back. The storm was subsiding; he could manage until dark. He removed his jeans, tied knots in the legs and hoisted them above the water line. The heavy, soaked fabric captured air, making as good a floatation device as could be had under the circumstances.

Logan watched the sun reach its zenith and drop to the rocking horizon before a shrimp boat lumbered by on its way to port. It chugged exhaust into the atmosphere and left a perfumed trail of iridescent film drifting on the surface behind it. The Mexican crew scurried to throw him a life ring and pull him aboard. The captain removed a cigarillo from his tobacco stained beard where his mouth might be.

"¿Como se llama?"

The red sun boiled the water at the edge of the earth. Sweat stink rose off the crew. The deck rolled solid under Logan's back. It was good to have a new start. He gagged and coughed before he looked up at the men surrounding him. Then he gave a little wink when he said,

"My name is Jonah."

Breinigsville, PA USA
07 October 2010
246896BV00001B/1/P

9 780982 616604